MW01478817

Margo's Child
Marjory May Wright

i

Contents

Dedication:

To all my Children and Grandchildren who cheered me
on.

.

Acknowledgements:

A special thanks to Jean Helmhoz's Creative Writing
class for their encouragement. Special acknowledgment
of appreciation to Shannon, my niece!   Thank You to
my grandson Larry Wright for helping with the editing
and everything!

Foreword

Foreword, by Dr. Paul M. Kingery, Associate Dean for Research, College of Education, University of Hawaii at Manoa

The depths of human experience are mined by the youngest souls who are exposed to the harshest of life conditions. We trust biological parents, and sometimes other caregivers, with young souls as a means of assuring their well-being. Sometimes this goes awry, however, when children are isolated by those with limited ability to love and care for them. Sometimes the children enter these difficulties with physical abnormalities that make matters even worse.

The signs of trouble are there in their faces, actions, and words, but don't tell the whole story. The caring observer will engage such a child, learn more, and offer assistance. The most troubling and intimate stories too often lie hidden within children as they grow to adulthood, even when telling them would bring healing. Such untold stories are created through painful life experience, one insult at a time. They can only be told a few sentences at a time, for the pain of recounting them is too great. Stories of the struggle emerge, in quiet moments in safe settings, a verse at a time, spoken to an intimate friend in barely a whisper. The fuller story is never completely told.

These dark tales of life that emerge paint the deepest colors into the never finished portrait of humanity. Without them we would not appreciate the small bits of light layered over them. Those who live in lighter conditions rely upon these young explorers who have mined the greatest depths to tell us what lies there. We must know their experiences to know what is possible, what can, and often does, happen.

This story was born in the heart of a young girl who was neglected and later abandoned by her parents. She carried the story within her for many years before it was slowly told. The story draws distinct flavor from the heart in which it was held for many years like wine aged in an oak cask. The main character, like many of us, is a fragile, abused little creature with physical imperfections struggling to overcome, to feel secure, to belong. Her every pain stemmed from the pain others carried in response to life events with limited resources, as an unbroken chain.

The author poignantly illustrates how ripples rise at intervals from every stone thrown, from every damage inflicted upon us, and how the waters of our spirits are calmed by repeated gestures of warmth, kindness, and love. The story she slowly draws out of her friend's life experiences resonates within the author as she later encounters other children who have struggled in similar ways. The story grows there within the author, and takes its own unique shape, becoming an amalgam of stories.

This talented new author strikes a harmonic chord in a dissonant world, and makes us want to sing. Our hearts are turned by her to the plight of other children. We learn that we care about them, that we want to hear their stories and to help them when we can.

*****

Prologue

After many seasons of sharing the lunch room table at the payroll office where I spent long hours during World War II, Korean War, and the Vietnam War; I was recognizing the heartfelt plea of a dear lady who had been denied the comfort of her parents love. Abandoned, abused, neglected, I suggested to my adult friend that her life story was a sad documentation which needed to be addressed and aired. Though she had been abandoned as a little girl, she had the remarkable strength of heart and forgiveness to care for her parents in her home in their old age. The cry of the sensitive heart still pleaded for affection she had never known.

After reading the continuation of "Margo's Child" in class last Tuesday the comment was made that it would be nice if "such and such" happened but it really would be too much of a coincidence to be realistic, and I agreed with the logical appraisal, being grateful for all the constructive help...Now I must tell you what happened that same Tuesday afternoon.

My foster brother and his wife came to visit us and they brought their granddaughter with them. Shannon was a frail child with lovely hair more golden red then strawberry blond – a gorgeous color almost defying description. The question flashed through my mind, what do I have in the house that might entertain and amuse this young visitor. I need not have wasted time with such a question because she had brought her own books and a puzzle, and immediately busied herself. I was amazed at this little one was already fourteen years old. Her love for books was very apparent and her mature answers to my interested questions impressed me. Then she volunteered to set the table for our supper – how thoughtful! Shannon was appreciative of the cook's efforts and most mannerly. After we had eaten and cleaned the kitchen I asked if she cared to go for a walk while her Grandparents looked at Uncle Weldon's paintings. I had an eager taker for my invitation – so off we went. Her pace was super fast. That body may have been small and frail but it was alive and going.

As we walked we talked...the first inquiry was, "what kind of classes are you and Uncle Weldon taking?"

"Well Uncle Weldon is taking a painting class and I am enrolled in a writing class."

"Oh, neat! I belong to an 'Author's club' at school – I write poetry."

"What are you writing about?"

"I am writing a story – the account of a child abandoned, abused and with scoliosis....do you know what scoliosis is?"

"Sure, it is curvature of the spine, the doctors discovered I had it when I was eight years old and I had to wear a brace for four years." "That is one reason why I am behind my classmates in school, the other reason is I had to have surgery, it sure was rough for awhile – the cast, eye surgery, and then my Mom and Dad got a divorce, that bothered me a lot." "I had a special teacher that seemed to understand and talked with me every day, she was the bright spot in my life, especially when my step sisters were so mean to me."

"How were they mean to you Shannon?"

"They wouldn't talk to me, and they wouldn't sit beside me even at the table, and when no one was looking they hit me and broke my dolls..."

"Did your Mother know this?"

"Yes, but she was afraid if she said anything it would make the kids more hateful."

"What about your Step Dad?"

"He didn't care, but my teacher cared and that helped."

"Shannon, I care too, and I want you to write to me, will you please do that?"

"I will Auntie Marj."

I could hardly take all this in – the similarities between Shannon and Lorraine, "Margo's Child." were almost unbelievable! Here was a frail, mistreated child, with golden red hair who loved books and found solace alone in the seclusion of her room, who had the good fortune to have a friend in her teacher. The scoliosis was an accepted fact of life by a little girl all too often mistaken for a boy.

A coincidence? Of course, but a coincidence indeed! This happening has strengthened my resolve to continue with my story as I had originally intended with the dedication to my family without whom this story would never have been dug out of unfinished business!

*****

The Interview

The old car rumbled and rattled as it turned the corner and was eased into a space too small for it's dusty, dented, once red body. The woman behind the wheel frowned at the sign on the building and almost read audibly: "Josephine County Elementary School, Grants Pass, Oregon."
The building was beautifully designed of light brick, and its size was impressive, and frightening to the woman, who sighed then spoke to the wide eyed child beside her.

"Grab your lunch, and c'mon."

The sidewalk and playground was alive with voices and laughter but the playing youngsters scarcely took notice of the car or its occupants. Not strong enough to open the door on the passenger's side the child slid out behind the woman, clutching the crumpled lunch sack that held a slice of bread generously spread with bacon grease.

The child half-skipped, half-ran behind the woman, holding the lunch sack with one hand and brushing brownish, ear length, uncombed hair from her fearful eyes. Every so often the jeans which were several sizes too large had to be hitched up, the drab plaid shirt missing sleeve buttons flapped limply over the frail body. This sorry wardrobe had been found in the last rented house, and was complimented by unlaced tennis shoes. The weary child reached for the comfort of an adult hand but was ignored. Then the big glass door was opened and the two stepped into another world. The woman's eyes scanned the long bright hallway identifying signs: Principal, Vice-principal, Nurse, Administration, Student Enrollment, that was it and she hastened to the doorway.

A smiling secretary's eyes surveyed her callers hiding the embarrassment she felt for them.

"Good Morning," she said.

Since there was no response to her greeting she turned toward the child noticing the terrible posture.

"Hello lad," she said.

"I'm a girl," was the child's quiet reply.

The secretary groaned inwardly, thinking what a way to start a day, and again focused her attention on the woman.

"May I help you?"

"Yes, I want to register the kid," replied the woman.

"Oh certainly," replied the secretary as she reached for an enrollment card and began to ask the familiar questions.

"Student's name?"

"Lorraine Hamilton."

"Address?"

"Happy's Trailer Park, 27292 River Road, Grants Pass."

"Phone?"

"None."

"Student's Age?"

"Seven years old."

"Date of Birth?"

"August 3, 1960."

"Place of Birth?"

"Ft. Worth, Texas."

"Mother's Name?"

"Margo, Hamilton."

"Father's Name?"

"Max Hamilton."

"Mother's Occupation?"

"Unemployed."

"Name of last school attended?"

"Shoreline Elementary, Watsonville, California."

"Last grade completed?"

"Well, sort of the second," replied the woman.

"What do you mean sort of finished?" asked the secretary.

"Well, she was in the second grade when we left New Mexico and almost finished with the second when we left California," explained the woman.

"Did you bring the last report card and school records?"

"Uh, no they were lost when we moved."

"Very well, we will send for them," responded the secretary.

"Don't be shocked at the grades, this kid isn't very bright," volunteered the woman.

At that comment Lorraine tried to become invisible behind her mother's skirt, hanging her head, and standing with one foot perched on the other.

"Are there any health problems the school should be aware of?" questioned the secretary.

"Oh no, everything is fine," hastily replied the woman.

"All our students are given an entrance physical by our school nurse and if there seems to be a problem the student is referred to the district physician," advised the secretary.

"That won't be necessary," concluded the woman.

"One other thing," continued the secretary, "We have a complimentary lunch program for qualifying families."

"We don't want charity," snapped the woman, "besides the kid has her lunch."

"But mama, I'm hungry," pleaded Lorraine.

"You have your lunch, and that is enough," said the woman with a warning look, and turned to leave.

"Wait mama, don't leave me, how will I get home?"

"You can walk, it's good for you," and with that the woman fled the office.

Ruth Haynes, the secretary looked in amazement and disbelief as Margo fled, hastened without a

3

backward glance from the office, leaving her little girl to fend for herself. Ruth's eyes quickly moved from the vanishing Margo to the face of Lorraine – the panic and dismay was indescribable. Ruth moved swiftly around the counter to Lorraine.

"Would you like to have me show you around the school?"

Lorraine could only nod her head in the acceptance and grasped the hand of Ruth extended. Ruth couldn't help but ponder the nationality of the dark skinned child and pity welled up in her as she noticed the bare feet laboring to keep the oversized shoes on her little feet and oh how she needed a bath!

As they passed the Counselor's office Ruth explained that Mrs. Kepka was a wonderful friend to all the children and this was a good place for anyone to come with their questions and problems. They turned and went down the hallway passed the kitchen and lunchroom, and Ruth informed Lorraine that all the students came to that room to eat their lunches, the restrooms were pointed out, and then they turned another corner to the wing where the classrooms were. Lorraine looked and listened in wide-eyed silence.

In the absence of placement testing, Lorraine was placed in the middle classroom to assign this little neglected bit of humanity. The slower paced class of Mrs. Erickson's would be a double advantage for the frightened child clinging tightly to her hand. Lorraine felt more comfortable in a less competitive atmosphere and Mrs. Erickson was a gentle mother of three and this babe surely needed some mothering.

As Ruth approached Mrs. Erickson's desk she greeted the teacher with a "Good Morning, Mrs. Erickson, I have a new student for your class."

"Wonderful," responded Mrs. Erickson.

4

"What is your name buddy?"

"I'm a girl," mumbled Lorraine.

Ruth quickly covered the blunder, "Mrs. Erickson this is Lorraine Hamilton who is transferring from California we will have to send for her records in the mean time she can get settled into class." "I see you have your lunch, Lorraine."

"Do you have a tablet and pencil?" inquired Mrs. Erickson.

Lorraine could only shake her head and lowered her cycs to the floor.

*****

Memory Lane

Margo fled from the Student Enrollment Office pursued by a demon with many heads...Where to hide? How to escape? Her thoughts whirled in a torment. Sitting inside the closed car only provided a hiding place from the eyes of the public and that was temporary. Margo started the old Chevrolet that had once been such a beautiful car and the pride and joy of Max. The demon sat beside her...she felt such a pang of guilt for abandoning her child and a stab of shame for depriving her of a warm lunch and disgust and anger because of the medical needs. But what did it matter now? Who cared? There was no way out of this black, slimy pit. There was no way back.

As the old red car with the dejected driver neared the Rogue River Bridge Margo contemplated putting her foot to the floorboard and crashing the guard rail but she instinctively knew the car hadn't enough power to break those steel railings. Instead of stepping on the gas, Margo stepped on the brake and stopped the car in a little parking area provided for viewing the rushing river. She looked at the height of the bridge and the roiling waters beneath and wondered what it would be like to die – she had seen two of her babies die – but what would become of Lorraine? What will become of Lorraine? The demon beside her said "jump", but her heart said, "I can't", and Margo put her head on the steering wheel and sobbed – deep racking sobs – it was safe to weep because Max couldn't see her, his reaction to weeping was violence, beating whoever shed a tear. Time was unaccounted for as Margo emptied her heart and soul of tears and as the storm within her subsided her mind went back again to a beautiful white stone, stately home near New Orleans. Her thoughts stopped at the pillars of the double gate, read again the old

English lettered sign fastened to the pillar on the right side of the drive: Judge Thomas Boesche. Then her eyes drank in the beauty of the giant trees lining the long drive and noticed with pleasure their branches touched over-head and the shady "tree tunnel" ended at the steps of the great white pillared house she had once called home. Margo's heart cried, "Oh Mama if I could just throw my arms around you again and tell you how wonderful life is, but it would only be a monstrous lie" "Oh mama, it is better you don't know." Her memories flung open the huge front door and she raced up the wide curving stairway to the second floor – down the hallway to her haven. The first thing her eyes sought as she stepped inside this gorgeous lilac room was the collection of photos of herself. There she was at one month, three months, six months, first birthday, first Christmas, first steps…first day of school, in ballet costume, first pony, first bicycle, first piano recital, junior-horsemanship competition, water skiing, high diving, ice skating at the arena, cheerleader, then her eyes moved to the right and there was the shelf with all her trophies to the left was the glass cabinet with all those beautiful dolls. Across from the window was the high-canopied bed framed by her collection of fans from all over the world. Her mind instinctively yearned to touch the closet and threw open the doors to reveal rows and rows of lovely dresses…it was always this way. Then she bounded down the stairs and into the kitchen where Freda, the nanny, was singing as she stirred and blended.

Margo could still hear her say, "There you are Miss Margo, I was waiting for you. These chocolate chip cookies are still warm let me pour you a glass of milk."

"Oh thanks Freda, I am starved, Mmmm they are so yummy" "What's for dinner Freda?" But before Freda could answer Margo would rush on "I hope Mom and Dad get home in time for the game, it's the last one of the year and we are undefeated so far, and then Max and I are going to the Norwoods' for the end of the season party." "Freda, next year at this time I will be at the U". "And someday I will be mom's law partner."

I could still hear Freda say, "Miss Margo, you are very bright and beautiful and it is going to be so lonesome around here without you, we are going to miss you honey."

Margo recalled that their school had won the pennant – they were the champs – Mom and Dad had made it home in time for dinner and had taken her in their car because Max would be bringing her home. Margo couldn't forget that Max had gotten very drunk again because he was competing with Hugh to see who could drink the most beer.

Margo had begged to drive home.

Max had boasted, "I can handle things just fine, Babe."

And when Margo again tried to persuade Max to let her drive he had opened the car door and pushed her in. Margo remembered being afraid to tell her folks for fear they wouldn't let her go out with Max again – they were very fussy about this drinking bit. And Margo was worried about what Max's folks would do because they were very strict about lots of things... they might even take the car away from him, but the coach couldn't kick Max off the team because this was the end of the season and Max had won the coveted Football Scholarship to the University.

Margo recalled breakfast that next morning and as her Mom and Dad asked about the party – she knew she had to tell about Max because they trusted her and she loved them so much. Max's folks had heard him stumbling and crashing around in the kitchen so drunk Max couldn't hide his situation. There had been restrictions imposed, Max had apologized to Margo's parents and promised them and his parents that he would not drink anymore. He was so sick and miserable it was an easy promise to make. And he kept his promise, until graduation night, but after the all night graduation party Max had gone home with a buddy so his folks didn't know about the broken promise.

When Margo had confronted Max about his excessive drinking and his promise that night he had laughed and said, "Baby, a fellow only graduates once."

Margo was remembering how the first semester at the University was such a busy, challenging time. Sorority pledges, early and late class schedules, lonesomeness being away from home for the first time, and her escape was the piano in the dorm lounge. How comforting it was to call home and hear the voices of the two people she loved. As for Max he had been accepted into the Fraternity of his choice, he could handle it he thought because he was well endowed with brains and ambition. The first semester they both made the dean's list. The second semester was more comfortable because Margo had the feel for the pace and schedule of classes and loved them, she practiced the piano daily and was improving her game of tennis besides getting in lots of swimming in the gym pool. Lately when she and Max went out for a hamburger he often ordered a beer, and when she protested he would wink at her, pat her hand, and said "Baby, I am big boy now." Margo was crazy about this handsome guy and tried to hide her disapproval and fear. The beginning of their second year at the U of Louisiana a can of beer always accompanied Max and by the second semester weekend beer parties at the Frat House were the norm. Max's grades slipped, there was a warning letter from the Athletic Department. Max made an effort to regain his status and reputation but his efforts were not one hundred percent successful. Margo tried reasoning with Max, pleading with him, she knew she loved him and he loved her. Margo remembered saying, "Max for my sake, for our sakes, won't you please quit drinking?" Max had hugged her and had promised to stop drinking. During the summer break they had announced their engagement, there was a gorgeous lawn party, pictures in the paper and plans for a wedding following graduation. Margo had mentally begun designing her wedding gown and making plans for the most beautiful wedding ever...Tina, the maid, would make her gown and wedding wardrobe just as she had all of her cloths since Margo was a little girl. Then came the third year at the U – and Max was back to the beer again more than ever. About Thanksgiving Max received a stern reprimand from the coach, and a warning letter from the Athletic Director. Next came an appointment with the Dean because of his grades...this angered Max. Margo could so easily recall the phone call late that Thursday evening when Max asked her to meet him at the Pub...

"Baby, I'm fed up with the hassle from the Coach, the dean, the whole crumby bunch. I don't need them and they don't want me, let's get married and take off for Texas. There is plenty of work to be had for good money in the oil fields."

"Oh Max, what about my folks, and your folks, and I wanted a real wedding?"

"C'mon Margo we can get along just fine without someone telling us what to do and what not to do, and we don't need a big fancy wedding and if you love me as much as you say you love me, you will come."

Margo started to cry again when she remembered the pain in her Mom and Dad's voices and heard them cry when she called to tell them that she and Max had eloped and been married and were headed for Texas.

Margo wrote from Texas, but as Max's drinking increased her writing decreased. The last letter Margo recalled writing was to inform her folks that they would be grandparents...then Max had been fired from his job, they moved to another town, she had a miserable pregnancy, and more drinking. Margo couldn't tell her parents about the way they lived in shabby shanties, often hungry, the constant drinking and terrible tantrums and she was ashamed to go back. What would become of Max? The only way she could ease her pain was to drink that detestable stuff too. She certainly didn't want her folks to come visit her and see the sorry mess…so they never knew they had a granddaughter.

Weeks and months and years became a blur of a crying child, dirty clothes not enough groceries, too much beer and heartless beatings, homesickness, and helplessness. Lorraine was four years old when little Clay was born. Max was proud of his first son and wanted to love his children but he couldn't stay sober long enough and by now he was resenting the money spent on the children's needs. Clay was barely a year old when he became very sick crying day and night. Margo had begged to take him to the doctor but Max insisted he was just spoiled.

Margo shuddered as she remembered Max snatching a feverish, crying baby boy from her arms and holding a hand over his nose and mouth to stop the crying. The crying stopped and so did the breathing. She remembered Max was shaking Clay to start his breathing but his little body was limp and turning blue. Max was frightened and wrapped Clay in a blanket and ran for the car to take the baby to the emergency room at the hospital. Assuring Margo he could handle the situation alone. When he returned he said there wasn't anyone at the reception desk when he entered so he laid Clay on a chair and left.

"Max, my baby! How could you?" "MY BABY! MY BABY!"

"Shut up woman," Max roared and slapped Margo across the face.

"Daddy where is my brother?" asked Lorraine.

"The hospital killed him," lied Max "I think we had better pack up and move on." instructed Max, "right now!"

Margo remembered the numbness and grief as she again packed their meager possessions, which by now easily fit, in her once handsome luggage. It looked so out of place now... it was the only nice thing she had left.

Max found a job in Lordsburg, New Mexico at a filling station and somehow miraculously by the time Lorraine started school and had held that job for two years. Margo dreaded telling Max that she again was expecting their third child and her doctor discovered Lorraine spinal curvature that needed attention but Max said "Not now." Then little Randy was born and Margo hoped that Max wouldn't celebrate too much and loose this good job. But Max did celebrate and ended up going to work very drunk, got into a fight with his boss and was fired on the spot.

Max declared, "I am tired of this job anyway." And thought he could look around in California for something better.... so with a new born babe in her arms Margo moved again, yet farther away from family, hope, and love.

Margo wondered what life in Watsonville, California would be like...but she was really too weary and hungry to care much. Max was a good talker and was hired at a local garage as a mechanic, they moved into a tiny trailer at the edge of town. Now Margo wished the rich sunshine would reach the terrible coldness she felt within her body. Max again brought home more beer than groceries.

Lorraine would beg, "Mama can I have something to eat?"

The cold cereal didn't do much to satisfy so Margo would give Lorraine a cup of beer so the child would sleep.

From the dingy trailer window Margo could see the truck gardens and artichoke fields – Watsonville was the artichoke capital of the world, and the fields were alive with people harvesting crops and the roads roared with trucks taking the bounty to processing plants. Maybe I could drive a truck or even gather artichokes if I put the baby in a back pack, so Margo felt a ray of hope as she contemplated asking for a job in the fields.

"Where do I apply for a job?" asked the slight mother with a fretful babe in her arms.

The husky suntanned foreman quickly surveyed the pale, gaunt woman with crying child in her arms and replied with a sake of his head, "You will have to find a place to leave the kid, we don't run a nursery out here," and turned back to tallying the boxes of artichokes being unloaded from the picking machine.

"Leave the baby?" Thought Margo, "There is no place to leave my baby, I don't know anyone and I don't have any money to pay for care…

The ray of hope in her eyes died as she realized her plight. "Oh Daddy, you would die if you could see me." "Daddy, you have so much, you have everything and I have nothing but I can't cross that chasm to you, I just can't." Then her thoughts turned to the possibility of asking for food stamps – she was hungry but Max had threatened to beat her if she asked for charity and the thought of a beating was sufficient to quell the thought or was it? Maybe Max wouldn't notice if she just brought home a few simple things and didn't say anything he probably would be too engrossed with his beer…. she remembered also a few nights before Max had not only brought home more beer than groceries but had added bottles of hard liquor.

Last night Lorraine had again begged, "Mama can I have something to eat?"

The little bowl of cereal didn't do much to satisfy that hunger, so Margo gave Lorraine a cup of beer again so the child would sleep in spite of her unappeased appetite and then she drank the remainder of the bottle so she too could forget...but even in her sleep there was torment because she dreamed of that little bundle left on a hospital waiting room chair.

*****

The Nightmare

Again and again Margo asked herself, "Where is the Max she thought she knew so well?" "What is the real cause of this endless drinking that produces this whirling, black nightmare?" "Why this hostility, this cruelty, this insanity, I can't cope with?" "Where is it all going to end?" "When will it end?"

These questions had haunted Margo ever since they eloped – all the years she had hoped he would wake up to realize what he was doing to himself, to her, to them, to their children.

All her pleading, "Max please go to the doctor for help with your drinking problem."

"I'm not sick and I don't have a problem," growled Max and turned back to the TV and his bottle of beer.

"Max, let's go to the clinic together and talk to the therapist, coaxed Margo."

"We're not going out together, we aren't going alone, we aren't going period...now or ever," was Max's defiant, bitter refusal.

"Why don't you just have a drink and shut up?" and his attitude toward Lorraine was unreasonable, cruel, and frightening, also.

At first he seemed to be proud of his darling little daughter and had applauded her first steps and laughed at her first words. As time went on he began to resent the money spent for baby food or new little shoes; he became jealous of the time Margo spent teaching or playing with their baby girl. He was quick to give a swift slap for crying or spilled milk, and if Margo intervened she too would get a fierce blow across the face. The abuse progressed to a hard kick with a work boot, or being locked in a dark closet, or sitting in a corner with a paper sack pulled over her little head. The beer was the demon in Max's hand but it was fast becoming the anesthesia to dull Margo's pain and the tranquilizer to put an abused child to sleep with.

"Max what became of your special dream to become your Father's partner at the family bank? And your dream to have a beautiful plantation? Or laughing children riding ponies in the back meadow? Max what happened to your dream? Our dream?"

Little Randy's cries roused Margo from her reverie – he was hungry and so was she. She gave the baby a bottle of milk and ate half a bacon sandwich and worried how she would tell Max there was no bacon left for his breakfast.

"I know, I will get more bacon. I am going for food stamps right now before Lorraine comes home from school," she told herself.

This decision gave strength and purpose to Margo as she picked up her little child and purse to begin the mile long walk to town. Margo made a mental note of the few things she would select today. Max did all the shopping because he didn't trust her with his paycheck, she didn't buy enough beer and besides he earned it he would spend it.

Margo could hardly believe her ears when she approached the Public Assistance desk and heard herself say, "I would like to apply for food stamps." Margo heard her voice but couldn't lift her eyes to face the person before her, and this person taking the application had no doubt but what this thin, weary-faced woman and child needed a generous portion of food.

Triumphant with her success her steps quickened as she sought the supermarket. Once inside it was difficult not to explore all the aisles with the wonderful selection of groceries but she must hurry and her purchase must be small so she could conceal it from Max, besides she already had her arms full with a squirming child.

16

Bacon was first then perhaps a small piece of cheese, and a little macaroni, and a small box of cereal. "That will have to be enough for today and least conspicuous." Concluded the happy shopper...now to race home before Lorraine gets there – she mustn't know so there will not be a possibility of a little girl talking and innocently starting trouble.

The day was warm, the weight of the baby and the groceries, and the length of the hurried walk left Margo breathless when she reached home but she had won the race with the clock and Lorraine. Now to quickly put these things away.

When Max came home he was dreadfully upset and complaining loudly about his boss who expected a lot and pushed his employees to the limit. Margo listened warily and hoped that as Max settled down with the evening paper and a couple of beers he would feel less sullen. Lorraine was headed for the kitchen to talk to her mother when she tripped over Max's extended foot and went sprawling on her face at her Daddy's feet.
"You clumsy oaf," roared Max, "Couldn't you watch where you are
going?" And with a sudden rage he grabbed the helpless child and hurled her across the room.
Lorraine cried out with pain and fright.
Max yelled again, "Go to bed, I have had enough of you for tonight."
"But Daddy, I'm hungry."
"Tough!" countered the uncaring father.
Holding her hands to her bleeding mouth and weeping as she quickly left the room. Lorraine slipped off her ragged tennis shoes and crawled into her bed to sob herself to sleep...hungry, hurting and frightened.

Margo knew it was useless to challenge Max's unfair decision so she poured herself a glass of beer to help dull the guilt and pain, and hurried to finish the macaroni and cheese she had fixed for their supper.

Max looked pleased with the meal on his plate, and took several hearty bites, then he scowled with a hard glint in his eye and commented, "I haven't bought any cheese, where did you get this?"

Margo's heart sank as she lowered her eyes to her plate.

Max roared, "Where did you get this?"

But before Margo could answer Max was on his feet and heading for the bedroom to get Margo's purse. It didn't take him long to find the food stamps and come stomping back to the kitchen, tearing the stamps in shreds as he came.

"I'll teach you to beg," he ranted and struck Margo across the head knocking her from her chair, as she fell he kicked her and walked away.

As Max passed the refrigerator he took a bottle of beer and headed for his chair in front of the T.V. The macaroni and cheese on the table mocked Margo and in spite of her hunger she knew she couldn't swallow another bite tonight so she carefully saved all the uneaten food and put it safely in the refrig for the morrow – it might taste better at lunch. As she placed the leftovers in the refrig she too took out a beer it would help lull her conscience to sleep. Her confused, tormented thoughts were ricocheting off the wall of reason. She should be weeping for a child who went to bed without supper again but Margo was hardly aware of the turning of her attitudes from pity and concern to contempt. The contempt for her own weakness was being transfigured to her helpless child. Feeling guilt, resentment, and hostility was replacing all of her feelings and coldness was creeping into her broken heart...futile frustration because she shouldn't turn back and she was fearful of what lay ahead. A whirlpool was pulling her down.

Max sat in front of the TV but he neither saw nor heard the images before him.... his rage ran rampant within him, he finished two beers and went for more, the door of memory tried to swing open but he slammed it shut with a silent curse. His wife who would have comforted him was now alienated and crushed, his child who could have delighted him and been the sunshine of his life was terrified and untrusting. But he would show them he was man of his house. He was in control. He hated himself, "but he was in charge," he told himself.

Margo looked forward to payday two weeks away and the days seemed to drag by. Lorraine kept a safe distance from her Daddy, busying herself playing with her little brother, trying to comfort and quiet his crying. His big blue eyes matched hers and his delight at her attention was apparent to her. Often her thoughts strayed to little Clay and her little-girl heart was heavy and sad and troubled. Lorraine held the bottle for Randy, kneeling beside his crib and reaching through to hold the diluted dinner that just didn't satisfy.

Max drank ceaselessly, never noticing he had a dear little son who was smiling, cooing, and hungry for nourishment besides a bottle. Margo tried to keep out of the way and usually only spoke when spoken to.

Payday came, Max brought home his beer but no groceries.

"Max we only have one can of tomato soup and a few crackers for our supper, and there is only a half bottle of milk for the baby."

"Well, fill the bottle up with water, he won't know the difference. I'm going to watch the fights and I don't want anyone bothering me."...Max was content with his generous supply of beer.

Margo shared that supply with her family, giving Lorraine a cup full and sending her to bed, filling the baby's bottle, then drinking a golden glass of guilt...what was wrong? What had awakened her? Coming fully awake Margo flipped on the lamp and rushed to the crib. Randy wasn't breathing, he had spit up the milk and beer and choked. She snatched up her limp, lifeless baby and screamed, a scream that penetrated Max's drunken, sleepy stupor.

"Max do something! Max, do something!" shouted Margo as she stumbled to the living room.

Max grabbed Randy and shook him by his feet, whacked him on his back, shook him again, but no response.

"Take him to the hospital quick," pleaded Margo as she ran for the soiled blanket to wrap the blue baby in. The ferocious shake of the adult's hand on the wee infant's body was sufficient to break the fragile bone structure. Something inside Max's intoxicated brain registered an extremity violated. He knew all limits had been exceeded and he feared! Max wasn't angry at the beautiful child that was struggling for it's lost breath but he was angry and frustrated of his inability to control a situation.

The situation seemed to sober him enough that he was able to negotiate the car into the street and out to the highway to follow the blue signs to the hospital. Even in his drunken state he knew there was nothing anyone could do for the still child beside him on the seat but who would believe his story – Max knew a rare moment of fear. As he approached the Emergency entrance he noticed there wasn't a soul in sight in the parking area and none near the door, so he stopped the old car a little past the doorway, picked up the proof of his selfishness, quickly laid the bundle beside the door and drove away without looking back. Something in the back of Max's brain told him he was guilty of two counts of murder...George Maxwell Hamilton, a murderer.

When Max flung open the door of their awful little trailer Margo was huddled on the floor sobbing.

"My babies! My babies! My babies!"

Max grabbed her by the arm yanked her to her feet and growled, "Turn that off woman, and get your stuff packed, we are getting out of here."

Lorraine had been awakened by the loud voices and was calling "Mama! Mama!"

Margo was afraid that her call would upset Max. Margo went immediately to Lorraine assuring her everything was all right, she must have had a bad dream and helped her to the bathroom. While Lorraine was in the bathroom Margo poured another cup of beer for the awakened child and took it to her. She helped Lorraine pull on her clothes and shoes then laid her back on the bed and covered her up hoping she would fall back to sleep while Margo dazedly made preparation for flight by night.

Exhausted with grief, fear, and panic Margo dozed. When she awoke she was aware the car wasn't moving. A quick visual survey revealed they were in a rest area, she knew not where, she was cold, Max & Lorraine were asleep, and her arms were empty.

A headline on the front page of the Watsonville News caught the eye of the Foreman of Central California Growers and Packers Association. As he read, "Dead infant boy found at emergency room door. Cause of death choking. Further examination reveals extreme malnutrition." Troubled thoughts furrowed his brow – he felt sure he had heard that baby's fretful cry and looked into the eyes of the desperate mother.

"Did I contribute to this ghastly tragedy?" He asked himself, "All in the name of efficiency and high yield production. This borders on murder and starvation in this land of abundance," he mused.

The man put his paper down and went outside to search the sky and his soul and could not find a comfortable answer.

Lorraine stirred in the back seat of the car and whispered, "Mama I'm cold 'n hungry" "Where are we, Mama?" "Where is Randy, Mama?"

The child's little voice awakened Max who answered the last question with a snarl and ignored all the others, "He got sick and the hospital killed him," lied the calloused father. "Now shut up your stupid chattering."

Margo reached into a sack on the floor and brought out a box of Cheerios, and divided the scant portion between the three of them. Lorraine liked Cheerios but she found it difficult to put the little pieces of cereal into her mouth as she pondered her father's answer as to the whereabouts of Randy.

Klamath Falls was quiet and pretty but so dreadfully cold at night at the higher elevation. Sleeping in the car didn't afford much warmth or comfort. Two mornings Max took Margo and Lorraine to the City Park and left them while he went to the Employment Office or made the rounds of different garages and businesses looking for a job. For Margo solitude at the park would have been welcome and enjoyable if she could have blanked out the events of the past week. She didn't even have the vitality to exercise to keep warm. Lorraine found the slides, swings, and merry-go-round interesting for a period of time but hunger brought her back to her mother's side.

The first day Lorraine had pleaded, "Mama, I am so hungry," and the answer had been a swift, slap across the mouth. So now she sat dejectedly on the bench watching the ducks and pigeons searching out edibles and wished she was a duck too. Lorraine silently wondered if her dad would bring a bag of donuts again but it seemed like such a long day and it was painful to wait. Fortunately as the hours passed the sun warmed the two bits of discarded humanity and watching the children play seemed to occupy their attention and help pass the dragging hours. Lorraine longed for the companionship of the children but none came near, her shyness prevented her from seeking out their friendship. The hunger of body and soul was keen.

The third day it rained and Margo was able to persuade Max to let them off at the Shopping Plaza so they could wander through the stores and shops to keep dry.

"I will be in front of Safeway at 4:00 o'clock" assured Margo and Max had driven off without an acknowledgement of the promise. Mother and child wandered through Woolworth's and for Lorraine it was like a fairyland.

"Oh Mama, look at the teddy bears, and can I have a doll someday?"

Margo had no answer for the child who had never had a teddy bear nor a doll but something about that doll sent her thoughts back though her home and for a moment she thought she was standing in the sewing room talking to Hilda – "Oh Hilda, is that going to be a new dress for me?"

"Yes child, isn't this a pretty pink? Your mother got enough material so that both you and my little Heidi can have matching dresses."

"Oh Hilda when will they be finished?"

"Well, if you don't stand still so I can measure you, they will never be finished, but I think you girls should be able to wear your dresses to school Friday – we shall see."

Content with the answer Margo and Heidi skipped out to the back yard to swing and to dream. Margo

remembered coming home from school that Thursday
night and the two girls raced to the sewing room to see
if their dresses were finished. They burst into the room
clamoring in unison,

"Are the dresses read?"

Hilda looked up from her mending and frowned,
"Dresses ready? What dresses?" "Can't you young ones
see I am mending sheets?" "Dresses what are you
talking about?"

"Oh Hilda, you know," and the two girls turned and
raced up the back stairs to Margo's room. Their
squeals and giggles could be heard downstairs and
Hilda smiled. The pink dresses were spread out on the
bed and beside each dress was a doll with a matching
dress.

"Oh Heidi, let's go give your Mother a hug – aren't
they cute?" And the girls ran and gave Heidi's mother
a huge hug.

Margo was brought back to reality by Lorraine's
insistent tug on her sleeve.

"Can I have a doll someday?"

"Quit pulling on me, and where do you think I'm
going to get a doll?"

"Margo felt anger rise up inside her because she
couldn't share her memories and because she was sure
there would never be the joy of a doll in Lorraine's
life...There were two sets of grandparents who would
have lavished their only grandchild with many dolls if
they knew they had a grandchild and knew where she
was but they didn't know. Neither did Lorraine know
she had grandparents it just wasn't mentioned.

Margo's disappointment boiled over into a caustic
reminder, "Keep your hands off things and for
goodness sake watch where you are walking."

The sharpness of her voice caused customers and
clerks to turn to see the origin of such harshness.
Margo gave Lorraine a shove and told her to move

on…next was Penny's and Sears. The little girl's heart yearned for the frilly blues and pinks of the dresses and the shiny black shoes but she knew better than voice a desire. Margo too, noticed the lovely skirts, sweaters and warm coats and felt a faint longing then she noticed her reflection in a mirror and she felt sick and disgusted and turned away. Their tour even included a hardware store…and now Margo took a short cut down the alley. Suddenly a door was flung open and she saw one of the stock boys come out of the back door of Safeway and threw away a large basket of fruits and vegetables into the garbage bin in the back of the building, then she turned back and hurried to the least likely source of lunch. The bananas, apples, and tomatoes were a welcome sight – ripe and edible. Margo thrust a handful into Lorraine's hands and carried what she could in her own and the two sat on the steps in the rain and gorged themselves.

Margo spoke warningly to Lorraine, "Don't you dare say a word about this, do you hear?" "If you do your Dad will beat us and then I'll beat you again." – "Do you understand?"

Lorraine had her mouth so full of apple all she could do was look up fearfully but comprehendingly and nod her head. Margo was thinking, "What a pity all this food and I don't dare carry any away with me, but tomorrow I will search out this bountiful bin again."

Margo made certain she was in front of Safeway long before 4:00 o'clock so as not to rile her testy husband, and it was a good thing she was because Max made his appearance before 3:00 o'clock. As the two empty handed shoppers climbed into the car, the impatient driver hardly waited for the doors to slam close before he had the old Chevrolet in gear and onto the street. As he drove Max was saying, "I overheard some fellows at the service station say that Weyerhaeuser Mill in Grants Pass is hiring so we might as well move on right now. Max was definitely in a hurry and not all that accustomed to driving in the mountains. Lorraine sat on the edge of her seat wide eyed and petrified as the car sped down the steep passes, finally she laid down and covered her head so she couldn't see the dreadful depths – it wasn't long until she was fast asleep. Margo was ever so thankful for the free lunch complements of Safeway because there was no sign of donuts, or any other kind of food... whether Max had eaten them himself or had forgotten - she would never know. The scenery was impressive but heading west and facing a setting sun was difficult – Margo thought, "It's like my life, I can't see what is ahead."

At Grants Pass, Mr. Howorth was proud of his well-kept court. He and his wife were choosy about their tenants. He opened the office door in answer to Max's knock and invited the unkempt caller to step in. This landlord prided himself on being a fair judge of character and often let his intuition and first impression guide his decisions. He felt feelings of doubt flicker through his mind as he sized up this man standing before him, offering a small deposit on a rental and explaining, "I'll be getting a job at the mill tomorrow and I will pay the remainder of the rent on payday." Mr. Howorth knew this was a long shot but he had seen the faces of the mother and child in the car when he opened the door to Max. Something in his keen business mind told him this was a risky bargain but the child's eyes haunted him and his tender heart pleaded for him to take the chance.

Margo and Max had quarreled because he wanted to trade her engagement ring for rent. Grieving for her dead child, grieving because of the abuse, grieving because of the haunting hunger, grieving for the helplessness of it all, grieving for broken dreams and promises, and grieving for the futility of every breath!! Crawling into bed late for much needed sleep, they were crawling away from the hideous results of uncontrolled temper.

The noon whistle at the mill pierced the air and penetrated the black depths of Margo's despair, jolting her to the consciousness of her surroundings. She lifted her head from her arms on the steering wheel and blinked at the brightness of the late summer sun. Crimson vine maple leaves and bright blue sky beyond caught her attention, then her eyes searched for the bridge and the roily river. It would be fast – it would be easy, but I can't disappear without giving Mom and Dad an explanation. They must know what happened, they must know about my babies, they must know about Lorraine, they must know that I kept silent because I loved them, they must not go to their graves wondering.

What shall I say? How shall I say it? How do I admit my mistakes, and weakness, and defeat? I don't have the price of a postage stamp and Max would fly into a rage if he suspected I had written to anyone. He doesn't want to contact my folks, nor his folks, no one. He is afraid I would tell it as it is. "Just you remember woman, what I have done with my life is my own business." Ranted Max the last time Margo had written – how long ago she couldn't remember – he had grabbed the letter from her hand and lit a match to it. I should have written another while I had the price of a stamp. If I asked for fifteen cents he would want to know what for and if I try to sneak it from his coin purse while he sleeps he might hear me and beat me. If I wrote a letter and hid it no one would ever find it – who is there to care? If I jump – if I end it all who is there to tell Mums and Daddy?

"No one ever had dearer parents than I have. Gentle and soft spoken just like my Grandpa and so caring. Easy to talk to and understanding yet expectations were high. And so much fun! Being an only child could have been a lonely existence but Mums and Dad made sure we did everything together as a family. They shared my every school activity, taking time out from their busy day to be with me and they were so proud of my every achievement. After supper we always went to the library, Mom and Dad sat in their recliners on each side of the desk and read their mail and the paper and I sat in Bumpa's big swivel chair on cushions so I could reach the desk and did my homework and then I would slide down and go to the piano and practice my lesson. Sometimes Mama sat beside me and we played a piano duet and sometimes Daddy got out his violin and played along with me and sometimes we all played together. I would snuggle up and go to sleep while he finished reading the paper. Mums always smelled so good and hugged so tight and was the best pal any girl could ever have. Surprise picnics, horse races across the back meadow and we would laugh until we nearly tumbled off our horses, The World's Fair, Disneyland, a week on a houseboat... It was all so long ago – or was it? Why didn't I just call and let them take me home? Oh no, their hearts would have been broken with our situation - they would have been humiliated, shocked, devastated and ashamed. Besides the one thing they insisted on was that I finish what I began. I tried but I was defeated in trying. It is not dishonorable to admit defeat. Would I dishonor those who gave me life if I took my life? How will I get a stamp? Without a stamp I will have vanished from off the face of the earth. What will become of Lorraine?

Margo was so entangled in the web of her defeat she couldn't see the paths of escape. The agony stifled her ability to reason. The inner darkness blotted out the light of hope. To admit defeat I must swallow my pride. I was so foolish to think I could help Max overcome that devastating drinking problem. I had dreamed that he would someday finish his education and help me finish too. His love for me turned to possessiveness – I know any love he had for me and his family has been obliterated by his obsession to drink. He must hate himself. I hate him - the man I once loved so dearly I now hate. I hate myself. I hate what I let him do to me, to us. I hate what I do to Lorraine. I want to love but I can't – I transfer all my disappointment, disgust, and loathing to a helpless child – there is no love left. I hate what I have done to myself and what I have done to those two heartbroken parents. I hate to hate, and fear the hate, and Max. Hate is a terrible, wicked thing and I want to drown that hate – all of it! Fear and hate have me trapped and there is only one escape..."

Margo sat rehearsing this dilemma over and over in her mind but kept running into the same dead-end – her next move hinged on a stamp....A rumble interrupted Margo's thoughts and she looked up to see the big yellow bus approaching, it shifted down for the bridge and proceeded with care. Voices of exuberant children laughing and talking could be heard above the motor's drone. School was out for the lower grades and Lorraine would be home soon, maybe she was on that bus. It would never do for her to be locked out because Mr. and Mrs. Howorth would surly see and doubtless make their disapproval known to Max. Then what would he do to Lorraine? Margo put the key in the ignition, awakened the sleeping car, and sped across the beckoning bridge for home.

*****

The Letter

Margo sat at the bare kitchen table slowly sipping a cup of hot black coffee, staring out the window at the little smoke curls rising from the chimneys of the surrounding homes and aware of the fall chill that had crept into their trailer from the nearby mountains. She shivered, shifted her position and continued her solitaire suffering and struggle...not noticing the cloudless autumn sky, nor the hills covered with trees in splendid fall apparel, nor the birds grouping for the miracle of migration. All this was lost to the woman who had picked up a pencil stub and had begun to doodle on the back of a brown grocery bag.

Both the motion of hand and dither of pencil followed a similar pattern first the sip of hot coffee that warmed the body but failed to ease the cold ache in the pit of the stomach; then circular tracing of the inside of the cup handle with the scarred, yellow pencil remnant, followed by little, tight circles trailing from the blunt bit of pencil. Circles, vicious circles, black circles that were closing in on her, from which there was no escape – no way out. Margo's thoughts alternated their focus from the bridge to the security and warmth of the old comfortable library back in Louisiana. There was a deep sigh, then the pencil ceased its' aimless wandering, controlled by tensed fingers it took a definite direction.

"Dear Mums and Dad – I love you both so much but..."

The pencils message was interrupted by a knock at the back door. Startled Margo came back to reality – but while pondering her next moves there was another more insistent knock...Margo quickly turned the brown bag over, set the nearly empty coffee cup on top of the bag and went to the source of the knocking.

Opening the door she was surprised to see a short, chubby, blond woman, "Hi, I'm Tillie your neighbor – I was wondering if I could bother you to help me? Our dryer is on the blink, so I hung my washing on the clothesline, in fact I was just hanging the last load of towels when the line broke. My car won't start, everyone else seems to be gone, and I have to get these clothes dried while the sun is shining – you know how it is in this part of the country it could rain tomorrow. Do you suppose you could take me to the hardware store for more clothesline?"

"Sure," replied Margo and she quickly gathered up the brown bag and pencil and hid them in a dresser drawer, picked up her empty billfold and car keys and met Tillie out by the old red car.

When the two neighbors returned with the new clothesline wire Margo started removing the wet clothes from the sagging line while Tillie went to get a pair of pliers.

"I'm sure lucky this line is over clean grass," panted Tillie, "or I would have to rewash everything...some good luck and some flexible bad luck," concluded the practical blond.

Having more determination then strength or skill the two women strained and struggled to secure and stabilize the replacement wire. Tillie's generous heart offered the use of the repaired clothesline anytime Margo wanted to hang her laundry out in the fresh air then she excused herself stating she had to finish the laundry, scrub and wax the floors, and by that time the bread would be ready to bake, then the clothes should be dry.

"Well you know how it is, woman's work is never done. Thanks again for all your help, let me know if I can do something for you sometime." Tillie smiled and bounced inside and closed the door.

Margo's gloom seemed to rise from the grass and encompass her again – the brief respite only seemed to magnify her misery – how she wished she had some clothes to wash, or some wax to polish the floors with, or some flour to bake bread. Realizing she probably would never have these things again, she walked indoors with feet laden with desperation and despair.

After again turning on the burner under the cold coffee pot she took her writing material from its hiding place and began again.

"Dear Mums and Dad – I love you both so much. I know you are grieving and hurting, but if I went home you would hurt even more being disgraced, shamed, and shocked. I cannot do that to you. I resent and abuse my child that I should love. I lash out at her because of my helplessness. She needs medical attention – so when you receive this letter please come get her before Max does something hideous again. What I am going to do is not your fault. Please forgive me...Margo."

The letter was carefully torn from the bag – but without an envelope and stamp it wasn't going anyplace yet – it must be hidden safely but where? Margo knelt and pulled her suitcase from beneath the bed and opened it. She lifted out a small leather bound Bible that her dear Grandpa had given her long ago. Folding the little brown note she tucked it inside the cover of the treasured book then clasped the keepsake to her bosom, bowed her head and wept.

*****

The Class Room
Monday

Lorraine sat entranced as her class took turns reading the story of a beautiful, delicate moth. Some of the kids read well, others hesitated and tried to sound out the unfamiliar words but Mrs. Erickson was patient and helpful – stopping every so often to enquire the meaning of a word or phrase. Then it was Lorraine's turn. The room seemed suddenly awfully quiet and she felt all eyes looking at her.

"Go ahead, Lorraine, it's your turn," prompted Mrs. Erickson as she sensed Lorraine's hesitancy.

Slowly and quietly she began to read and to her delight she was able to pronounce the words of the short paragraph without any help. She felt the flush of accomplishment warm her face.

Next was social studies and a discussion about the chapter on Brazil which the class had read. Lorraine tried to absorb the answers given to the questions and felt very inadequate as she sat unable to respond to the questions. She was aware someone behind her was whispering about her but she tried not to be distracted.

Then it was recess time. Lorraine lingered behind the others to ask if she could stay in and read.

Mrs. Erickson smiled, and said, "You need to go on outside and get some fresh air and exercise."

Mrs. Erickson really wanted more time to evaluate her students.

Lorraine wandered outside and felt the warmth of the late summer sun but didn't experience the warmth of a welcome to join any of the games in progress. The merry-go-rounds were full and spinning, the swings were all in use, so she stood dejectedly and watched the activity from afar. Someone mentioned getting a drink, and it occurred to her that she too was thirsty. The

33

long, cool drink was comforting and satisfying – then the school bell ended the recess.

The third grade class was quiet and intent on their arithmetic assignment, especially the new child. She really felt over whelmed by the problems and Mrs. Erickson sensing the frustration walked back to Lorraine's desk and told her not to worry because she would help her later.

Then turning to the class she announced, "It's time to put your books in your desks, and line up to wash your hands, quickly and quietly please.
Only five minutes before the lunch bell rings."

Those were welcome words to Lorraine's ears and she soon found herself being propelled by a small tide of exuberant humanity towards the lunchroom. Timidly Lorraine looked around for a place to sit and saw Ruth beckoning her to come to a vacant table.

"How did it go this morning?" inquired Ruth.

"Okay," murmured Lorraine.

"Good, I am sure you will like Mrs. Erickson. Here is a carton of milk and an apple to go with your sandwich," offered Ruth secretly wondering what the sandwich consisted of.

"What is your name?" ventured Lorraine.

"Oh my dear, I'm sorry I didn't introduce myself, I am Miss Haynes, can you remember that?"

Lorraine nodded and ventured a wee smile.

"Enjoy your lunch and I will see you after school," were Ruth's parting words as she returned to her busy office.

Lorraine kept her eyes on her lunch, too shy to speak but hoping someone would come sit beside her, but the new child was ignored and left alone except for the stares of the curious. Lorraine thought about the milk and apple and wondered if she dared tell her mother about it. As she considered the consequences a lunch room monitor came by to remind all the stragglers they had to clear out of the lunch room to make room for the next class, so Lorraine meandered to the hallway and was leaning against the wall looking out the door when a teacher came by and told her all students had to go outside.

"No one is allowed in the hallways during recess, why don't you go play soccer with the boys?" urged the teacher.

"I'm a girl," quietly responded Lorraine, causing the teacher to look at this "rag-bag-moppet".

She stopped to watch a little knot of girls playing hopscotch when the apparent leader of the group sniffed and informed her, "We don't want any dirty boys playing with us."

"I'm a girl," retorted Lorraine.

But giggles was the only reply. Lorraine sought a secluded spot by the building where she could absorb the warmth of the bricks and watch the games she longed to join in.

Mrs. Erickson had decided to make arrangements for Lorraine to spend ten minutes of every recess to catch up on missed assignments, she would tell her little pupil in the morning, sensing the child's eagerness to learn.

The last bell of the day was ringing and Lorraine could hardly believe the day was over so fast. She followed the throng out to the side door where all the buses were lined up and sure enough there was Miss Haynes waiting for her. What a relief to hear Ruth tell the driver to stop at the Riverside Trailer Park...but what would Mama say about her riding the bus? Fear rode home with Lorraine.

Squealing brakes and the unique throb of the diesel engine announced the arrival of the familiar yellow school bus.

The chatter temporarily subsided as Mr. Adams turned partially in the driver's seat, cleared his throat and announced, "This bus will be here at 8:15 in the morning and remember this is a blind corner so for goodness sake stay back off the road so I don't have to practice my first aid skills. Okay kids, see you in the morning."

Four boys and two girls of varying ages and sizes rushed from the bus ahead of Lorraine with their hands full of books, papers, and jackets.

As the last little student lurched forward and hesitantly stepped from the bus, Mr. Adams called out, "Goodnight Sonny," and closed the door never hearing Lorraine indignantly mutter, "I'm a girl, I'm a girl."

She cautiously looked around and realized the bus stop was not visible from their mobile home – that was a relief. Lorraine had not seen her mother's car at the bridge. She didn't know Margo wasn't home. With doubtful steps and pounding heart she detoured around the end of the Manager's tool shed and discovered a pile of sand. A big blue dumpster shielded the sand pile from the rows of trailer houses but she could see the cars and trucks as they sped around the corner beyond the long row of mailboxes. The school bus had disappeared around the bend long before Margo's old car stopped beside their trailer. Not a person to be seen and with a slight twinge of conscience Margo visualized a little figure trudging beside the busy road.

Turning to the interesting pile of sand Lorraine picked up a short, fat stick and tested the sand... probing a neat hole into the damp mound...with every thrust of the stick she repeated, "I'm a girl, I'm a girl, I'm a girl." Having momentarily slacked her frustration her thoughts turned to weightier matters she had to face. "Will Mama whip me for riding the bus?" "Will Daddy kick me or send me to bed without my supper for eating the apple and drinking the milk Miss Haynes gave me?"

"Will they let me ride the bus in the morning or do I have to walk? … Maybe, I don't know the way, and I would have to cross the high bridge." Thoughts of that bridge made her suddenly aware of the fact she could hear the roar of the river across the road, it sounded scary and it made her shiver. With every worry and fear that materialized another hole was jabbed into the unresisting hill of hidden horror. The stick was poised for another worried attack on the pile of black sand when Lorraine heard and saw almost simultaneously the company bus as it rounded the corner. She knew her Dad would be getting off that bus and she hoped he hadn't seen her. Making a frantic dash for their trailer she darted around parked cars, garbage cans, and shrubs hoping to gain entrance to the front door undetected. Opening and closing of the front door was muffled by the blare of the TV while Margo fixed supper. Lorraine had just closed her bedroom door when she heard her Dad slam the back door. Weak with fright she flung herself across the bed and waited. As the pounding of her heart subsided her thoughts returned to school and the prospect of reading from that beautiful, new book and the promise from Mrs. Erickson to help with arithmetic. The thought of Mrs. Erickson's sweet voice and gentleness comforted the hiding child and she slept.

Lorraine's nap was ended by her father's angry voice. She was immediately awake and listening apprehensively to, "Don't you dare touch my beer woman, there is just barely enough to last until pay day on Friday and this is only Monday – if I catch you snitching I'll break your arm," Max roared, pounding the table with a clenched fist for emphasis. "And where is that kid? I'm ready to eat."

Lorraine moved as stealthily and silently as a shadow and slid into her chair as her Dad had finished filling his plate with wieners and sauerkraut. The child with smudged hands went unnoticed while Max savored the first bites of food on his plate.

When he finally noticed the little girl sitting quietly waiting to be served, he growled, "Well, where have you been?"

"I've been in my room," carefully answered Lorraine.

"What on earth were you doing in your room after school?" queried the ever-suspicious father.

"I was sleeping," apologized Lorraine.

"Sleeping? You got in trouble at school and was sent to your room right?" questioned the frowning father.

"Uh-Uh, I was just tired and fell asleep."

"I'm hungry, Mama," ventured Lorraine, stating a fact and wanting to end the suspicion-laden questioning.

Now Margo was convinced by Lorraine's weariness that she must have walked home but she decided not to ask or make comment lest it upset Max – however, she was briefly ill at ease with herself.

As soon as Lorraine finished the meager portion on her plate she slid from her chair and went outside to explore the immediate vicinity of her new home, then back to the therapeutic sand pile. Somewhere close by she could hear children playing – their laughter carried on the evening breeze – it sounded inviting but she feared rejection again so chose to remain in the company of the accepting mound of earth…until darkness prompted Margo to step to the door and shout for the lonely child to come in. As Lorraine passed her Mother's chair in front of the TV she paused, took a deep breath and hesitantly informed her that the bus came at 8:15 in the morning, but Margo did not acknowledge the child so she was unsure if she was heard or not but was afraid to repeat the information lest it bring reproach or worse, so she hastened to her room and it was but a brief interval before The Sandman and the sandy child held a rendezvous.

Tuesday

Max slammed the door shortly before 7:00 o'clock as he went to catch the company bus. Lorraine was instantly awake, even though she was very used to the habitual slamming of doors by her father. She lay still for just a moment listening then heard the company bus stop and then drive away. Being fearful that she would miss her bus and not sure just what time it was the eager student slid out of bed and pulled on the sad, sandy garments of yesterday then ventured to the kitchen. Surprisingly her Mother was making another bacon-grease sandwich for Lorraine's lunch and a bowl was placed on the table beside a box of cornflakes. Lorraine longed to share the little joys of yesterday with her mother but fear sealed her lips and she locked the little kindnesses safely in her heart with her dreams.

Lorraine was the first child to arrive at the bus stop but the last to board the bus because she refused to push and to be the first in line. As she walked down the aisle all eyes were on the unwashed, uncombed child and no one offered to make room for her. An empty space at the rear of the bus seemed to swallow the frail, bent child as she took refuge on the high brown seat. Eager anticipation was this little girl's companion as the bus closed the distance between home and school.

Lorraine stretched to lookout the window but was only able to see tree tops as the bus jostled along, stopping and starting to gather up clusters of students – all ages, all sizes, all dispositions. As the seats filled it was inevitable that someone would fill in the empty space and have to share Lorraine's seat...two little kindergarten girls tumbling, giggling and tee-heeing engrossed in their own private joke, really not aware of the third occupant. Lorraine wondered what was so funny but her anticipation of reaching school soon overrode her curiosity. In fact the deafening din of voices trying to out-shout any other wasn't able to reach Lorraine's imagination nor dull her dream of discovering the mystery and magic held between the lovely book covers in her desk.

The three mile ride ended with a squeal of brakes and the swoosh of the door opening for the boisterous departure of all this human exuberance. Lorraine lingered until last, clutching the well-worn bag and quietly following the thundering herd into the spacious hallway. Ruth was standing in the entryway watching for her little self-appointed charge and smiled a welcome that equaled the sun in warmth.

"Everything okay?" asked the adult.

The question was answered with a shy smile and a nod of the head.

"Great, see you in the lunch room at noon."

Ruth's brief greeting sent Lorraine's spirits soaring to heights she couldn't comprehend and caused her feet to try to skip with the oversized shoes.

The results were less then graceful and caught to secure and stabilize the attention of a group of older boys who loudly jeered, "Yeah look at the donkey dance," and fell in behind her, mimicking her every step changing the fleeting moment of joy to fear.

At the hallway corner where she attempted to turn to go to her room the boys gathered around and blocked the way.

"C'mon donkey dance, do a jig for us, ding-a-ling."

Every time Lorraine attempted to walk away they shoved her back into the center of the ring...

"Dance for us do-do," chanted the tormenters.... the sight of an approaching Hallway Monitor dispelled the taunting toughies freeing the frightened child who started to run to her room.

"No running in the hallways," warned the Monitor.

Lorraine walked with pounding heart wondering if she would ever reach the safety of Mrs. Erickson's presence.

"There you are my dear, I was waiting for you," welcomed Mrs. Erickson.

Lorraine only half smiled a little afraid that this friendly moment might be snatched from her.

Mrs. Erickson met her student at her desk and assured her there would be a few minutes to read. Glancing down at the sand grimed hands the patient teacher patted Lorraine on the shoulder and suggested that as soon as she had put her lunch in her desk she could wash her hands and then begin reading. Would the promised moment ever arrive? Lorraine sighed a deep sigh of satisfaction as she finally was seated beside her teacher with the book open in her hands. If the world would only stand still for a moment for this child...and so she began to read.

Recess time should have been a fun time – a time to laugh and play and enjoy the friendship of classmates but it was a miserable time of rejection and cruel taunts – of "stinky freak", followed by a sharp shove then aware they must not be heard by the Play Ground Monitor the kids began a whispered chant and marched around and around Lorraine, repeating "Stinky freak, stinky freak, stinky freak, stinky..." The ringing school bell rescued the child with the wounded heart, she was relieved to return to the classroom.

As promised Ruth met Lorraine in the lunch room, "How is everything going?"

Lorraine shrugged her shoulders unaccustomed to such care and concern.

"Do you like oatmeal cookies?"

"Uh-Huh."

"What kind of sandwich do you have today?"

"I dunno."

"Well, let's peak and see."

As Lorraine parted the slices of bread and revealed the unappetizing spread, Ruth managed a gracious, "Oh, bacon drippings, well that is different." "Now I must run along, I will watch for you when you leave tonight, until later Chickadee."

Ruth sought out Mrs. Erickson and together they plotted how they could arrange for Lorraine to see the school nurse the next week in spite of the Mother's protests.

Lorraine pleaded to remain in the last recess to study and was granted her wish, except Mrs. Erickson asked her to help carry some papers to the office going the long way around, a subtle way of adding some exercise to the day's curriculum.

All too soon the last bell of the day was ringing and Lorraine was again on her way out to the bus – Ruth was by the door and promised, "I'll see you in the morning," and wondered how any one of such miserable circumstances could smile so sweetly.

At home the sand pile was a silent, welcome companion, neither accepting nor rejecting but comforting in a passive way. Mrs. Erickson had crossed off Tuesday on the big calendar before they left school and Lorraine pondered what Wednesday would bring – one thing she knew for sure she would get to read again first thing in the morning and this brought a peaceful anticipation.

Wednesday

Wednesday dawned overcast and windy but Lorraine was again first to be at the bus stop, shivering and glad for the busses arrival knowing there was the world of wonderful books waiting for her at the end of the bumpy ride. Apprehensively she wished she didn't have to walk that long hallway to reach her room lest the rowdies of yesterday would mock her again but the thought of Ruth waiting for her helped allay her fears though not completely because her thoughts were playing a vicious game of tug-of-war between fear and joy. In her imagination she suddenly took hold of Ruth's hand and together they walked past fear.. why not? She would do it!

The abrupt jerk of the buses' brakes brought Lorraine back to the moment at hand. The brief reverie had given her strength to face that dreaded hallway regardless...Her eyes sought for Ruth and when their eyes met tears of relief welled up in the little girl's eyes giving the impression of large blue pools ready to run over. Silently Lorraine reached for Ruth's hand just as she had imagined and without a question Ruth clasped the child's frail, gritty hand in hers and together they silently walked the length of the hallway. She couldn't help wonder what had prompted this act of confidence and need but she felt it was better not to ask. At Mrs. Erickson's door Ruth gave the little hand an extra, warm squeeze and parted with, "I'll see you at noon Chickadee..." Lorraine returned the squeeze, the appreciation and trust in the tear brimmed eyes was ample expression of gratitude...what more could one want.

Mrs. Erickson was genuinely glad to see her "early bird" student and gave Lorraine a warm hug – noting the swimming eyes but deciding a question or comment might be embarrassing.

"Are you ready to read?"

"Yes."

"Good, you have time to go wash your cold hands with warm water and soap while I arrange the chairs."

Lorraine had just turned off the warm water and was reaching for a paper towel when the door of the restroom flew open and three older girls burst in complaining loudly about their teacher then they spied Lorraine drying her hands...

"Oh, here is that stinky freak."

"We don't want any boys in our restroom."

"You better get out before we call the Monitor."

"I'm a girl."

"No, you are a smelly, dirty freak."

As Lorraine tried to slip past the troublesome trio they started kicking her and shouted, "Get out trash."

The humiliated student was too ashamed to mention the encounter to Mrs. Erickson – anyway she was used to swallowing her hurts...

It was a joy to work with such an eager pupil but Mrs. Erickson pondered the discrepancy between mental acuity and appearance. She knew there were many outgrown garments in her children's closets that would surely fit this little ill clad body but how to circumvent the mother's fierce refusal for help? She must develop trust of child and then parent someway.

Lorraine was again reluctant to go out at recess time partly because of harassment and partly for eagerness to learn but Mrs. Erickson compromised by suggesting that Lorraine go get a drink of water and walk out to the swings and back...the child needed this exercise and a break from studying and Ruth needed an opportunity to trade sandwiches in the wrinkled brown bag – a bacon

44

grease sandwich for peanut butter on homemade whole wheat bread... a secret kindness.

Another lunchtime endured and the last recess survived. Lorraine was elated that Mrs. Erickson had suggested that she take two library books home with her reminding to wash and then asked if she could take a couple sheets of her writing tablet also and the wish was granted...Lorraine carefully folded the paper and slid it inside one of the books and then tucked a blue crayon in her jean pocket. Mrs. Erickson was already crossing off Wednesday on the calendar and the class day ended.

Lorraine went directly to her room when she reached home sitting on the floor beside her bed she hungrily read her books then took the crayon from her pocket and began to draw pictures on the tablet to portray the stories she had just read. Lorraine shivered as she sat engrossed with stories but content with her warm world of words.

A chair scraped across the floor, tipping over with a crash, followed by Max's angry voice. Lorraine couldn't hear what this outburst of temper was about but it sounded like the same fuss she heard last night before going to bed. Her Dad was mad because his beer supply was almost gone. This was only Wednesday and payday wasn't until Friday night. Lorraine heard, "And woman don't you dare drive the car, there is only enough gas to get down town to the station."

Lorraine turned her face to the wall and pretended to be asleep just in case the flames of fury spread from the kitchen – in fact she pulled the covers up over her head and waited, she knew she wasn't going to get up until her father left the house for work. Her thoughts turned to the pictures she had drawn the night before and she couldn't decide whether to give Ruth the drawing of the girl in the swing or the child on the trotting horse. Maybe she should let Mrs. Erickson and Ruth choose which one they wanted, but what if they both like the same one? She didn't want to hurt their feelings. "No I will decide, I will give Ruth the girl in the swing and Mrs. Erickson can have the child on the horse." Her decision was punctuated by the slamming of the back door. With relief she pushed the covers off her face and breathed in the cold air. She lay quiet until she heard the green jitney rumble away then she scrambled from bed and into the clothes she left on the floor, shivering the night before in the unheated house. There wasn't much light either – the sky was heavy with scudding clouds pushed by a brisk wind.

Thursday

When Lorraine went to the kitchen to eat her cold cereal she could hear her Mother in the bedroom blowing her nose, she would liked to have gone to offer comfort but feared the rejection she so often experienced instead she picked up her lunch sack and the two library books with the surprise drawings carefully folded and hidden in the biggest book and ran to the bus stop.

At school Lorraine felt shyness overwhelming her as she approached Ruth who was waiting at the usual doorway. Without a word Lorraine slipped the picture from the book and handed it to Ruth.
"Is this for me?"
"Uh-Huh."
"For me to keep?"
"Uh-Huh."
"Did you draw this all by yourself?"
"Uh-Huh."

"That is very well done – I am going to frame it and hang it in my office."

"O.K."

"Thank You, Chick-a-Dee."

The artist and secretary walked together to Mrs. Erickson's room, each engrossed in her own thoughts but glad for each other's company. Ruth aware of the coatless child and eager to switch lunches contemplated how she could further help and Lorraine was eager to present her labor of love to Mrs. Erickson, but Mrs. Erickson was talking to a mother of one of the students.

"Oh, oh, Mrs. Erickson is busy, you can just put your things on your desk and go play until the bell rings, see you at lunch time."

Lorraine put her lunch and books in her desk. And went out into the hallway to wait, but a Hallway Monitor shooed her outside with the reminder, "everyone outside until the bell rings."

"But I'm cold."

"Well, put your coat on dummy."

"I don't have one."

So the shivering child stood close to the building until the bell rang.

Lorraine didn't think recess time would ever come so she could present her teacher the special pictures with privacy...but the magic moment did arrive and she walked shyly up to Mrs. Erickson's desk and laid the picture at her elbow as Mrs. Erickson made a notation in her grade book. Mrs. Erickson caught the action out of the corner of her eye and looked over at the picture and then up into the face of the expectant child and then back at the picture.

"Sweetie, did you draw that picture yourself?"

"Yes, 'm"

"All by yourself?"

"Yes 'm"

"It is lovely."

"It's for you."

"Are you sure?"

"Yes 'm"

Mrs. Erickson reached her arm around the frail artist and squeezed her, adding a warm "Thank you, thank you I will matt this and put it on your class room bulletin board for everyone to see."

Turning to the child smiling with rare pleasure, "you have time to go to the restroom and wash your hands with warm water and walk down past the Nurses Station before we settle down to reading. Sorry our plans were upset a bit this morning, some interruptions just can't be helped." "Wash your hands good and take long steps. I will be finished here when you return."

The "lunch fairy" didn't even have time to switch sandwiches – because she had seen Lorraine in the hallway – she just switched sacks, sandwich and all and disappeared going directly to the Nurses office to make an appointment for Lorraine first thing the following week.

Lorraine had just passed the Nurses Offices and entered the long hallway when she met a fourth grade boy coming out of the Principals Office – daring and devilish he stuck out his foot and tripped her sending her sliding head long on the hard floor. The culprit opened the door to the basement and vanished from sight. That belly flop knocked the wind out of Lorraine and she lay stunned for a moment and before she caught her breath Ruth came around the corner and saw the prone figure of her little friend. Lorraine was picking herself up when Ruth reached for her.

"What happened?"

"Someone tripped me."

"Do you know who it was?"

"Uh-Uh."

"Was it a girl or a boy?"

"A boy."

"Where did he go?"

"I don't know."

"Are you hurt bad?"

"Uh-Uh."

"Let's go see the Nurse to be sure everything is okay."

"Oh no, Oh no, I'm not hurt and Mrs. Erickson is waiting for me."

"Are you sure?"

"Uh-Huh."

"Well I will walk back with you and you let me know if you see the person that tripped you."

Lorraine's hands and knees smarted from the fall but she never complained as she snuggled up on the chair with her book next to her caring teacher.

At the last recess Lorraine was just going out the side door for a quick run to the swings and back when the bully who had tripped her came along and began to taunt, "Tattle-tail, tattle-tail, if you tell again I'll push you into the swimming pool."

Lorraine was confident he meant what he said.

Friday

Friday dawned cloudy and blustery, and puddles of water were proof that there had been showers during the night. The feel of autumn hung like a promise in the air.

Lorraine heard familiar sounds from the kitchen confirming that her Dad was still eating breakfast – she could smell coffee and hear his spoon clanging against the cereal bowl. Sighing she turned over and reached under her pillow for the new library books she had brought home from school. Inside one was a story she had written about the puppy she dreamed of having someday... it was easy for this child to live in a world of daydreams and make believe. Besides the library books was a math workbook which Mrs. Erickson had let her bring home. Lorraine reached for the workbook to double check the problems she had done the night before – no effort was too great to obtain a gold star at the top of the page. In fact the need for that star was almost as great as the need for food at the moment.

Ironically the child had the protection of a large plastic bag furnished by Mrs. Erickson for her books but there was no protection for her frail body from the damp wind that hurried clouds across the sky and cleaned the ground of early fallen leaves. The shelter of the bus was welcome to the coatless child.

Ruth groaned audibly as she watched her little friend step from the bus wearing the same garments of the past week and with no protection, but the child's smile was warm though shy regardless of her discomfort. It was apparent this unfortunate being didn't measure her esteem nor joy by the same material yardstick that shallow thinkers employed. Lorraine had a source of deep strength that propelled her up and over adversity.

"I wrote a story for reading class today, would you like to read it?"
"I sure would, how would it be if I read it in Mrs. Erickson's room where it is more quiet?"
"Is it a true story?"
"No, it's a wish story."
"But wishes sometimes come true, don't they?"
"Maybe, I don't know."
Ruth leaned against the wall and read the neatly written wish story while Lorraine put her things in her desk and herself wished fervently she could make this sweet, simple wish come true!

"Honey girl that is a good story – a real good story. You wrote so neatly, and there weren't any misspelled words either. I bet you get a good grade on that paper."

"Good job, Sweetie. See you at the lunchtime."

Ruth threw a kiss and returned to her office wishing she could bathe and clothe this little wonder.

Lorraine took her math workbook to Mrs. Erickson first announcing that she had done the whole page.

"Did I do them right?"

"Well, let's see..."

And Mrs. Erickson with a red pencil went from row to row without pausing to make any marks – when she reached the last problem and still hadn't made a check mark Lorraine took a deep breath because she had been holding her breath while the pencil made its searching journey down the page. When the well-earned 100% was written in red at the top of the page she sighed and when the coveted gold star was placed beside the date, stars came to life in her blue eyes.

"I read both of my library books last night too."

"That is great. You may take two more books home tonight, and you may also take your Math workbook home again and you can do as many pages as you like because this book is for practice and make up credit, O.K.?"

"Okay."

"Now you just have time to go to the rest room to wash your hands before the bell rings."

When it was Lorraine's turn to read her story during reading class she fidgeted with shyness and could scarcely be heard and when Mrs. Erickson praised her effort the little author blushed with pride and embarrassment and hastened to her seat. She heard kids whispering about her after she sat down. Cruel judgment and cruel envy – she was already familiar with that aspect of life.

The lunchroom was alive with youthful chatter and laughter but the rejected child appreciatively ate her peanut butter sandwich alone as usual unaware of her benefactor.   Understandably lunch was her favorite meal of the day.

It was already nearly time for afternoon recess and Mrs. Erickson was reminding the class that after recess they would have their weekly art session – this sounded interesting and Lorraine looked forward to this special activity with eagerness.

Because the other third grade teacher had come to discuss a problem with Mrs. Erickson it was suggested that Lorraine go outside to the play shed for some exercise. The covered play area was a welcome cover from the shower but did not afford any warmth. Lorraine had reached the play shed before the Playground Monitor arrived. Some of the older girls were jumping rope when Lorraine happened in but they immediately stopped, gave her a sharp shove knocking her to the pavement then began lashing her with their jump ropes. All she could do was cover her face with her arms for protection from the stinging ropes.   The taunts of "stinky freak" sunk deeper then the flailing ropes.   The Playground Monitor was detained elsewhere and never did come and Lorraine was afraid to move for fear she would be shoved to the pavement again and they might slap her across the face with their ropes....
"If you tell on us we will get you good next week," warned the attackers, and unfortunately her clothing hid the red welts inflicted on legs, back, and arms. When the bell finally rang a little girl was left to limp alone back to her class.

Mrs. Erickson saw the red eyes and tear stained face and though she privately questioned Lorraine she could not get any answers. This distressed the caring teacher and she made a note to pursue this further on Monday. In the mean time all she could do was give the hurting child a squeeze and continue with a project of colored craft paper, leaf patterns, scissors and glue. Lorraine became engrossed in selecting a bouquet of various colors of paper and lovingly cut an assortment of leaves to be arranged as a bouquet on the sky blue background.

All too soon Mrs. Erickson was saying, "Time to put things away and clean up before the last bell rings."

Lorraine was so deeply engrossed in her artwork she had forgotten temporarily about the play shed episode and also had lost all track of time. Mrs. Erickson was already crossing off Friday on the calendar and hurrying the slow pokes to get their desks cleaned off. Lorraine hurried to the library table in the back of the room to select the books she would be taking home. Her eyes surveyed the rows of books for the thickest ones so she would have plenty of reading material – having made her choice she slipped the books and the Math workbook into the plastic bag just as the last bell sounded.

Lorraine waved to Ruth as she rushed through the side door and ran for the bus through the gently falling rain. When the bus reached the trailer court there was the usual farewell messengers of, "See you Monday," "Don't forget to bring your arrow heads."

Jostling and giggling one by one the students stepped from the bus lazing along in their warm coats, kicking rocks into the puddles, unmindful of the shower. Lorraine was the last off as usual and she made a beeline for the front door not relishing the cold shower that was quickly reaching her skin.

She went directly to her bedroom. Taking the books from their sheltered bag she laid them on the bed and leafed through the library books looking at the pictures, then she sat on the floor with her back against the bed and workbook and pencil in hand began to work the addition and subtraction problems.

The back door slammed announcing her Dad's arrival home.

"I'll go down and cash my check before supper."

Lorraine knew that meant a new supply of beer, and the door slammed shut as he went out. She heard the car start, then stop and the door slammed again with a terrible shaking bang.

"Woman have you been out with that car? It has a flat tire!"

"Do you want to eat before you fix the tire?" cautiously asked Margo avoiding answering the question.

"Nope, I'm going to fix it now before it gets dark."

Max went to the refrigerator and took the last bottle of beer opened it and gave the door a vicious slam as he stomped out. Lorraine was glad she was out of sight. She had scarcely turned back to her arithmetic problem when there was a knock at the back door. Now who could that be? They never had visitors. Then she heard her Mother open the back door.

"Hello, Mr. Howorth, won't you please step in?"

"Is Max here?"

"Oh yes, I will have Lorraine go get him, won't you please have a seat?"

"Aren't you folks a bit cool without any heat?"

"It is getting cold."

"Hey Lorraine, come here."

"Coming."

Lorraine left her workbook and pencil on the floor and went to answer her Mother's call.

"Go tell your Dad, Mr. Howorth is here to see him."

"O.K."

Lorraine went out past the storage shed to the carport where her Dad was changing the tire.

"Dad, Mom said to come, Mr. Howorth is here to see you."

"Well, tell her to go away!"

"But, Mr. Howorth is waiting."

"Get out of here you stupid brat," and Max followed that order by throwing the bottle of beer he had in his hand striking Lorraine in the forehead, and sent her sprawling with blood streaking down her face.

When Max realized he had thrown a bottle still half full of beer he was furious and roared as he lunged for the child, the bottle, and throwing the tire iron at Lorraine.

"I'll drown you in the river, just let me get my hands on you." Max tripped over the jack handle and fell head long with another threatening oath on his lips.

As Max crashed, Lorraine scrambled to her feet and started to run.

"So help me I'll throw you in the river."

Lorraine disappeared around the end of another trailer house, running as fast as her legs would carry her. She reached the country road, fear told her to keep running and don't look back.

*****

Wild Ride

Margo and Mr. Howorth heard the shouting accompanied by the sound of tools clattering on the concrete and immediately hurried out to the back steps to see what was happening. Max was just picking himself up from the concrete.... Explaining he had tripped over the car jack on his way in to see Mr. Howorth.

"Are you hurt?" inquired Mr. Howorth.

"Naw just skinned up my shins but nothing to bellyache about."

"Where did Lorraine go?" asked Margo.

"Doggone if I know, she took off like a scared rabbit when I tripped."

"Sorry about the flat, do you have everything you need to fix it?" inquired Mr. Howorth.

"I'll just put the spare on and fix the flat tomorrow, thanks."

"Well, I just stopped by to collect the rent since this is pay day."

"Yeah, I know. I was going to cash my check when I discovered the flat, as soon as I finish changing the tire I will go get some money and I will be right over."

Mr. Howorth noticed the smell of beer on Max's breath and the red bruise on Margo's face and wondered if somehow they were related, but left without making a comment or asking more questions. It was still drizzling a cold October rain and the house was too cool and damp for comfort. He wondered if he should have some Propane delivered...but it was too late for a delivery tonight. He turned with a friendly "See you later," and headed for his warm house.

Max picked up the lug wrench and finished removing the lug nuts, slipped the flat tire off, pulled the bald tire from the trunk and pulled the spare tire from the trunk and slipped it into place, tightened down the lug nuts, then finished the bottle of beer... the last bottle. He had to get more in a hurry.

Going into the house to wash his greasy hands he hollered at Margo, "Come on and go with me, we can have a quick one at the bar."

"Where is Lorraine?"

"How do I know?"

"She is probably off playing in a puddle someplace, she will come home when she gets ready."

"We won't be gone long, come on get a move on."

"Can't we eat first?"

"No, the old man is antsy about his rent I don't want him over here again checking up on me."

Margo reluctantly turned the heat off under the kettle and suggested they leave the lights on and the door unlocked so Lorraine could come in, knowing to refuse was only asking for more abuse. As Max started the engine, Margo looked in all directions hoping she would get a glimpse of Lorraine but when she didn't, she secretly hoped the little girl had come in the front door and was secluded in her bedroom. Gravel flew as Max spun the wheels and roared out the driveway, the thought of another beer changed this bedeviled human into a maniac. Reluctantly Max stopped at the service station to put gas in the nearly empty tank because he knew the station would be closed before he got back. It didn't take long to put in a little fuel in the thirsty tank.

Margo knew they could cash the paycheck at Safeway but it was smarter not to open her mouth lest she have another fist in her face. Max passed several taverns, driving to the outskirts on the far side of town where the cars in front didn't look much better than the one he was parking at the side of the tired looking building.

The smell of sweaty bodies, stale beer, and heavy tobacco smoke mingled with rancid grease from the grill was not the most welcome aroma, especially when she was so hungry. But it was warmer here than at their trailer.

Max cashed his check than ordered two tall draft beers, it wasn't food but it did help take the edge of her hunger pangs…Max gulped his mug of beer down with such haste Margo wondered how anyone could swallow that fast. Now he was ordering two more beers. By the time Margo had finished the second huge mug she forgot to worry about Lorraine.

When Max ordered the third round Margo protested, "but Max said you only live once and I am buying." Margo tried to calculate how many groceries she could buy with what they were drinking but her thought process didn't function all that well.

When Max ordered another refill Margo said, "No Max," and started to get off the stool.

"Where do you think you are going?"

"Home."

"Not without me, you aren't. Now get up here and sit down before I break your arm."

"We will go when I am ready, and I'm not ready…understand?" So another refill was finished and then another.

The bar tender finally told Max, "No more refills tonight buddy."

"What's the matter isn't my money any good?"

"Your money is fine but you have had enough - come again another day."

"What do you mean come again? You are throwing me out of your dump, and you say come again." "I'll never set foot in here again." "Come on let's get out of here, we and our money aren't welcome." Max swaggered with uncertain steps to the door.

Furious Max backed the car out of the parking spot and roared onto the street – it was raining harder now then when they arrived hours before, and it was completely dark – the shorter days and rain-laden skies gave a wintry appearance.

"Max we turned the wrong way."

"I'm driving this car, and I know where I'm going, so just shut up!"

With that emphatic comment Max tromped on the gas and roared down the old road still seething at the bar tender's refusal to serve him another drink. His wild driving had a sobering effect on Margo who sat wide eyed and petrified as they sped along this unfamiliar old highway. They should have been home by now but still Max persistently plowed thought the dark away from civilization. Margo saw a sign that convinced her they were headed south toward Medford or maybe Klamath Falls.

"Max, we are headed south, we are miles from Grants Pass."

"Woman, you just keep your fat mouth shut, I know what I'm doing and where I'm going, I don't need any of your stupid help."

And to prove his point Max pressed harder on the gas pedal just as they approached a curve.

Margo screamed, "NO MAX! MAX DON'T!!"

The old car could not make the corner at that high speed and slid on the rain slick pavement crashing into a huge maple tree. The noise of crashing metal and breaking glass was deafening but there was no one to hear. The steam from the ruptured radiator hissed with a final burst of energy then all was still.

*****

Runaway Girl

Lorraine's heart pounded so hard in her ears she couldn't hear her ill fitting shoes slapping against the black top as panic pursued without pity – she continued to run from the nightmare that began in the carport and could end in the cold, muddy river, but her pace didn't slacken. Nearly a mile from home the road divided, to the left she could see the tall smoke stacks of the mill opposite the river. Glancing to the right she chose the unpaved road leading away from the river and up a narrow valley nestled between tree covered hills.

Low clouds were swiftly drawing the curtains of the day as the rain continued its nightlong assignment. Lorraine had gone around a gentle bend and down a slight hill when suddenly she was aware of headlights coming toward her. They had just become visible over a distant hill and spelled terror…was her Dad looking for her? Were the police looking for her and going to take her back to her Dad? Stopping abruptly she slid in the loose gravel and was only momentarily aware of the sharp rocks cutting into her hands and knees, but this interruption of pain only added momentum to the fleeing body. Scrambling to her feet she made a frantic lunge for the far side of the ditch, she clawed the muddy bank with her hands and found marsh grass for a hand hold enabling her to crawl on hands and knees the length of her little body to a clump of bushes where she fell, almost afraid to breath as gravel from the passing car spayed her hiding place, the lights were so bright she could see all around, had they seen her?

The fugitive lay still, listening for the sound of the returning car and sobbed softly to herself, "Oh Mama, Daddy is going to throw me in the river, I'm so scared!" After the bright car lights had washed over her it seemed darker than before. Minutes passed and as

Lorraine waited, to her it seemed darker than before. Minutes passed and as Lorraine waited, her eyes began to adjust to the deep dusk. A wind stirred the bushes and Lorraine shivered as she got to her feet and carefully went back down the short embankment to the roadway.

The runaway girl's pace had slackened to a slower but determined trudge. Who considers a destination when fleeing danger? Fear and hunger were her only companions and she crested the hill where the car had so suddenly appeared earlier. From the viewpoint she could see a few distant lights scattered across the valley floor, she could not hear the roar of the river so it had to be a safer place to go. The little traveler would have been amazed had she known the nearest light was more than two and one – half miles away. Mud and water squished around her toes inside the sodden shoes bathing the ugly blisters as she started down the long, winding road with her eyes fastened on the welcome lights.

For some reason the distant glow caused Lorraine to think of Ruth and Mrs. Erickson – candles of hope in her dismal little world – she wished she knew where Ruth lived. But as her feet moved so did her mind and she remembered the events of the playground earlier that day and how terrible it hurt when the girls beat her with their jump ropes and how sick she felt in her heart that none wanted her around. And that big boy might throw her in the swimming pool like he threatened to do and she knew she didn't want to go back to school anymore.

The farther down the hill she went the harder it was to see the lights, she had been walking such a long time. Near the bottom of this long, winding hill were large groves of trees on both sides of the road right next to

Lorraine.   At the pastures edge an unseen old mare nickered a welcome.   A scream stuck in her throat as she bolted to escape.   Unknown to this city bred child the rancher's horses were standing in the shelter of the evergreen trees and one friendly mare was just acknowledging the presence of the visitor.

Running between the groves of trees was like running through a tunnel because there seemed to be a speck of light ahead.   As she cleared the stand of cedars her eyes once again found the beckoning lights of the nearest home but the lights were spinning around her.

Desperately she cried out, "Oh Mama, my head hurts so badly!"

Weakness, fear, and hunger tripped the lost child and she fainted.

*****

Unexpected Guest

Lady raised her head instantly attentive, expectant with one ear poised forward and the other turned back, then both ears bent forward, she turned her head from side to side listening beyond the music which softly filled the room. Maria was nearly at the end of her knitting row when Lady whined low and trotted to the front door.

"All right girl, I'll let you out just as soon as I finish this row."

Lady sat by the door waiting with her ears probing the beyond. Maria glanced at the grandfather clock in the corner – it was 20 minutes before nine – tomorrow was going to be another heavy day in surgery and she felt the urgent need for a good nights rest. Surgeries weren't usually scheduled for Saturdays but some things don't wait. All the while she was knitting her mind was in the hospital room with that miniature man and marveled at the amount of pain and fear such a little boy could endure...pain and fear that were mirrored in his big brown eyes, pain and fear that trembled on his lips, that registered in the stethoscope. This abused child struggling alone with the pain and fear of the present and fearing what every new footstep he heard would bring. Because fear can be deadly Maria had ordered special nurses to stay with this little tyke. As she had stood at his bedside tucking the teddy bear into his arms she hoped this little pillow pal would be as effective at removing psychological scars as surgery was at mending physical wounds. When she patted his hand goodnight she envisioned a future day in a courtroom before a judge on this tykes behalf.

The final strains of Rigoletto were playing, strange how she found solace in the hauntingly beautiful melody of this tragedy, then the record player clicked off. Just one more inch and she would lay her needles down – only the clicking of the needles and the ticking of the great clock could be heard – then Laddie's long, deep howl penetrated the serenity of the quiet house. Lady barked in answer. Maria threw her knitting on the end table as she dashed for the door. Lady rushed past as Maria flung the wide door open and flipped on the porch and yard lights. At the outer perimeter of light Laddie stood pleading in the rain beside a small, dark image.

Maria followed Lady to Laddie's side gathering up her pink velour robe with one hand as she ran in slippered feet. Quickly kneeling beside Laddie she was astounded to realize this little, limp, wet lump was a child.

"My word, way out here in the country and at this hour of the night."

Laddie whined and Maria praised him with a sincere "Good boy, Laddie, good dog!"

"Where did this wee person come from?" "What ever happened?" "Who is it?" "Where did you find this babe, Laddie?"

Maria was no stranger to the police bringing children to the hospital but this was something else, and she knew most of her questions would never have an answer. As she gently turned the child over, Lorraine moved and moaned. "It's all right little one everything is going to be all right, we will get you dried and warmed in a jiffy." Lorraine couldn't run, she couldn't even struggle but maybe she didn't really want to – the voice she heard was quiet and kind like Ruth's and Mrs. Erickson's, but she was still so afraid.

Maria gathered up the shivering, drenched child in her arms and carefully made her way back to the house with a wagging escort on each side. When she stepped under the porch lights she looked down into a little face covered with blood and mud and was distressed to see the deep, swollen gash in the forehead which was still oozing. A pair of blue eyes blinked weakly and fearfully as they met the caring eyes of Maria. Lorraine sensed there was warmth and shelter inside that big house, but who was in there and what was going to happen to her? Pushing the big door open with her arm Maria and the rescuers stepped inside.

It was warm and it smelled good but what was going to happen? Maria hurried down the hallway to the comfortable, warm kitchen and laid Lorraine on the braided rug by the heat register in case she fainted again, she wouldn't fall. Stepping to the cupboard she took down a sparkling glass turned to the refrigerator and took a pitcher of orange juice and poured a half glass of juice, then sitting on the rug beside the child she lifted her with her left arm and held the glass with her right hand while Lorraine sipped the refreshing drink. While Lorraine slowly drank the strength giving beverage Maria was assessing this smelly, shabby, and scantily clad child and wondered how one could walk in such miserable misfits...what kind of environment had produced this and why? The same time Maria was evaluating the little person in front of her, Lorraine's eyes searched the room over the top of the juice glass. That big knot in her stomach was still there but it wasn't choking her anymore.

"How do you feel now?"

"My head hurts!"

"I bet it does, that is a nasty gash!" Maria could see it went back into the hairline. "This orange juice should help you feel better, would you like some more?"

"Uh-Huh."

Lorraine sniffled and Maria handed her a tissue then refilled the glass which the thirsty child quickly emptied.

"I am Miss Maria, what is your name?"

"Lorraine."

"Lorraine who?"

"I dunno."

"Lorraine is a pretty name, I like that." "Maybe you can remember the rest of your name after awhile."

Lorraine didn't answer but she feared if she gave her full name it would be easier to send her back to her Dad. Maria wondered if this child had a mental block because of the wound or if it was a psychological block from fear. Well, a name at this point was immaterial.

"Can you remember, were you in a car wreck tonight?"

"Uh-Uh."

"How did you get hurt?"

Lorraine began to sob, Maria knelt on the rug in front of Lorraine and hugged her close.

"What happened, how did your head get hurt?"

Between sobs she managed to say, "Daddy hit me."

"With what?"

"A tool to fix tires."

Maria felt anger and disgust rise inside of her. "Was this at your home?"

"Don't let my Daddy get me, don't let him throw me in the river, please don't let him!"

Maria got the grisly picture and was instantly aware of this child's flight for safety, but from where and from who???

Holding the sob wracked child close, Maria assured her, "No one is going to get you, absolutely no one is going to hurt you here, I won't let anything happen to you." "Laddie and Lady won't let anyone hurt you either." At the mention of their names the two dogs wagged their tails in confirmation…

"Let's go take those wet clothes off and get warmed up in the shower and after that mud is washed off we can see to fix that nasty cut on your forehead."

Carrying Lorraine to the utility bathroom Maria stopped in front of the mirror.

"Lorraine, do you know that girl." "Let me take a picture so someday you will see what a mud-baby you were."

Maria knew such a picture would carry weight if charges were filed against a parent or if she asked for temporary custody.

"Don't you think a picture is a good idea?"

Lorraine gave no answer but offered no resistance. Stepping across the hallway Maria took her Polaroid from the closet then stood the mud-baby beside a chair for support and got a good front view then stepped to the side for a side view.

"There, in a few minutes you can see the pictures I took of you, now let's get you out of those cold, wet clothes." "Getting a closer look at Lorraine's forehead under the florescent lights Maria voiced an opinion that had formulated earlier. "Really I think we should take you to the Hospital Emergency Room to have your cut stitched and bandaged and have an anti-biotic so you don't get infection considering all the dirt that is in the wound."

Lorraine pushed away from Maria, screaming, "OH NO, hospitals kill you." The terrified child struggled to free herself from Maria's arms.

"Why do you say that Lorraine?"

"Because the hospitals killed my little brothers."

Maria was speechless with wrath and horror as the enormity of the lie focused in her mind's eye. Maria knew better than force this issue and terrorize this waif any further. "Lorraine we will stay right here, I think you and I can take care of this problem with a little help from Aunt Dagne and Uncle Rolf, O.K.?"

Lorraine didn't answer but she relaxed her rigid outstretched arms.

"Now out of those clothes and snuggle into this warm towel while I make a phone call."

"Are you going to call the police?" "Are you going to send me back to my Daddy?"

"No, No, No I am not going to call the police, and no one is going to send you back to your Dad, I am going to call Aunt Dagne and Uncle Rolf to come help us get your head fixed."

"Will it hurt me?"

Maria knelt in front of Lorraine and looked directly into her distrusting eyes, "Honey girl, your head is very sore and when we touch it to put the medicine and bandages on, it may hurt a little, but we will be very careful and no one is going to hurt you any more than we can possible help. The medicine may make the sore sting a little but that won't last very long and it is very important that we do put medicine on so you don't get a nasty infection, O.K.?"

"Uh-Huh."

"Let me help you get out of those horrid, soggy clothes, and wrapped in this towel." Miserable as those garments were Maria recognized that they were Lorraine's only security and she was very reluctant to let go. "There, now doesn't that feel much better?"

"Uh-Uh."

Maria hugged her and said, "You will feel better soon, and I will just lay these wet things on the washing machine, and I'll set your shoes on this plastic bag." Maria had never seen such oversized, ugly shoes on any little girl's feet before and hoped never to in the future. "Now do you want to sit on my lap while I call Aunt Dagne?"

"Uh-Huh."

Maria dialed the familiar number of her dear neighbors and suspected she might be waking them.

On the third ring Dagne answered. "Hello, Aunt Dagne this is Maria, I hope I didn't waken you."

"No."

"Good. I have a different kind of S.O.S. tonight. Can you and Uncle Rolf come right over? I have a little wounded, runaway that really should be in E.R. but under the circumstances I think we had better suture the wound here. I don't have anything here so please have Uncle Rolf bring his emergency kit and an antibiotic. I am in the utility bathroom. This babe is caked with blood and mud and I have to get down to child so we can see what we are doing. The lights are on so just let yourselves in the back hallway...see you in a minute Aunt Dagne, Goodbye."

Maria took a bottle of Tincture of Green soap from the cabinet over the sink then stepped to the shower to turn on the water.

"Are you going to burn me?"

"Goodness no Lorraine, I am not going to burn you and you may feel the water with your hand before you step into the shower to make sure it is the right temperature."

"Are you going to drown me?"

Again Maria was on her knees before this suspicious little victim, tipping her face until their eyes met, "Do you really think I am going to hurt you?"

"Uh-Huh."

"I'm not going to hurt you, I just have to get all this mud and dirt off of you so we can see to fix that cut so you won't have a bad scar or get infection."

Maria knew in her heart that someone somewhere had purposely hurt this innocent, helpless little bit of humanity, and her heart felt heavy.

"Lorraine, I want to be your friend, and I want you to be my friend."

"O.K. now tell me when the water is warm."

"Not warm enough," said Lorraine.

"Tell me when it is just right."

"There."

Maria's eye did not miss the welts on Lorraine's back and the heels – she washed ever so gently. But beyond the welts, bruises and blisters Maria was aware that this babe was not standing straight, was it the trauma of the injury and weariness or was this permanent posture?

Folding a wash cloth she handed it to Lorraine, "Here hold this tightly over your eyes while I wash your hair – let me know if I hurt you." As the color of the water changed so did the color of the child. Turning off the water Maria couldn't help exclaim, "You look so much better and I know you feel better, don't you?"

"Uh-Huh."

Taking some of the warm towels from the dryer Maria folded one and put it on the table and sat Lorraine on it, then handed one to Lorraine so she could dry her tummy, legs and feet while Maria dried her back. Maria had finished drying the little bent back and was wrapping the towel around the wet head when there was a tap on the door, a gentle "woof" from the hallway welcomed the summoned callers.

"Come in, come in", greeted Maria through the utility room door.

"Uncle Rolf, do make yourself at home in the kitchen for a few minutes and Aunt Dagne I need your help please."

As Aunt Dagne stepped into the warm, steamy room she closed the door behind her, exclaiming, "Well, it looks like you girls have been playing in the water."

Maria looked down at her stained and drenched robe, Lorraine's eyes met hers and Maria winked, a shadow of a smile played at the corners of Lorraine's mouth while Maria chuckled and Aunt Dagne added her hearty, musical laugh.

"Aunt Dagne, would you please go upstairs to my room and get a warm sweat shirt from the bottom drawer of my dresser and in the left corner there should be some little footies, then in the back closet is a short, white terry beach robe. Everything will be too big but they will be warm and take care of the present situation."

While Maria was waiting for the "make-do" wardrobe, she took a closer look at the gash on Lorraine's forehead – it was a least three inches long and was going to take a lot of stitches and it was deep. Aunt Dagne returned with an armful of things.

"Goodness Miss Maria all I found was a white sweat shirt, white sock, white robe, white everything – don't you have any clothes with color?"

"Oh, yes, down in the stack somewhere, but white is fine, it's clean and warm and that is all that is important now."

"Thank you my friend."

The sweat shirt came way below Lorraine's knees and before Maria turned the sleeves back Aunt Dagne waved Lorraine's arms making the long, empty sleeves dance, "I think we have a puddle puppet, or a diddly duck."

Lorraine chuckled out loud which was an unfamiliar sound to her ears.

"Are you warm now?" asked Maria as she pulled the cozy footies onto Lorraine's feet and wrapped the beach robe around her.

"Uh-Huh."

"How would it be if you sat on this chair while I pick up all these wet towels?"

"Uh-Huh."

Aunt Dagne was already busy wiping up the puddles around the shower.

"Uncle Rolf, I think we are ready for your help," called Maria as she placed warm, dry towels on the table.

"Well, look at Snow White," exclaimed Uncle Rolf as he entered the room.

"Uncle Rolf this is Lorraine," introduced Maria.

"That isn't Lorraine, that's Snow White, can you shake hands?" asked the gentle giant, as he extended his big hands and grasped the child's little hand between his. "Do you think you and I and this teddy bear can help Miss Maria fix your forehead?" he asked as he unwrapped a big beige and brown teddy from a towel and handed it to the amazed child. All Lorraine could do was gasp and nod her head in wonderment.

Uncle Rolf whistled when he saw Lorraine's forehead and commented, "That's an awfully big owie for such a little girl, do you want to hold a mirror and watch us?"

"Okay," "but, first we have to trim the hair away from the cut so you will have a little bald spot up there, shall we call you Baldy?" said Maria.

"Uh-Uh, call me Snow White"

"Well, where are all your Dwarfs?" said Uncle Rolf.

Lorraine shrugged hers shoulders for want of an answer.

She watched with fascination as the hair was trimmed back away from the wound, then when Maria was ready for the Novocain injections she explained, "I am going to put some medicine in the cut to help take the pain away."

"Snow White is brave, Miss Maria, she is going to squeeze the teddy bear close to her and hold my hands with her hands while we think of a good name for teddy." "Can you remember the names of the Seven Dwarfs and maybe one of those names would fit this bear?" "Help me to remember."

"Uh-Huh."

"Well, there was Doc, and Sleepy, and Grumpy, and Sneezy, and, and."

"And Happy, that's the name I want," said Lorraine.

"Great, now you have a Happy Bear."

Maria had finished the last injection and there wasn't a flinch or fuss – thank goodness she had a small, sharp needle. Not watching this part of the repair was helpful because just the sight of a needle is enough to make some children cry. Now came the suturing but

Maria's skilled hands and practiced eye met this challenge calmly.

Uncle Rolf sang the Seven Dwarfs song "*Hi Ho, Hi Ho and off to work we go.*" in his deep baritone voice, then he tried "Somewhere over a rainbow blue birds fly, birds fly over the rainbow, why then oh why can't I?"

"Because you don't have wings," piped up the little patient.

All the while Uncle Rolf and Aunt Dagne were standing by holding Lorraine's hands and encouraging her to lie very still.

"I am ready for bandages," announced Maria – "one for Lorraine and one for Happy Bear, they were wonderful little patients." "Aunt Dagne, I bet we could all eat, I think there is some chicken noodle soup in the pantry, and some fresh apple sauce in the refrig."

Lorraine's eyes opened wide with anticipation at the mention of food – it had been such a long time since lunch.

Uncle Rolf again handed Lorraine the mirror so she could see the bandage and she was pleased that Happy Bear also had a sympathetic bandage. With camera in hand Maria suggested, "I think we should take a picture of Snow White and Happy Bear with their bandages."

"Say, I think I would like to have my picture taken with them too," said Maria.

"All right, Maria smile," replied Uncle Rolf.

"Soups on," called Aunt Dagne.

"Coming."

"Aha, did you hear that? Soups on and it sure smells good enough to eat, what about you Snow White, are you as hungry as I am?" queried Uncle Rolf as he stood Lorraine on the floor.

"Uh-Huh."

"Well, bring that Happy Bear and let's go see what Aunt Dagne is up to." "C'mon Miss Maria," "Oh, yes

I'll be there just as soon as I let the dogs out for some fresh air."

Aunt Dagne was ladling steaming chicken noodle soup with whipped eggs added for additional nourishment into blue bowls when Lorraine slowly looked around the corner, "There you are beautiful, blue eyes, and we are using bowls to match your eyes."

A dish of applesauce was at each place, a plate of sliced, homemade bread, butter and a pitcher of cream were on the center of the small table.

"Miss Maria, what would you like to drink tonight?"

"I think I will have a glass of milk to help me sleep, please and Lorraine would you like to sit here next to me, Aunt Dagne to my right and Uncle Rolf across the table."

"Thank you, first let me get another chair for Happy Bear so Snow White won't have such a lap full, besides he might eat too much," chuckled Uncle Rolf.

Lorraine pulled the extra chair close and was pleased to have her bear friend seated next to her.

"There now, I have quite a family around my table tonight – Uncle Rolf will you please say the blessing."

Lorraine watched as the adults bowed their heads and she did likewise.

"Gracious Father, accept our gratitude for thy provision and for blessings that we don't even recognize. Amen"

"Blue eyes, let Aunt Dagne tuck this napkin under your chin tonight and goodness, I think you need a couple of catalogs to sit on so you can reach the table."

Lorraine had already tasted her soup and welcomed anything that would speed the filling of that painfully empty stomach. Nothing had ever tasted better to the gaunt child.

"Lorraine, I know your head is still hurting real bad so I want you to take this medicine to help take the pain away, and it is best if you take it now before you eat your applesauce and bread and butter, it will also help you sleep better too."

"Where am I going to sleep?"

"Upstairs in the guest room."

"Will my Daddy come and get me?"

"No Lorraine, your Daddy doesn't know where you are, anyway the house will be locked so NO ONE can get in."

"He might see me in the window."

"No, little one, the shades are pulled, and the drapes are closed so no one, absolutely no one can see into the house."

"Are you going to take me to the police?"

"No my dear, I would like to have you stay right here, is that Okay?"

"Uh-Huh."

"Is Aunt Dagne and Uncle Rolf going to stay too?"

"No, they will go home tonight and Aunt Dagne will come back tomorrow, but how will it be if Laddie and Lady sleep on the rug next to your bed tonight?"

"Okay."

"Can you swallow this pill for me?"

"I dunno."

"Have you ever swallowed a pill before?"

"Uh-Uh."

"In that case we will take a spoonful of applesauce, hide the pill in it and then pop it into your mouth and just like that the pill goes down. Ready?" A slight nod of the head gave consent, and she swallowed. "Well, what do you think about that Mr. Happy Bear?" "Lorraine swallowed her first pill tonight – no fuss, no muss. Now she will feel better."

Aunt Dagne and Rolf exchanged distressed glances over Lorraine's head, pondering the cause of this child's wild, frantic fear. As everyone ate their apple sauce, Maria filled Aunt Dagne in on the unexpected schedule for the morrow and how the unusual events of the evening that necessitated Maria's relying on Aunt Dagne.

"Don't your worry, Miss Maria, I will be here bright and early in the morning – in fact Uncle Rolf and I will have breakfast with beautiful blue eyes. Uncle Rolf has some errands to tend to in the morning but he doesn't need me. Now let's tidy up the kitchen before we leave. You must get some rest." "If you don't mind Uncle Rolf I might add an errand to your list for tomorrow." "Miss Maria you just give me your list in the morning and I will gladly take care of it for you.

Lorraine listened to this exchange of conversation and understood that Maria had to go to work and that Aunt Dagne would be coming and she felt comfortable with the plans the adults were making involving her.

Maria was already putting food away and Aunt Dagne was rinsing the dishes and putting them in the dishwasher, and Uncle Rolf carried the extra chair back to the utility room, when he returned he announced "I think it is time for you girls to go to bed, Snow White can you tell me goodnight so I can go home?"

"Uh-Uh," was Lorraine's quiet reply.

He held out his hands to bid Lorraine goodbye – he would liked to have gathered this unloved child in his arms and given her a big grandpa hug but he feared it may frighten her more so he just held her hands and grabbed her shoulder and gave the Happy Bear a pat on his head, with an admonition, "Don't you snore tonight and keep Snow White awake."

"Are you ready Aunt Dagne?"

"Just as soon as I give this blue eyed babe a goodnight love" "See you in the morning Flicka."

"What's Flicka?"

"That's little girl in Swedish." "And shall we have Swedish pancakes for breakfast?"

A nod of a little strawberry blond head was sufficient reply.

Uncle Rolf was already going down the hallway singing, *"Hi Ho, Hi Ho It's off to bed we go."* Lorraine held Aunt Dagne's hand as she and Maria followed Uncle Rolf and Aunt Dagne to the door.

"Thank you for everything!"

"Thank you for letting us help."

Laddie and Lady were lying on the back porch and as Uncle Rolf walked by patted Laddie on the head with "You're a good dog Laddie, you learned your lessons well."

"Good night everybody"

"Good night."

As Maria turned to go back in the house she called the dogs to her,

"How would you two like to keep Lorraine company tonight?" "I think Lorraine would like that, wouldn't you?"

"Uh-Huh."

"Lorraine, I am locking this door, it has two locks on it, and see I can't open it, it is locked tight." "And all the shades are pulled...now let's go double check the front door. Yes, it's locked tight and there is no way I can open it until I unlock it." Maria took Lorraine from room to room assuring her that all the drapes and shades were closed."

"Now, let's go find a soft pillow to put our heads on and together the two went up the wide stairway followed by faithful guards.

Lorraine's fears and doubts were mingled with curiosity as she climbed the wide, carpeted stairs. She had never been in a house with an upstairs and she was not at all sure what to expect.

"How come you sleep up here?"

"Because all the bedrooms are up here."

"Why are they up here?"

"Because there is a beautiful view of the mountains from up here. The judge that had this old house built wanted to see the sunrise over the eastern mountains in the morning and the sunset over the western mountains and valleys in the evening. And I like to see the moon rise over the mountains on a sparkly, clear night. I will show you tomorrow how gorgeous the view is from here."

A soft, pink light at the top of the stairs cast quiet, sleepy shadows inviting the weariest of mortals. In one hand Lorraine clutched Happy Bear and with the other she held Maria's caring hand ever so tightly – and her feet almost resisted the next step. When they reached the landing at the top Maria had Lorraine turn around at the balcony railing and showed her where she had just come from helping her acquaint herself with the new surroundings.

Maria switched on a brighter light so Lorraine could see the long, wide hallway, then she reached inside the first door and turned on the bedroom light.

"This is the green room, in the day time you can see the meadow from here, I'll close the drapes."

Maria turned out the light and stepped across the hallway and turned on another light, "This is the for-get-me not room, in the daytime you can see Aunt Dagne's house from here, and we can close these drapes too." Next is a bathroom and we will leave a light on in here so you can see where you are going. Maria went to the next room and turned on the light, this is the pink room and here is an aquarium of little fish," Maria stepped over and closed another set of drapes. When Maria turned on the light of the yellow daisy room Lorraine let loose of Maria's hand and put her little hand to her mouth with an "OOOOOOOH!" of wonder, because there were dolls everywhere! Clown dolls, Raggedy Ann and Andy dolls, Strawberry

Shortcake Dolls, Blueberry Muffin Dolls – beautiful, loveable, huggable dolls on chairs, on the davenport, sitting on the floor, dolls everywhere. Maria closed yet another set of drapes. She left the light on while they went to the end of the hallway. Maria turned on the last set of lights, revealing a lavish, large room. "This lavender room is mine and I will show you the mountains from here tomorrow, now how would you like to choose a doll to take to bed with you and Happy Bear?"

Lorraine's eyes were like blue saucers as she looked up into Maria's face in silent wonder, then those astonished eyes surveyed the room and came to rest on Strawberry Shortcake baby with lace, ruffles, bonnet and hope.

Maria wondered which one would appeal to her little guest... "Which one do you want, Lorraine?"

Lorraine could only point, almost afraid this vision would vanish as quickly as it had come.

"Go ahead and pick her up, she is yours."

"To keep?"

"Oh yes, my dear, to keep."

Lorraine brought Happy Bear and the new Strawberry Shortcake doll up to her face in a little girl embrace. The sudden joyful fulfillment of desires and dreams of such possessions of her own filled her being 'til there was no other way to express her emotions. Lorraine looked up into Maria's face with wide eyes filled with wonder and awe. Lorraine wanted to say "thank you" but the words wouldn't come.

Maria saw the pale lips quiver, a mute mouth open and close, and the self-conscious swallow, and understood the struggle, so she just knelt close to the over-whelmed child and whispered, "It's all right, I understand, the words are stuck down here," pointing to her heart, "they will come out another time, these little friends are going to like sleeping on your pillow".

"How would you like sleeping in the pink room next to mine?"

Lorraine could only nod.

"Those fish are quiet fellows, they don't say much." Maria was glad the aquarium was here as it would give Lorraine something to concentrate on besides her fear, the light was soft but would illuminate the surroundings. As Maria turned down the comforters she reassuringly explained, "I will leave your door open, and my door will be open, there will be night lights in the hallway and in the bathroom, and if you need me just call, I will hear you. How would you like to use this little padded stool to make it easier getting in and out of bed? You can slip off that robe and lay it on this chair, now let's try the stool and see how it works."

With one big push Lorraine climbed into bed and settled her head on the soft pillow with a new soft friend in each arm.

Maria snuggled the blankets up around the child and her sleeping companions then, bent to kiss a cheek that had rarely been kissed.

"Good night sweetheart, I'll see you in the morning before I leave for work. Lady and Laddie are going to lie here by the door and keep you company tonight."

Lorraine sighed and turned a head full of ringlets, the bed was so soft and the fragrance of lavender scented linens pleased her senses so much she breathed deep several times to inhale the sweet, foreign aroma and in so doing her tense little body relaxed and invited sleep. The medication had subdued the pain so she at last knew comfort and rested.

Maria glanced at herself in the mirror as she hurried past and groaned inwardly – she had already showered earlier but she was certainly in need of another. As she slipped off her robe and surveyed the blood and mud stains she wondered if there was any hope for the garment but she wouldn't think about that tonight. The little face on the pillow in the pink room haunted her. That beautiful babe, beaten and banished. What had twisted the mind of a human being to torture this treasure of a tot?

Maria was weary and anxious for needed rest but sleep shunned her. A question had formed in the back of her thoughts earlier, now it was crowding all else from her mind, where had she seen that child before?

*****

Swedish Pancakes

Awakening automatically Saturday morning, as was quite usual, Maria noticed it was seven minutes before five as she turned off the alarm. Hastily switching on the bed lamp she reached for the note pad and pencil, which were beside the phone on the nightstand. It had long been her custom to immediately jot down errands and reminders thus freeing her mind of all little encumbrances so she could focus instantly and clearly on other matters. Heading the list was the notation,

"Have Dagne call Penney's."

"Call Chief Bennett and Judge Spencer."

She tore off the top sheet and laid it on her purse. Having showered and dressed quickly she hurried down the hallway. Pausing at the doorway to Lorraine's room she could hear the child's soft, regular breathing, whispering to the dogs she motioned for them to follow and led them downstairs, opening the back door for them to go out.

Maria had just filled the coffee maker when she heard Rolf and Dagne's car in the driveway and turned on the porch light.

As she set four juice glasses on the table she heard a soft tap on the back door and responded with, "Come, come."

"Gutten Morgin fair lady," called Rolf as he held the door open for Dagne who had her hands full.

"Good Morning to you both, how did you fare with such a short night?"

"Oh, not bad, not bad at all, remember we are hardy Scandinavians, but what about you?"

"Sleep was scant, but I am doing surprisingly well, the adrenalin must still be pumping. I will spend ten minutes on the trampoline in therapy and twenty minutes in the pool and that should really clear all cobwebs from the corners, then a good breakfast to fuel this Frenchman. That will give me ample time to review my patient's chart and the procedures before the scheduled eight o'clock surgery. I wanted a minute to talk with you before I call Lorraine. Will you be able to bend your schedule next week to stay with Lorraine until she is well enough to return to school? If returning to school doesn't pose a safety problem, that is. I am going to seek custody of this tot."

"It would be a pleasure to get acquainted with that little dear, and when she does return to school she could get off the bus at our house and stay until you get home."

"Rolf could you endure three errands?"

"Of course my dear, we are in this thing together, just tell me what you want done."

"Wonderful, Aunt Dagne, as soon as breakfast is over would you please do me the favor of making a list of all the clothing this child will need for the present, then call Terry Moore the Manager of Customer Service at Penney's and have her fill the order so Rolf can pick it up later. I will give him a blank check. I know Lorraine will be too fearful to go to a store for awhile." "And perhaps a call to the library would be a good idea too, have our friend Miriam select some books and records, here is my library card Rolf, and the third request is a stop at the Variety Store next to Penney's for some coloring books, crayons and a doodle tablet? Can you think of anything else we could get to keep a little girl happy and contented this weekend? And is there anything else we should discuss before I waken our mystery girl? It is awfully early but I feel it is important that she is awake before I leave and I want to check that wound."

"Now Maria, don't you fret, this Grandma can think of lots of busy things to keep little people happy, go waken our girl so we can see how her head is doing and she can have juice with you before you go."

Dagne started taking the ingredients for her Swedish Pancakes from the cupboard as Maria went down the hallway. On her way through the living room Maria turned on the stereo and sounds of music drifted through the house. As she stepped through the doorway of the pink bedroom Maria spoke softly to the sleeping child hoping not to startle her as she awakened.

"Good morning Lorraine, can you open your eyes?" Maria rubbed the little hands as she continued to talk, "Is that Happy Bear still asleep too? Come on little sleepy heads." Maria turned on the small bedside lamp as Lorraine opened her eyes in momentary bewilderment, "You better tell Happy Bear it is time to get up."

At the mention of Happy Bear Lorraine turned her head so she could see her pillow pal, then reached out to touch it to make sure it was real and not a dream.

"Let's put on this robe and footies. How does your head feel?"

"It hurts."

"You will have more medicine with your breakfast which will make that hurting head feel better. First let's go to the bathroom and wash your face and hands then we will go see Aunt Dagne and Uncle Rolf and find out how breakfast is progressing."

"Will my Daddy come get me?"

"No, your Daddy doesn't know you are here, and we are not going to tell him."

Taking Lorraine's hand in hers Maria and child went down the stairs.

"Where's Laddie and Lady?"

"They went outside for some fresh air and exercise, you will see them in a little bit. Both of them stayed by your door all night like I told them to."

"Well, good morning Snow White," greeted Uncle Rolf as the two entered the kitchen.

"Good morning little Flicka," said Aunt Dagne. "Now I better pour some orange juice so Miss Maria can go to work."

Maria picked up Lorraine and Happy Bear, and snuggled both on her lap. Her sensitive fingers felt the patient's cheeks and forehead and could not detect a fever, and she was satisfied with the appearance of the wound, noting there did not seem to be an excess of swelling. The bandage was dry and that was great. Reaching for her orange juice she took a sip then turned her attention back to Lorraine.

"Do you think you can help Aunt Dagne take care of the house today?"

Lorraine's "Uh-Huh" was followed by an expectant, comfortable glance at Aunt Dagne.

"Fantastic! You and Aunt Dagne are in charge of the house while I go to work, and Uncle Rolf takes care of his errands. I am not sure what time I will be back, so please don't plan lunch for me but I do know I will be home in time for supper."

Maria gave Lorraine a warm squeeze and kissed her forehead. Lorraine could not remember ever having a hug and kiss and found the warm embrace very pleasing.

"See you all later," called Maria as she hurried out to the garage.

"Good bye Maria, hope you have a successful day. Lorraine and I will wave to you from the dining room window."

"Remember, you gave me a blank check, you might come home a pauper," joshed Uncle Rolf.

"I'm not much worried," and the back door closed.

Lorraine and Aunt Dagne waved to Maria as she drove past the house, then Aunt Dagne suggested, "Uncle Rolf will you please help Lorraine get her hands washed while I finish setting the table, the first batch of pancakes will be ready to eat before you can get back to your chairs."

"Oh, I don't know about that," challenged Uncle Rolf, "We can splash pretty fast. So they raced Aunt Dagne. Lorraine wasn't used to this kind of loving fun and camaraderie and hardly knew how to respond but the happiness and laughter were so contagious she found herself smiling shyly and enjoying the game. "We won, we won," announced Uncle Rolf as he and his racing partner scurried back to take their places at the table.

"You sure did, and the winners get the first pancakes. What would you like on your pancakes, Flicka, applesauce, blueberry jam, honey, or maple syrup?"

"I dunno, what do pancakes taste like?"

"Is this the first time you have ever eaten pancakes?"

"Uh-Huh."

"Well, in that case," said Uncle Rolf, "Let's start out with just butter on the first half so you can get a good taste of Aunt Dagne's special pancakes - she makes the best pancakes in the whole, wide world, the very best. Here let's cut this first one in half, then we will put a thin slice of butter in the middle and you can spread it around with your knife until it's melted all over, then you cut a piece and pop it in your mouth. There, do you like that?"

"Uh-Huh," and the pancake disappeared.

"I knew it, that half of pancake melted - it's gone. What you do you want on the other half?"

"Butter."

"O.K. More butter," and that half pancake disappeared too.

"What shall we try on the next one?"

"Blueberry jam."

"That's a good choice - Aunt Dagne made that jam from the blue berries in our garden."

That pancake disappeared also. Aunt Dagne put the third hot pancake on Lorraine's plate, delighted to see an appetite. It was a pleasure to see this child eat so eagerly.

"Well Snow White, how about some of this luscious applesauce topped with whipped cream?"

"Uh-Huh."

"I picked these apples from the orchard and Aunt Dagne made this delicious chunky applesauce, I think I will have some too."

"Would you like some more milk Flicka?"

"Uh-Uh, I'm full."

"Good, we don't want anyone leaving the table hungry." "Well Snow White, do you think you like pancakes?"

"Uh-Huh."

"Wouldn't you say Aunt Dagne is the best cook in the whole, wide world?

"Uh-Huh."

"Thank you, thank you, you know flattery really keeps the cook cooking."

"Uncle Rolf, while I clear the table and put the dishes in the dish washer would you do me a favor?"

"Sure thing, what do you have in mind?"

"Take Lorraine to the utility room and weigh her, get her height, and trace an outline of her feet on a piece of paper."

"Is that all?"

"Yes, and I am guessing she is only 51 pounds," remarked Dagne.

"O.K. Snow White let's go see how much you weigh, how tall you are, and how big your feet are."

As Maria drove by the lighted dining room window she waved and beeped the horn a quick three toots, she wasn't sure if Lorraine could see her wave but she knew she could hear the farewell. The car lights beamed on a gravel road in Oregon but her thoughts focused on the beautiful campus at the University of Louisiana. As the car's headlights searched out the familiar driveway Maria contemplated how that child had been able to find her way the night before. And as her mind searched the past she couldn't ignore that feeling that she knew this little one from somewhere, this beautiful elfin tot that she felt so comfortable with. Maria hardly dared contemplate the possibility of gaining permanent custody of Lorraine. Her dream of having a child of her own had died when that Air Force plane had been shot out of the sky over the jungles of Korea. Her dead dream had been replaced by a driving dedication to the countless unfortunate youngsters who suffer from every imaginable misfortune.

As the car wheels turned forward, crushing the gravel beneath, Maria's thoughts turned backward crushing her heart again - she seldom traveled this painful past because it left her spent and empty but when she did she tried to gather the happy moments and run back to the present salving the wounds with work. She remembered pushing the lab door open, her arms full of books, a little out of breath because it was so far from her last class across campus. As she glanced frantically for a seat before the professor started the evaluation of the last lab procedure (he was such a bear about late arrivals) someone was taking the load of books from her arms and leading her back to a seat. She managed a smile and a whispered, "Thank You," just as the professor cleared his throat and began. This courtesy was repeated for several weeks before there was even an exchange of names; such a quiet, reserved, courteous gentleman, and maybe a bit shy? But then so was she. The friendship grew slowly, sweetly and serenely - both were dedicated to their studies and a vision.

Warren was specializing in Neuro-surgery and Maria was specializing in Orthopedic Surgery. They talked and planned and dreamed of marriage, a home, a family after graduation — but after graduation the Korean War erupted and Warren was drafted. There had been the letters - few but precious because the demands on the skilled surgeon were strenuous.

Maria was thrilled to be offered a position on the staff of the Children's Hospital in Boston and welcomed the opportunity to apply her skills and knowledge - the heavy schedule helped Maria fill the long lonely days and she always wrote a letter every day regardless how late or how tired. Then there was the opportunity for additional training and a job at Children's Hospital in Denver. This was a real honor to be accepted and a definite challenge. She loved her work and the satisfying results of a job well done. Denver was a beautiful city — Colorado was a beautiful state, perhaps this would be a good place to settle. Warren wouldn't have any problem establishing a practice, so she would work and wait and dream. Then the telegram came and Maria's world turned dark and cold. She did not want to accept the message - this was a nightmare from...
Which she would awaken from to find everything was all right but the dream was dead — forever dead. Warren was gone forever.

Maria turned her energies and frustrations and sorrow into her work, she would have to make a new world for herself and lock her dreams safely out of reach, to be touched and wept over rarely, and then go on. The notice of the new Children's hospital being built in Grant's Pass caught her attention followed by a letter of inquiry and then a visit followed yet another, and now this she thought, as she parked her car in the spot reserved for Chief of Staff. At the pools edge, Maria tucked her long, coiled, blond hair securely under her bathing cap and plunged into the cool depths hoping to wash away the residue of the sad reminiscing and come up with a clean, clear conviction.

*****

Peanut Butter Cookies

Back at the big, country house Uncle Rolf had weighed, and measured Lorraine, drawn outlines of both feet just in case there was a discernable variance in foot size. He gave the figures to Aunt Dagne, but the outlines he had carefully folded and tucked in his denim vest pocket and told Dagne the measurements.

"You were right on, our Lorraine is exactly 51 pounds and she is 38 inches tall," exclaimed Rolf.

"Thanks, I will have to ensure Lorraine gets the proper diet," said Aunt Dagne.

While Lorraine busied herself beside Lady and Laddie, stroking and watching them Uncle Rolf filled the dog's dishes with dry food and then he refilled the water dishes. Now that he and his four legged friends were fed his thoughts turned to entertaining Lorraine while Aunt Dagne made the necessary list and made the phone calls.

Aunt Dagne had completed her phone calls and came to tell Uncle Rolf he could pick up the orders anytime after 10:00 o'clock, then handed him a separate little list which he evaluated then tucked into his vest pocket with the foot outline, "Good idea, and I will call home before I leave town in case you think of something else."

"This farmer had better be trotting along. See you later gals," Uncle Rolf bent down and kissed Aunt Dagne goodbye and patted Lorraine on her shoulder...

"Are you going to tell my Daddy where I am?"

Uncle Rolf's eyes met Aunt Dagne's over Lorraine's head.

They silently groaned, and then he sat down and placed Lorraine on his lap.

Tipping her little face up to look at him he gently reminded her, "We are not going to tell your Daddy anything — we don't know who your Daddy is, nor where he lives, and he doesn't know where you are."

"Lady and Laddie are right here on the back porch and they won't let anyone near you."

"Can Lady come in the house with me?"

"Well, of course she can come in, now remember no one is going to hurt you here."

"What if my Mommy comes?"

"Your Mommy doesn't know where you are either, so she won't come."

"Let's bring Lady in and I must go or I will never get home in time for lunch. Have fun."

Lorraine and Aunt Dagne waved to Uncle Rolf as he drove past the back door then Aunt Dagne closed and locked the door.

"Well, little Flicka let's see how much we can get done before Uncle Rolf gets back. How about starting upstairs in the bedrooms, you can help me make your bed." So the two "keepers of the house" stopped in the pink bedroom and made the bed, then they went to the lavender room. "Miss Maria has already made her bed, we will feed the fish and go stir up some cookies, do you think you could help me with that?"

"Uh-Huh."

"Have you ever helped make cookies before?"

"Uh-Uh."

"Well, this will be a fun thing for both of us."

Even though Aunt Dagne knew the peanut butter cookie recipe by heart she still got out the cookbook and opened it to the proper page."

"Flicka can you read the ingredients we will need?"

"Uh-Huh," and she began reading.

"Well, you sure can read - you did more than try, you did it. That is super."

All the while Aunt Dagne was busy getting out the mixing bowl, mixing spoon, cookie sheets and spatula. Now read off the list of things again and we can begin. So the child read, and the adult assembled the necessary makings.

"All right Flicka you can turn off the mixer again. Good girl, now we will take this teaspoon and put the dough on the cookie sheet, then you can take this fork, dip it in this bowl of flour and press the dough down like this and then turn the fork the other way and press again like this. Good, good. This pan is ready for the oven and while it is baking we will get the second pan ready."

And so the two baked a double batch of peanut butter cookies and a big batch of chocolate chip cookies.

"Now it is time for the cooks to get their reward," and so Aunt Dagne set little plates and glasses on the table.

She poured milk for each of them and put two of each kind of cookie on the plates for sampling.

"You did an excellent job little one, just wait until Uncle Rolf and Miss Maria come home and taste these goodies... they will be surprised." When they had finished their little break, the cookie jars were filled and the extras were put in cookie cans and frozen.

"Maybe we should start a kettle of soup for Uncle Rolf - he will be hungry and he loves homemade soup. First I had better take a loaf of bread out of the freezer. How would you like to wash the carrots and celery? I will move the step stool up close to the sink so you can reach." And so while Lorraine brushed the carrots and celery Aunt Dagne was busy peeling onions and garlic to add to the meat already simmering in the big kettle. Lorraine was so enthralled with all this new activity not to mention the prospect of more good food she really forgot her fears and anxieties, and that is just what Aunt Dagne wanted to accomplish. Knowing that being busy was the best antidote for fear of any kind.

Aunt Dagne was just adding the last of the scrubbed vegetables when she exclaimed, "Here is Uncle Rolf already, I didn't expect him for another hour or more, but this is great, he can have some of your warm cookies…. look here is Miss Maria too, they can have cookies and coffee while the soup simmers."

Lorraine scrunched her shoulders up in a momentary, silent expression of pleasure, then a cloud crossed her face as she asked again, "Is my Daddy coming too?"

"No, dear little Flicka, your Daddy is NOT coming, it's just Miss Maria and Uncle Rolf. Let's go open the door for them."

Lorraine followed uncertainly as Aunt Dagne hurried to open the locked door.

Miss Maria was followed closely by Uncle Rolf, both had their arms full of packages.

"Oh Aunt Dagne, something smells scrumptious!"
Uncle Rolf chuckled, "Any good Swede would know that's a cookie smell, why do you think I postponed most of my errands? Had to come sample 'em you know."

"Well, I want you to know our little Flicka is a good cook."
Lorraine smiled a little self-conscious smile and ducked behind Aunt Dagne, who reached back and put her arm around the hiding child.
Maria, I am so glad Uncle Rolf was able to reach you, we didn't want you to miss this special occasion, I'm sure the other business can be put on hold for a little while, as long as the surgery was completed."

"Oh, thank you for calling me home, I really didn't want to miss out, I guess I just felt compelled to push on."

Maria led the way down the hallway to the living room and laid her bundles down on the floor by the davenport, Uncle Rolf set his on the big, round coffee table, then went back out for another armful. Aunt Dagne stopped by to put coffee cups, plates, napkins, and cookies on a tray then brought the refreshments in and placed them on the end of the coffee table. Uncle Rolf set his second load down on the floor and raised his hand,

"Wait, one more thing," and he hurried down to the library and returned with the camera, and sat close to Aunt Dagne.

Lorraine had never, ever seen so many packages and this innocent child never guessed that all of this generosity had anything to do with her. She just was eager that Miss Maria and Uncle Rolf would hurry and taste the goodies she had helped to create.

Three pair of adult eyes met in anticipation yet in wonderment that this little one displayed absolutely no curiosity about the many bulging sacks that were heaped about the table and floor.

Lorraine's enthusiasm couldn't be restrained longer as she carefully picked up the plate of cookies and stood before Maria, "We made these for you and Uncle Rolf."

"They look lovely and the whole house smells delightful, I bet they are delicious, thank you.

Then Lorraine stepped to Uncle Rolf's side and asked, "You want a cookie?"

"I was beginning to think you would never give me one, but is one all I can have?"

"Uh-Uh, you can have more. We made lots," and she raised serious eyes to meet the smiling eyes of Uncle Rolf.

"Lorraine, these cookies are delicious — you did a super job."

"You should have heard Flicka read the recipe to me — she reads like a grown up."

"Snow White, you will be as good a cook as Aunt Dagne before you know it."

Lorraine carried the cookie plate back to Maria and Uncle Rolf took a picture of the proud cook.

Maria put her arm around the little hostess and drew her down on the sofa beside her, "Can you guess what is in this sack?"

"Uh-Uh."

"Well, let's set this cookie plate down then you and I had better go quickly and wash our hands after holding cookies in our fingers. Excuse us, we will be right back."

Returning to the sofa Lorraine at last had the flush of anticipation and excitement realizing she was to be involved with a package. The adults were anxious to see how the phone order had been filled and waited with interest to witness the child's reaction.

Maria handed Lorraine the package and suggested, "Let's see what is in here."

Lorraine opened the sack wide, peeked in slid her hand down to feel the contents, and carefully lifted out a light lavender jumper dress & a ruffled, white blouse. Her eyes were wide with wonder as she touched the soft corduroy fabric.

Maria helped her hold it out at arms length so she could look at it, then asked, "Do you think you like that? Do you suppose it will fit?"

"Lorraine nodded and whispered, "I like it."

"You can try it on in just a minute, but let's see what else is in this sack." So Lorraine repeated the process and pulled out a pair of pink leotards, a corduroy skirt and a pink print top with a big white teddy bear on the front.

A whispered "Ohhh," And her eyes searched the eyes of the adults for an answer and saw only love.

Lorraine continued to open and empty sacks of their secrets revealing more skirts, sweaters, tops, dresses, a gorgeous mauve, quilted, hooded, jacket, undies, pajamas, slippers, a robe, and a pair of pink shoes with velcro closures.

"What would you like to try on first?"

Lorraine picked up the first item she had removed and caressed the soft fabric again.

"O.K. Let's go see how it fits," and Maria picked up undies, slip, socks, and shoes while Lorraine carried the prize dress.

When they returned Uncle Rolf said, "Oh my goodness, I don't have a Snow White anymore I have a beautiful lavender Lorraine."

"I'm still Snow White."

"What a lovely little Flicka, your eyes are bluer then ever..."

All right lavender Snow White let's see how those shoes fit and Uncle Rolf bent down to see just where the little toes ended, then felt all around the shoe for wrinkles and slack. Satisfied with his choice of footwear Uncle Rolf had Lorraine stand by Maria while he took another picture.

Lorraine looked at Maria with pleading eyes, "Is this mine to keep?"

"It is all yours, yours to keep."

"Will my Daddy take it away from me?"

"No, your Daddy won't take it away from you - he doesn't know where you are, remember?"

Maria stood Lorraine in front of the full length mirror so she could watch herself being dressed until the last button had been fastened as she held her hands to her face in awe of the reflection.

On bent knees Maria took Lorraine's little arms, whispering, "You are so beautiful" then drew the child into her arms and held her briefly.

"Before you try on the other clothes, let's see what is in the rest of these sacks."

Lorraine opened the smaller, plastic bag and peeked in, "What is it Flicka?"

She pulled out a hairbrush, comb, a variety of hair clips, toothbrush, and bath powder. "You can put those things in your bathroom when you go up to bed.

"Now what about this sack?"

Again the cautious peek, then an enthusiastic digging as Lorraine removed a big coloring book; Math activity book; puzzle book; crayons; pencils; a lined tablet; plain scribble tablet; just all the neat stuff little students treasure.

The tote bag from the library was last and heavy but so easy to unload... there were four big books and several tapes.

"Do you like to read Lorraine?"

"Uh-Huh."

"Wonderful, so do I, we can read together after supper. Do you like your new things?"

The overwhelmed child could only drop her eyes and nod her head.

"Flicka, come see me," beckoned Aunt Dagne. Speaking low she said, "Miss Maria bought the clothes for you and Uncle Rolf bought the other things, I think they would like a big hug."

Catching the spirit of the moment Lorraine ran to Uncle Rolf and giving him a hug and murmured, Thank you." Then walking slowly and purposefully to Maria she pressed close, with eyes lowered she whispered, "I wish you were Aunt Maria."

Maria reached out her hands lifting Lorraine's face until their eyes met for a deep soul searching moment each expressing unspoken words of love from unfathomable depths. Lifting the child onto her lap Maria snuggled Lorraine close, tears filling her eyes.

"I would love to be your Aunt Maria. . . .Tia is a pretty word that means Auntie, how would you like to call me by that special name?"

Lorraine nodded thoughtfully.

"Can you say it?"

"Tia" formed quietly on the child's lips and a little smile crept around her mouth.

"That sounds great - I like that. Now that I have a new, short name how would it be if I give you a new shorter name also?"

Lorraine looked up expectantly, enjoying this little serious game.

"Lorraine is a beautiful, long name, but Uncle Rolf calls you Snow White and Aunt Dagne calls you Flicka so may I call you LoRie?"

A nod of acceptance followed and a contented hush settled in the room with the ticking of the grandfather clock.

Faint strains of music drifted from the library as from another land and Lorraine sighed as a babe that has cried from the depths of fear and despair and has found comfort. Her breathing was quiet as she nestled her head against Maria savoring the warmth of her arms and the sweetness of her perfume. So much had happened so fast she cast her eyes around the room to assure herself this was not a dream. Maria clasped her arms tightly around the frail little body and knew she had found the answer to the void in her life and would fight the most desperate of battles to keep this child. The thought of Lorraine returning to the horror she had known was unthinkable. Aunt Dagne was already making plans for things she and Lorraine could do together, welcoming the opportunity to teach and share with such a responsive student. Uncle Rolf too, was strolling down the "thinker's path" of possibilities mentally diagramming the potentials.

The three adults knew their lives had been altered and would never take the same direction again . . . because of this child. How it was all going to come about they were not sure, but the force of their love and their concern and motivation was strong and could accomplish difficult tasks — challenges were to be conquered.

The great grandfather clock struck a solemn 12 o'clock, bringing Aunt Dagne instantly back to reality. "Oh, my goodness, the soup!" and she hurried to the kitchen to check the progress of the simmering lunch.

Uncle Rolf stood and inhaled the tantalizing aroma that met his nostrils with the assessment, "That doesn't smell like a disaster to me... in fact it smells almost as good as those cookies. How about it Snow White do you think you can handle a bowl of soup?"

"Uh-Huh."

"I think I'll go keep the cook company and see if the fire needs another piece of wood."

"Do I have to take my dress off?"

"No sweetie you can wear it and after lunch Aunt Dagne will help you try on all these other things to make sure they fit. I think I have an apron in the kitchen drawer that will do nicely to cover your dress while you eat so nothing accidentally gets splashed on it, and I think I will look for one for myself too."

*****

Special Arrangements

Gathered around the kitchen table spread with steaming bowls of hearty soup and thick slices of homemade bread, Maria wished her heart felt as comfortable as her stomach. With her body fortified she felt ready for her afternoon appointments and was prepared to "do battle" if necessary.

Maria parked her car in the Visitor's Parking Space in the shadow of the red brick Police Station. Confidently approaching the Information Desk she informed the clerk, "I am Dr. Maria Goetche, and I have a 1:30 appointment with Chief Bennett."

"He is expecting you, please come this way."

"Good afternoon, Dr. Maria."

"Good afternoon Chief Brad."

"It is most unusual for you to be on my home territory, it seems it is always the other way around. How can I help you?"

"Has anyone reported a missing child in the last 24 hours?"

"No, why?"

"My big Laddie found a little girl and brought her to my door last night, soaked, cold and starved."

"He is a marvelously intelligent animal and so well trained. And what about the girl?"

"She was bleeding from a deep head wound, petrified with fear that her father would find her and throw her in the river as he had threatened. Scantily clothed, filthy, malnourished and when I bathed her I found numerous scars and bruises of the type that would indicate extreme abuse! When I suggested taking her to the Hospital Emergency Room for suturing she panicked and informed me that", "Hospitals kill you. They killed my little brothers." "She could not remember her last name, which I think was a self-preservation mental block because she appears very intelligent and responsive. I suspect she has been abandoned."

Reaching into her purse Maria brought out the pictures she had taken. "This is Lorraine as we found her last night, this is Lorraine after the shower and emergency suturing in my home office, with the help of Dr. Rolf, and this is Lorraine this afternoon."

"Jeepers, Maria."

"As frightened as she was last night I could not justify adding to her horror by doing anything except giving her the much needed care and a measure of security and assurance. If anyone comes to inquire or report this missing child please detain them in one of your special jail cells. I am going to seek custody of this child, in fact I have an appointment with Judge Steven Spencer at 2:30 in the Court House."

"Thank goodness, for people like you Dr. Maria! I don't think you will encounter any opposition to a custody decision, and you can be absolutely sure I will detain any person or persons making inquiry! That child is in the best of hands and I will be in touch with you. Good luck!"

"Thank you Chief Bradley - we are in this thing together."

Judge Steven Spencer had just parked his car when Maria pulled in long side of him so they walked into the Court House together. They were professional friends of long standing and respected each other for their interest and effort for the sake of humanity. Maria testified often on behalf of a neglected or abused patient.

"Dr. Maria, this must be urgent to call me in from a game of golf."

"This is urgent, and I am sure you will agree with me."

After listening to Maria's account and seeing the pictures Judge Spencer whistled and remarked, "That little waif was most fortunate to end up on your door step."

"Oh, and I didn't tell you she also has Scoliosis which has apparently gone untreated so there is some special care ahead for her."

"Dr. Maria I can't think of a better place for that little Lorraine to be and I will most definitely give you custody, temporary for now of course, and we shall see what the future brings. I will keep in touch with you, and I hope to meet this little gal soon."

Maria stood and shook hands with Judge Spencer, "Thank you so much for taking the time to listen to another problem. It is comforting to know I have authority to protect this child. And I really am sorry to have interrupted a relaxing game of golf."

"Oh Maria, I was just kidding. Sylvia and I already played a round of golf this morning and this afternoon we are going to pick our winter apples before the deer sample all of the fruit."

"The farmer in the heart of some of us just won't be quiet, will it? Please remember me to Sylvia, and thanks again for all of your help."

"It is my pleasure! And if I can be of further help please don't hesitate to call anytime, even at home if need be."

"Thank you on behalf of the hurting and homeless."

Maria turned her car back up the hill toward the hospital so she could check the progress of the little patient who had surgery that morning. Another two hours went quickly as she not only confirmed the progress of the new patient, but had a reassuring visit with the parents before making late afternoon rounds.

With a satisfied sigh Maria hurried to the parking garage. Her thoughts preceded her to her country refuge.

A flurry of wagging tails welcomed Maria as she drove into the yard, and singing greeted her from the kitchen as she opened the back door.

Such a delightful sound, "I'm home."

"Come join us," sang Aunt Dagne and continued singing Mairsey Doats in her lovely soprano voice.

Maria applauded when she finished, and Lorraine volunteered, "Aunt Dagne is going to teach me that song too."

"Then the two of you can sing it together for me."

"Tia, you must learn it too then we can all sing, even Uncle Rolf."

That sounds like a happy idea — and I am all for happy ideas!" concluded Maria.

"Good, I have another happy idea," ventured Aunt Dagne, "Let's put on our sweaters and walk out to the orchard to get some big apples to bake for our supper. That should taste pretty good with fried chicken, don't you think?"

"A walk sounds perfect to me, Aunt Dagne, just let me change my shoes."

"Will my Daddy find me?"

"Flicka, there is no way your Daddy can find you, he doesn't know where you are. Tia and I will hold your hand and Lady and Laddie will go with us. Now let's put our sweaters on. The heat is turned down low under the Dutch oven, the potatoes and squash are baking and we all need some fresh air."

Maria took her big fruit basket from the utility room and headed out the back door. Lorraine looked around fearfully for any sign of danger and wasn't sure what was ahead of her down the path, but Aunt Dagne began to sing again, the dogs raced ahead, and Lorraine gained confidence grasping an adult hand in each of hers.

Long shadows were cast in the orchard by the late afternoon sun, and Maria commented on the possibility of a gorgeous sunset. A pheasant called from the meadow and Lorraine cried out, "What was that?" as she grasped Maria's arm.

"That was a pheasant calling."

"What is a pheasant?"

"It is a beautiful big bird that lives here, and he was probably calling to his hen, telling her it was time to find a sheltered place to sleep."

"Will it hurt us?"

"No, pheasants are our friends, because they eat bugs. We will see one sometime. Look at these huge apples, we must put them into the basket very carefully so we don't bruise them. Do you like baked apples?"

"I dunno."

"Flicka, I just know you will like my baked apples, filled with brown sugar, cinnamon and a dab of butter, then when it is all baked we will put some good thick cream on it."

"Little LoRie, Aunt Dagne does wonderful things to food, including baked apples."

"Flicka, you can help me fix them."

"O.K."

Their basket was filled with shiny, red, giant apples but instead of picking it up Maria suggested, "Let's wait and watch the sunset." The two adults knelt beside the fascinated child and watched. "So beautiful, so silent," whispered Maria, "There it goes out of sight for another day."

Lorraine had never shared a sunset with anyone before and she was speechless with awe and wonder. Though the sun had vanished from sight the western sky was aglow with soft red and gold hues, there was a momentary hush in the orchard as if every bird and insect was observing a silent respect for the completion of another day. Maria, Dagne and Lorraine remained motionless just watching the kaleidoscope on the horizon.

Maria whispered again, "Listen, it is so beautifully quiet, but in a moment we will hear the birds begin to call, who will be first to hear them?"

Lorraine's eyes and senses came alive at the prospect of this new game, and she began listening in a new way. "There," she whispered, "I hear it."

"Isn't it lovely? That's a Quail," informed Maria, "And hear the Flicker, he has a sharper voice, we have lots of bird friends here."

"Will we hear the pheasant call again?" inquired the interested child.

"Maybe, not tonight, he's probably talking real low and quiet to his hen so no one else can hear," explained Maria, "but we will hear him again because he loves to crow early in the morning just as the sun comes up, and when the sun shines on his feathers he is beautiful."

"Who else lives out here?" questioned the little nature student.

"In the fall and winter the bright, noisy Blue Jay, Ruffled Grouse, the shiny black Crow, Canada Geese, Mallard Ducks, and my little Juncos. Sometimes an owl comes by to visit ...but in the summer time there are many, species of birds and the orchard and meadow are alive with their songs," replied Maria the bird lover.

Tia, can I come again and visit your friends?"

"Of course LoRie, I love to come here to watch and listen, and we shall come together."

"My Daddy can't find me here, can he?"

"LoRie you are safe here - your Daddy doesn't know where you are and he will not find you."

"Little Flicka, this is a perfectly safe place but your Daddy wouldn't know you anyway with all your new clothes and ponytail."

Lorraine reached up and felt her new ponytail then tested the pockets of her new sweater with doubting hands. She had a hard time convincing herself she really had a ponytail and that she really was wearing a new, warm sweater just like she dreamed about. Being surrounded by adults who talked to her and loved her and cared for her was such a different experience, except for Ruth and Mrs. Erickson she had never known such kindness. A sigh escaped her tense body as her dreadful fears kept colliding with solid reassurances. She shivered.

Maria and Dagne picked up the laden fruit basket between them and Maria offered her other hand to Lorraine and the three turned their steps toward the house. A curling plume of smoke rose from the kitchen chimney.

"There is going to be a beautiful moon tonight and probably a heavy frost," observed Maria, "I'm sure glad the wood shed is full."

"And the freezer, and the fruit room, too," continued Aunt Dagne, "There isn't anything anymore comforting than a full pantry."

Though Lorraine didn't know where all of this provision was she absorbed the fact that there was ample provision for the coming winter and all was well.

Back at the house Aunt Dagne selected four even sized apples for their evening dessert and four more for the following day. Lorraine stood on the step stool at the sink watching the scrubbing and coring of the apples. After placing the apple in a baking pan Aunt Dagne mixed the sugar and cinnamon and gave Lorraine a large spoon and showed her how to fill each cored center. Then Aunt Dagne cut a sliver of butter and topped each apple before setting the full pan into the waiting oven.

Maria had set the table while the apples were being readied for the oven, so all they had to do was wait with patient anticipation. The smell of the simmering chicken was already teasing their senses.

"LoRie, while we are waiting for supper to finish cooking shall we read a story together?

I think Aunt Dagne is going to read the paper."

"O.K."

"Which one?"

"Heidi."

"Have you ever heard the story?"

"Uh-Uh."

As Maria opened the book she commented, "I like this story and I think you will too," and so she began.

The timer for the oven buzzed and Aunt Dagne went to the kitchen to take the apples from the oven, and check on the chicken. The sweet smell of baked apples preceded Aunt Dagne as she came back to the living room but she had scarcely sat down and picked up the paper when the dogs announced the arrival of Uncle Rolf.

"That was good timing commented Aunt Dagne - everything is ready including my appetite."

Maria acknowledged the call to eat with, "As soon as I finish this paragraph we will get washed up for supper, it smells so scrumptious"

*****

Elves

Uncle Rolf burst through the back door like a hungry man in a hurry - "Hello everybody! It smells like the elves have been busy in yonder kitchen with the help of my "Miracle Chef".

Beaming with the familiar praise, Aunt Dagne commented, "Your timing was perfect, the elves must have told you."

"Ah, indeed! But they did more than tell me, they bustled me around like a bunch of miniature whirlwinds. One took off my cap; two helped me out of my coat; three turned on the shower; four scrubbed my back; five laid out my clothes so if my socks don't match you can blame them; six sang 'Rub—a dub-dub three men in a tub'; seven tied my shoes; and eight hustled me out the door," chuckled Uncle Rolf with a big grin.

Lorraine and Maria had entered the kitchen just as Uncle Rolf began to give this nonsense account, and Maria asked so seriously, "Didn't you invite your helpers to join us for supper?"

"Well of course, but they were so busy with a jug of fresh cider and the glass jar of Aunt Dagne's cookies they just mumbled a thank you with their mouths full and waved goodbye .... busy little rascals. I told them not to leave any crumbs on the table or floor lest Aunt Dagne hide the cookie jar next time. Anyway, this way I can have their share of supper," and Uncle Rolf winked at Lorraine.

Lorraine searched each adult face for confirmation of this spoof but being so unaccustomed to joking she was afraid to smile at the amusing picture her imagination portrayed of the helpful elves, and just ducked her head as she stepped behind Maria.

"What about it Snow White, did you ever see an elf skating on a bar of soap in the shower?

"Uh-Uh."

"It can make you dizzy watching them go in circles," concluded Uncle Rolf most seriously as everyone sat down to the table.

"I really think you are dizzy from hunger and hard work if the truth were told," commented Aunt Dagne

"That is a fact, my dear, I cannot deny it."

Uncle Rolf bowed his head and in his quiet, gentle voice prayed, "Gracious Father, accept our gratitude for thy provision for our bodies needs. Amen."

Aunt Dagne passed the platter of chicken to Uncle Rolf commenting, "To the king of the elves and all those wonderful helpers of earth folk."

"Thank you queen of the elves," replied Uncle Rolf.

"Vaccinating and tagging and registering 47 head of rambunctious, bawling cattle does help work up a giant appetite. However, it was a pleasure working with Jeff Gregson and his boys. They have a beautiful herd of healthy cattle and a well-kept ranch which they are justifiably proud of. Jeepers those animals are gorgeous. But enough of cows let's talk about the cooks and keepers of the fire. Snow White, what did you ladies do this afternoon?"

Lorraine suddenly felt self-conscious as attention was focused on her, and looked at Maria for reassurance, "Tell Uncle Rolf where we went this afternoon and what we heard."

Lorraine took a deep breath and with animated eyes began to give an account, "We picked a basket of apples and heard pheasants calling and quail talking."

"Were they speaking Swedish?" teased Uncle Rolf.

"I dunno."

"No Snow White, birds speak their own language in every part of the world. Did you see any deer?"

"You will have to leave the dogs at the house if you want to see our beautiful Bambi, because the dogs think it's a great game to see how fast the deer can run," explained Uncle Rolf.

"Have you read the story of Bambi," asked Maria

"Next time we go to the library we will check out that book," promised Maria.

Lorraine suddenly remembered the story begun before supper and hastened to inform Uncle Rolf, "Tia is reading the story of Heidi to me."

"Do you like that story Snow White?

"Uh-Huh."

"Good, someday you can read it to me, okay?"

"Uh-Huh."

"Good books are like friends, if you read well you will always have good company," explained Uncle Rolf.

That is a wonderful truth," agreed Maria, "there would be a lot more contented people if they discovered the magic world of good reading."

"Not to change the subject," interjected Aunt Dagne, "but are you on duty tomorrow Maria?"

"Just morning and evening rounds."

"Well, how would it be if we took Flicka to the park with us and you meet us there?"

"OH, NO," cried the alarmed child, "My Daddy might get me."

"Flicka, remember your Daddy wouldn't recognize you with your pony tail and all your new clothes, besides Uncle Rolf and I would each hold your hands and no one could get you."

"NO, NO, my Daddy might grab me when my back was turned." Her eyes wild with fear were frantically assessing a hiding place as she slid from her chair to make a dash to escape from the plans...

Uncle Rolf quickly and quietly reached out his gentle arm and lifted the alarmed child onto his knee, "Snow White, we will stay right here tomorrow. We don't want you to be worried and afraid. O.K.?"

"Uh-Huh."

"When you are afraid you must run to us so we can help you and you must tell us when you are afraid," counseled Maria, "We want to help you and keep you safe."

"Snow White I see a pan of baked apples on the counter, are those the ones you picked?"

"Uh-Huh."

"Flicka filled the centers for me. Are you ready for your dessert King of the Elves?" queried Aunt Dagne.

"I certainly am."

Uncle Rolf whispered in Lorraine's ear, "Do you want to help Aunt Dagne serve the apples?"

"Uh-Huh."

"Since I am King of the Elves, are you going to bring me the biggest one?"

Consoled and reassured, Lorraine gave her usual "Uh-Huh" response as she slid off Uncle Rolf's lap.

Supper was finished, the kitchen tidied, and Uncle Rolf and Aunt Dagne had left for the night. Lady and Laddie were stretched full length in front of the fireplace while Maria finished reading the chapter she had begun before supper. Feeling the stress of the long day her thoughts turned toward a soft, welcome pillow and a good nights rest.

"LoRie, would you like to help me lock the doors and turn out the lights before we go upstairs to take our baths and go to bed?"

"Uh-Huh."

Maria included Lorraine as she locked the doors and closed the drapes hoping this would give the child the reassurance of security. Together child and adult climbed the wide stairway followed by the devoted dogs. Maria drew a shallow tub of warm water with bubble bath for Lorraine hoping to keep her bandage dry until it was changed on the morrow, and also aware that a tub bath would help remove another layer of grime stain from this little girl's fair skin. A shallow tub of water for the purpose of allaying the fears of this fearful waif.

Finally tucked in with Love Bear and doll and the dogs stationed between the bed and door, Maria leaned down and hugged child, bear, and doll in one big embrace. "Sleep tight angel, see you in the morning."

"Night." was the tiny response as the little body burrowed under the covers.

Showered, brushed and relaxed the comfort of a bed was at last a reality for Maria. The day had been very rewarding and correspondingly long. There were many problems yet unresolved but at least there had been a constructive beginning. She must take a day at a time and not let her thoughts race ahead of actuality and facts. Deep sleep interrupted the unresolved question of "Where had she seen Lorraine before?" Her mind and body longed for and welcomed release from stress and struggle.

The grandfather clock in the darkened living room had struck the quarter hour, then the half hour, followed by the three quarter hour but no man regarded nor recorded the approaching hour in the hushed house. Sleeping mortals are unmindful of anything except the comfort of sleep itself....

The noise of pain and panic exploded in the pink bedroom.

"NO DADDY, NO, NO DADDY - LET ME GO DADDY - PUT ME DOWN DADDY."

Lady and Laddie burst into a frenzy of barking accented by Lorraine's screams of terror.

Maria was awake and running in one swift motion reaching Lorraine's bed where the little girl was thrashing wildly fighting the nightmare that haunted day and night.

"LoRie, LoRie," Maria called as she untangled the struggling child from the blankets.

"LoRie, this is Tia, wake up, everything is really all right."

Lorraine opened her eyes wide in fright and disbelief, "My Daddy was going to throw me in the river. He'll get me and hit me again."

"LoRie, that was all a bad dream. See you are safe in your pink bedroom, I am here, Lady and Laddie are here, no one else is here except Love Bear and Strawberry Shortcake."

Lorraine was crying and trembling uncontrollably...

"Let's go get a drink of warm milk and a graham cracker, it will make us feel better... hand in hand Lorraine and Maria went to the kitchen and heated two mugs of milk. While Lorraine and Maria sipped their warm milk Maria started reading another chapter of Heidi. When milk, crackers and the third chapter of Heidi were finished the two retraced their steps up the impressive stairs but when they reached the pink bedroom Lorraine shrank back as though she still saw the dreaded phantom figure of her nightmare.

Maria knelt before the suffering child and asked, "Would you like to sleep in my big bed with me tonight?"

"Uh-Huh."

In the darkened living room another hour had passed and the grandfather clock struck the quarter hour, the half hour, and the three quarter hour no one noticed nor recorded the approaching hour because woman and child slept.

*****

Love Heals

Maria's hand reached up in a sleepy, automatic motion to turn off the alarm before it sounded, turning on only the night light in the base of the lamp. She moved silently so as not to disturb Lorraine who lay clutching Love Bear and Strawberry Shortcake. The child breathed evenly and deeply, exhaustion from fright acted as an anesthesia and gave the little one healing rest.

Showered, combed, and dressed Maria picked up her purse and coat, walking silently on the carpeted floor - whispering for the dogs to follow. After letting them out for fresh air Maria took Lady back up to her room instructing her to "Stay" so if Lorraine awakened she wouldn't be alone and alarmed.

Maria plugged in the coffee pot, lit the fire in the Franklin Fireplace in the corner of the kitchen, then pulled on a sweater and stepped out on the back porch to admire the heavens. She breathed deep of the cool, clear air and stretched her arms high as though she were reaching for a moon beam. Mr. Moon cast soft shadows across the yard and Maria marveled at the brightness of the moonlight she would love to have strolled down through the orchard to the creek, but she dared not entertain such a luxurious thought this morning.

There was a silence observed by both bird and beast as though they were holding their breath waiting for the first rays of the new day. Maria heard the crunch of tires on the graveled driveway and took another appreciative look at the sky before the approaching headlights changed the scene.

Rolf parked the car, turned off the headlights but when he and Dagne got out of the car they stood silently soaking up the serenity and beauty of the overhead scene, they stepped up onto the porch and went slowly into the house without saying a word as if their voices would shatter the moon's magic spell.

Going in the door Dagne patted Maria's arm in a silent greeting, and Rolf commented almost in a whisper, "It's wonderful to be alive - I hope that scene is permanently fixed in my memory - the best things in life really are free - and by the way good morning Maria."

"Good morning and a cup of coffee to you too," Maria replied as she poured three cups of coffee.

Uncle Rolf put another piece of wood on the fire before sipping the steaming, fragrant drink.

"Did you have a restful night?" inquired Dagne.

Maria frowned, "Finally, with a noisy interruption, we went to bed early, all seemed well and sleep was waiting for both of us. Then panic and pandemonium erupted in the pink bedroom sometime before midnight. LoRie was having a hideous nightmare of her Daddy throwing her in the river. Her screams and the dogs barking had me on my feet in seconds. A mug of hot milk with graham crackers plus a chapter or two of Heidi seemed to quieten the fears, however, she finished the night in my bed." "We must get her to start talking."

"Doubtless there will be more bad dreams and outbursts," observed Rolf, "but if she can talk about the dreams, and her feelings, and feel secure while she is doing it, stability will come. Time and love are healers."

Maria sighed, "Time, a lot of time. Though I had not considered sending her to school this week, I'm not so sure she will be emotionally ready to go next week either. This fear is real and very deep."

Rolf was frying bacon.

Dagne looked up from the biscuits she was making and commented, "It would be a pleasure to dust off my teaching skills. I even have a desk and chair her size that would fit nicely in the sewing room - I could stitch and tutor and she could study in a classroom full of dolls.

Maria smiled, "That sounds perfect and practical and prudent," they all laughed.

Maria hurried up the stairs singing a little nursery rhyme her Mother had sung to her as a child.

"Good morning, Merry Sunshine, how did you wake so soon? You frightened all the stars away and scared away the moon." The moon, the moon, OH, the moon," murmured Maria to herself, "If it isn't already too late." Hurrying to the window she pulled aside the drapes and looked out. There it was hanging lower in the sky but still visible and beautiful.

Maria started singing the little ditty again as she gently shook Lorraine,

"Good morning, Merry Sunshine, open your eyes LoRie, are you there?"

Maria would love to have let the child sleep but she feared LoRie might feel abandoned and confused if she went off to work and left her sleeping.

"Things will be different later when she is settled, secure, and understands the pattern of my schedule," she rationalized.

"LoRie, can you wake up? It's time for breakfast. LoRie are you awake?"

"Uh-Huh."

"Are you hungry?"

"Uh-Huh."

"Before you get dressed, let's slip your robe and slippers on and go out on the sun roof and look at the gorgeous moon."

"O.K."

Stepping out onto the balcony Maria felt Lorraine's hand tighten on hers in fear, so Maria squeezed the little hand in return, then pointed to the North Star, The Big Dipper and the Milky Way. "Doesn't it look like the man in the moon is whistling?"

"Uh-Huh," Lorraine thrilled to this new experience.

"That's enough star gazing for this morning, it's chilly out here and Aunt Dagne will be waiting for us."

Lorraine went down to breakfast, washed and shining wearing a green knit skirt and top and a big green bow tied around her pony tail looking very much like a little bit of Ireland.

"Well, I declare if an Irish Lass hasn't come to pay us a visit," observed Uncle Rolf. "Do you think the Irish and the Swede's can get along this morning?"

"I dunno."

"My you look fresh and pretty Flicka. Do you like omelets?"

"I dunno."

"Is this the first time you have eaten one? asked Aunt Dagne.

"Uh-Huh."

Uncle Rolf laughed, "If we Swedes like them the Irish will too, don't you suppose?"

"Uh-Huh."

"What should I call you now that you are all green?"

"Snow White."

"But you aren't white."

"I'm your Snow White."

"Good enough - you will always be my little Snow White," agreed Uncle Rolf and gave her a tight squeeze.

The omelet had vanished - all four plates were empty and Uncle Rolf was putting butter and honey on a biscuit, "What about it Snow White, do you have room for this?"

"Uh-Huh."

Handing the warm biscuit to Lorraine, Uncle Rolf reached for another for himself and commented, "The Irish and Swedes agree that was a mighty fine breakfast, right Snow White?"

"Uh-Huh."

Maria rose from her chair, "I must be going, thanks so much for a delightful breakfast, and I will see all of you later today, and tonight LoRie gets a fresh new bandage."

Maria hugged Lorraine and asked, "Are you going to wave from the dining room window again?"

"Uh-Huh."

"Good, I will be looking and waving too. Good Bye."

"Quick Flicka, let's wash the sticky off of your fingers before we go to the dining room, we can beat Tia if we hurry."

"There, we made it in time, I see the headlights coming."

Maria beeped the car horn and was gone.

Uncle Rolf helped Aunt Dagne clear the table and put food away while Lorraine sat at the table busy with crayons and color book. Uncle Rolf put another piece of wood on the fire, went out to the freezer and brought in a small ham to thaw for supper, then went into the living room and began to play the piano.

"Let's go into the living room with Uncle Rolf," suggested Aunt Dagne when she had finished setting the Jell-O.

Lorraine responded by putting her crayons in the box and taking her project with her to the coffee table near the piano. Sitting on a cushion next to the coffee table made an excellent "coloring studio" and gave her a view of the keyboard and the musician.

Looking up from her work Lorraine saw a flash of green in the big mirror across the room then realized that flash of green was her own image . . . reaching up to check the ribbon and feeling the softness of her dress she shivered with satisfaction.

Aunt Dagne was seated on the bench beside Uncle Rolf and they began to sing in beautiful, perfect harmony. Lorraine had never heard anything like that before and sat with her crayon poised in mid air absorbing the vibrations of piano and peace.

Love heals, time heals, and music heals.

After lunch Aunt Dagne asked Uncle Rolf if he would like to go for a walk down in the orchard. "Oh you bet I would," responded Uncle Rolf, maybe we will see our Bambi Deer. What about it Snow White, are you ready for some fresh air and sunshine and a visit with the deer'?"

"Uh-Huh."

"Sweaters everyone, and let's leave our barking friends in the house so they don't chase our deer friends away," instructed Uncle Rolf

Hand in hand, man, woman and child quietly approached the orchard.

*****

Investigation

Monday morning Ruth hurried to the school office to hang up her coat and put away her lunch and the extra lunch she had fixed. She smiled in anticipation of Lorraine's pleasure at having a chicken sandwich, chocolate cake and a golden delicious apple. Hearing the bus engines whine as the driver's downshifted to turn into the "loading zone", she hastened to her self-appointed meeting place in the hallway.

A multitude of students all sizes, ages, and description milled past but not a sign of Lorraine. The last bus pulled away and Ruth couldn't believe her eyes. She went out the door to make sure Lorraine wasn't being bullied or detained by someone, but no child. Feeling extremely disappointed, Ruth stopped by her office to inform her assistant she was going to Room 3A and went directly to Mrs. Erickson's room.

"Good morning Ruth, how are you?" inquired Mrs. Erickson.

"I'm troubled, Lorraine wasn't on the bus. I don't know if she missed her bus, or if she is sick, or if there is another problem. I worry about that tad-pole," fretted Ruth.

"We have reason to be concerned, that's sure," sympathized Mrs. Erickson.

"If she missed the bus, I am sure her Mother wouldn't bring her . . . . Maybe Lorraine is walking - she loved school so much," rationalized Ruth.

"Is there someone who could drive out and see if she is walking? I would go only I should be in my room at this time of day," continued Mrs. Erickson.

"I'll go," volunteered Ruth, "An Aide can cover for me, and I am sure Mr. Bowman will give his approval," concluded Ruth as she turned to retrace her steps.

Stopping at her desk she verified the address given on Lorraine's enrollment card, slipped on her coat, picked up her purse and headed for the Principals office.

Mr. Bowman had been made aware of Lorraine and the unhealthy atmosphere surrounding her presence the day she enrolled, so now Ruth's proposal of making sure she wasn't walking quickly met with the Educator's approval.

Ruth's eyes scanned both sides of the road as she drove out of town, crossed the bridge and headed for the Trailer Court along the river. When she didn't see her little friend along the road, Ruth turned her car into the Trailer Court driveway and approached Unit #9 warily. The car was gone, there were no lights, and all seemed awfully quiet. Ruth reasoned if someone was ill and sleeping it would be better not to disturb, so she headed back to the school greatly perplexed and feeling ill at ease.

Ruth had returned just minutes before the class bell rang and went directly to Mrs. Erickson's, room to give her the facts. They looked at each other with unspoken defeat.

Back at the big country house Rolf and Dagne had just finished carrying the little desk and chair up stairs, rearranging the furniture so this special desk would be in front of the south window for light and warmth and a view of the orchard.

Lorraine was standing in the doorway watching and listening to Aunt Dagne explain, "We are going to have school right here with all the dolls, wouldn't it be clever if they learned to read and write too?"

Lorraine's mouth managed a hint of a smile but her eyes were alive with the make-believe concept of teaching the dolls. Uncle Rolf had just brought in a large blackboard with a stand. The sewing machine table-cabinet would do double duty as a teaching station and sewing center.

"How about that Snow White, that's a pretty spiffy classroom, don't you think?"

"Uh-Huh."

Lorraine was enthralled with the thought of class and dolls all in one room!

"Aunt Dagne is the best teacher any doll or Snow White could ask for... she might even teach you to speak Swedish," chuckled Uncle Rolf.

"Well, teacher, is there anything else I can do before I leave?" asked Uncle Rolf.

"Thank you, I think everything is taken care of. Will you be home for lunch?" asked Aunt Dagne.

"Probably not, perhaps I had better take a lunch so I don't starve to death before supper," replied Uncle Rolf, "I can fix it."

"Oh I will help you, that is the least I can do for a working man," countered Aunt Dagne.

With his lunch pail and thermos in hand Uncle Rolf hugged Lorraine and Aunt Dagne, "See you girls tonight." He was whistling as he went out the back door to the pickup.

Aunt Dagne and Lorraine waved to Uncle Rolf as he drove past the house, he returned the wave and beeped the horn and was gone.

"Flicka, I think the nicest way to start a school day is with some music, so let's begin at the piano."

And so class had begun.

Maria made her morning rounds and gave varied instructions to the nurses who stood in awe of this gentle, talented woman who treated them with such respect and her patients with such compassion. Maria's calendar was full and the schedule heavy but she was pleased there were no surgeries scheduled for the day. Picking up the phone she called Chief Bennett of the Police Department.

"Good Morning Chief, this is Maria Goetche, any report of a missing child yet?

"No Maria, no reports here, nor for miles around. I have called every city and there is nothing," replied Brad Bennett. "How are things going for you and the child?" he further inquired.

"There is much trauma and fear, which is to be expected. I have excellent help and support. Dagne is tutoring at home until the child over comes the fear of leaving the security of her new home," explained Maria.

"That sounds great. Of course your schedule will be altered, but it appears all is under control," praised the Chief.

"I certainly don't mind having some changes in my life, if I can save one little life from disaster it is worthwhile. It is a joy to have this child, she views everything with wonder and amazement," concluded Maria.

"It will be most interesting to follow this case, and I shall inform you if I get any information," replied Chief Bennett.

"Thank you again - I most surely appreciate your interest and help, Good Bye," said Maria.

Next Maria called Judge Spencer.

"Hello, this is Maria Goetche"

"Oh Good Morning Dr. Maria, any new developments?"

"Not a thing, Judge. I just spoke to Brad Bennett and none of his searching's have yielded anything. He has sent out inquiries to all the surrounding area and all he has is a blank," replied Maria.

"Well, lady, you have temporary legal custody. The document is signed, sealed, and delivered, and if you would like I can have the court clerk file it when she files other documents this afternoon," assured Judge Steven Spencer.

"Thank you, thank you, I appreciate the offer, that would be a real help." replied Maria.

"But there is one more thing I need before noon, if at all possible," continued Maria.

"And what is that?"

"A copy of the custody document," replied Maria.

"The clerk will leave it at your office this morning," assured Judge Spencer, "and if there is anything else I can do please don't hesitate to ask."

"You doubtless will be hearing from me. I will be in touch. Thanks again. Good bye."

Maria made one more phone call before turning her attention to her arriving patients.

"Good morning, Mr. Bowman, this is Maria Goetche."

"Oh good morning Dr. Maria, how may I help you?"

"Would it be at all possible to see you during lunch break today, like quarter after twelve?"

"Why of course, will you have had lunch?"

"Well, no."

"May I order a tray from the cafeteria for each of us? We could eat in my office while we talk," suggested Principal Bowman.

"That would be ideal, thank you. See you later. Good bye," and Maria hung up the phone.

Time flew by and Maria had just seen her last patient for the morning - it was nearly noon and she was hungry. She was so glad Mr. Bowman had suggested lunch in his office, it would save precious time.

Parking her car in the visitor's parking spot in front of the school, Maria hurried to the Principal's Office.

Glancing at her watch as she stepped up to the open door, Maria commented, "I made it with a minute to spare."

"Hello, Dr. Maria, come in, come in. That was perfect timing, I just returned with the trays. How have you been and what good things do you have planned for our students this year?"

"I've been very well, thank you. I think loving my work gives me extra immunity to the 'bugs'. I have some interesting things to talk to the students about and I have some new films which they will love and learn a lot from, but my visit today is about something different."

"O.K. I am listening," replied Principal Bowman.

"Do you know this child?" asked Maria as she reached into her purse and took out the pictures of Lorraine which she had taken on Friday night and Saturday... handing the first ones to Mr. Bowman she explained,   "This child was found by my big Laddie and he brought her to my door Friday night. She has a deep gash on her forehead, plus numerous bruises and wounds on her body which indicate extreme abuse not to mention malnutrition. The only name she could or would give me was Lorraine and she informed me her father had hit her in the head with a tire iron as well as threatening to drown her. I checked with Chief Bennett and he has had no report of a missing child in this immediate vicinity nor the surrounding area."

Looking at the picture Mr. Bowman exclaimed, "My word, Maria, when this child didn't get off the bus this morning our receptionist drove out to the home to make sure she hadn't missed her bus and was safe." Scrutinizing the picture more closely Mr. Bowman commented, "Yes, this child was just recently enrolled. Our receptionist brought her admission to my attention immediately because it was apparent that this girl qualified for complimentary school lunches, which the mother emphatically declined. Further the mother was insistent that a physical was not to be given by either our school nurse or visiting doctor. Ruth, our receptionist, was so concerned about this neglected student she collaborated with Lorraine's teacher to switch lunches at recess time, she also saw to it Lorraine had milk and fruit. When Ruth opened the confiscated sandwich she found the bread spread with bacon grease. And of course this little girl was so inadequately clothed and dirty. It makes me sick to have the means to help these unfortunate children and then have my hands tied by proud and/or ignorant parents. There are ways around this barrier but it takes time to get the authorization so as not to be liable for a law suit."

"Working with the public as you and I do we learn to view the frustrations as a challenge, don't we? The bittersweet side of our professions," agreed Maria. Since this child was cast on my doorstep, I cared for her and kept her. Thankful that it was my doorstep and not someone else's. After checking with Chief Bennett I talked to Judge Steven Spencer and asked for legal custody. Under the circumstances, of course, he could only give me temporary custody, and here is a copy of the order which you will need for your files. And now I need your help."

"Anyway I can, Dr. Maria."

"I need to know who this child really is, and where her parents live. Also this child is petrified at the thought of leaving the safety of the house, she has nightmares where she is running from a father who is trying to throw her in the river. My dear friend Dagne has offered to tutor her, so I would like to talk to her teacher and make arrangements to take her books home and also have her work graded and supervised by the school so she will get proper credit."

"That sounds reasonable enough, and I agree it is most fortunate Lorraine was brought to your household." agreed Mr. Bowman.

"I didn't mention that Lorraine has Scoliosis which must be treated as soon as possible," continued Maria.

Mr. Bowman smiled, "I can recommend an excellent surgeon from our Children's Hospital..."

Maria smiled in acknowledgement of the compliment.

"It occurs to me," said Mr. Bowman, "It might be a

good idea to have Dr. Rolf bring the Search and Rescue Team for a demonstration one of these days.

"No doubt that could be arranged, Dr. Rolf loves the animals and loves to teach, and it would be very educational for the student body. But I will let you do the inquiring," answered Maria.

"By the way, here is an 'after' picture of Lorraine. This one is after a shower and suturing and swathed in my sweat shirt; and this picture is after a telephone ordered wardrobe," advised Maria.

"My word, one wouldn't know it was the same child! What a transformation!" exclaimed Mr. Bowman, "A real Cinderella!"

"It was necessary and it was fun and she is so appreciative, a real sweetheart,' answered Maria, "I wish she was mine, I hope she will be." Glancing at her watch again she stood up, "Thank you for lunch, that was appreciated."

"It was my pleasure Maria. Let's go to Mrs. Erickson's room first since it is closest," and they started down the hallway. "You will find Mrs. Erickson very understanding and helpful. She is a real jewel," commented Mr. Bowman, "And speaking of jewels there is Mrs. Erickson and Ruth now."

"Mrs. Erickson and Ruth Haynes, I would like to introduce you to Dr. Maria Goetche." Maria extended her hand and greeted both ladies with a cordial, "I'm glad to meet you."

Mr. Bowman continued, "Both of you ladies will be happy to know Dr. Goetche has Lorraine safe in her care."

"You have?" both exclaimed in unison.

"Come in to my room," invited Mrs. Erickson, "I want to hear about this."

Seated around Mrs. Erickson's desk, Maria again recounted the happenings of the weekend and showed the pictures.

"What a relief to know where she is and to know she is in good hands," sighed Ruth.

"My exact sentiments," echoed Mrs. Erickson, "How can we help?"

Maria explained Lorraine's terrified refusal to leave the premises and the arrangements that had been made for tutoring.

Mrs. Erickson beamed, "There isn't a more qualified person to instruct and guide Lorraine during this traumatic adjustment. Would you like to use our books until she can be persuaded to return to school?"

"That was one of the reasons I came today," replied Maria. "And would you be willing to grade and record her work so she gets full credit?"

"Oh, of course," answered Mrs. Erickson, "And may Ruth and I come to the house to visit her?"

"I think that would be a splendid idea, in fact why don't you bring her books to her this evening if it's convenient?" replied Maria.

"That is an excellent idea, I will do just that," commented Mrs. Erickson, "And I am so relieved to know she is safe."

You can say that again, she has been in my thoughts all morning," countered Ruth.

"Thank you both so much, you are most welcome to come anytime and I am confident your visits will help Lorraine reenter her school world." Maria, ever conscious of fleeting time, again checked her watch and stood, "I hope I am home this evening when you come so I can see Lorraine's reaction, but if not, Dagne will fill me in."

Mrs. Erickson and Ruth graciously accompanied Maria as she walked down the hallway.

Mr. Bowman turned to Ruth, "Dr. Goetche has a legal custody document for our files, and she would like to see Lorraine's enrollment card for name, age, and address data and whatever else would be useful to her, in fact, why not just make a copy of the card, and while

128

Dr. Goetche is here get a new address so our records are updated."

Ruth stepped to the file cabinet and withdrew Lorraine's card from the folder and handed it to Maria.

Maria read aloud, "Lorraine Hamilton, Space #9 River Road Trailer Court.   Father: Max Hamilton. Mother: Margo Hamilton."

Maria became silent as she began thinking to herself, "Margo Hamilton. THIS IS MARGO'S CHILD!" Maria stood silently scanning the card in her hand but not really reading - her mind racing in several directions at once. Mr. Bowman, Mrs. Erickson, and Ruth looked at each other astonished and perplexed but none spoke, as Maria looked aghast but unseeing at the card in her hand.

After what seemed an eternity of silence Mr. Bowman cleared his throat, "Is there a problem or something we can help you with, Maria?"

Instantly aware of her surroundings and regaining her composure Maria met the eyes of each of her companions and smiled, "Thank you, this is sufficient information for today. It's very apparent we have a mystery on our hands, and I probably will have much to share with you later, but first I must do some background work. Suddenly involvement is thrust upon me. Mrs. Erickson and Ruth I hope to see you this evening."

Extending her hand in a firm, warm handshake Maria bid each one good bye with a sincere, "Thank you." and hurried to her car.

*****

Visitors

Upstairs in the big country house a little girl with strawberry blond hair tied in a pony tail sat at a small desk sharing her seat with a teddy bear and a Strawberry Shortcake Doll laid across her lap.

Aunt Dagne had given Lorraine an assignment in a Math workbook for third graders and Lorraine was devouring the problems persistently. When Lorraine had finished the assigned page she took the book to Aunt Dagne who was sewing a clown doll. Aunt Dagne, anxious to know how her special student had done, laid down her sewing project and corrected the page with Lorraine.

"Flicka, you get a star - I am so proud of you. Now would you like to go to the blackboard and spell some words for me?"

And so the spelling words filled the blackboard. "We must save those words for Maria to see when she comes home," admonished Aunt Dagne.

"Now it is time for a little bit of fresh air. Do you like to jump rope?"

"I dunno."

"Have you ever jumped rope?"

"Uh-Uh."

"All right we will do it together, Uncle Rolf made us each a jump rope with smooth handles. Which color do you want?" asked Aunt Dagne as they went out the back door.

"The red and yellow one," replied Lorraine.

And so the day of learning progressed.

Dagne and Lorraine let the dogs in then went to the big, warm kitchen to put the tea kettle on the stove and begin supper when a car drove into the yard, followed closed by another. Aunt Dagne had never seen those cars before, and her immediate reaction was apprehension.

"Where can I hide Lorraine?" she thought.

Lorraine's own panic was heard in her question, "Who is that? Is that my Daddy coming to get me? Don't let him get me!"

Dagne paused and hugged Lorraine but before she could answer the child the front door bell rang. "You wait here," was Dagne's nervous instruction, and she turned to go answer the ring.

Because Dagne had hesitated and was walking slowly, plotting a course of action in her mind, the callers rang the doorbell again a little more insistently. Cautiously Dagne opened the door and there stood Mrs. Erickson and Ruth.

"Oh, for goodness sake Marguerite, I couldn't imagine who could be at the door. We have a case of the jitters around here," explained Dagne.

"I bet you have!" replied Mrs. Erickson, "Dagne I would like to introduce our school secretary, Ruth Haynes."

"How do you do," replied Dagne, "I have seen you probably at the super market, do come in ladies."

Mrs. Erickson explained, "Maria stopped by the school today to get Lorraine's books and we offered to bring them - the perfect excuse to see our little girl, you know. Ruth and I have become very protective of her as well as deeply interested in her welfare. She has won our hearts."

"I understand perfectly well," replied Dagne, "Our sentiments exactly. But you probably won't recognize the Lorraine who lives here."

"Maria showed us the snaps she had taken before and after - so we do have a little advance warning," smiled Mrs. Erickson, "but we are anxious to see living proof."

"Flicka come, you have company. Can you guess who is here?" called Dagne.

"Flicka?"

"She is so shy and frightened," interjected Ruth, "We can go where she is and not worry her anymore."

"Of course, and the kitchen table is a relaxed place to have a cup of coffee," agreed Dagne as she led the way. "Flicka, guess who came to see you and look what they brought you," announced Dagne. "Well, where is she," asked Dagne looking around the room, "Oh I bet she went upstairs to her new classroom, she is enthralled with her classmates and the idea of school; come, I will show you," invited Dagne as they climbed the stairs.

But the room was dark and when Dagne switched on the light only the silent stare of the dolls greeted her. "This is our class room," explained Dagne. "Psychologically this environment may be very therapeutic," she continued, "and quiet! Maybe too quiet."

"This is a situation few children would even dare day-dream about," whispered Ruth, and for our little chickadee it's perfect - no one to torment and harass."

"There are some meanies, out there," agreed Dagne. "By the way you might as well leave the books here on the desk; you have had your arms full long enough."

Flipping off the light Dagne went to Lorraine's room, "Flicka, are you watching the fish?" But no answer here either.

"Well, let's go have a cup of coffee, and perhaps our girl will get over her shyness and come out of hiding," suggested Dagne.

As Dagne was filling their cups for the second time Maria came home and agreed to the quiet approach of waiting. Before joining the coffee drinkers around the table she ran upstairs to leave her things and change her shoes, and couldn't help looking in all the rooms in hopes of finding the hiding child. Pulling up her chair and helping herself to a scorpa she commented wistfully, "I was so in hopes this would be a happy occasion for everyone concerned, but emotions, especially fears are difficult to cope with."

In a few minutes Rolf also drove in. When he had heard the events of the last hour he reasoned, "Well, let's have Laddie find her."

"Well of course, the dogs are in the utility room," replied Dagne.

"Here Lad," called Rolf, "Come on boy. Here Lady."

When neither dog responded Rolf went to see if the door was closed. The door was open and the room was empty.

Slowly Rolf returned to the kitchen, pondering the depth of Lorraine's fear, he really wasn't worried about her safety with the two dogs for companions but he was concerned about her emotional health. He poured himself a cup of coffee and joined the others at the table. The silence hung heavy in the room so when he bit off a piece of crisp Scorpa the crunch filled the kitchen, and each adult felt the crunch of dismay and despair for this hurting child.

Rolf laid down half of the Scorpa and cleared his throat. "I have a little idea that just might work," he stated. "It's apparent Lorraine is afraid of what she doesn't know, and that is who came in the two strange cars. When you ladies are ready to leave, I want each of you to say your goodbyes out by the cars and mention everyone's name in a happy, exuberant manner, toot your horns as you leave and then Dagne and Maria can come back to the kitchen and start supper, make biscuits, cookies or whatever and I am going down to the orchard to check on the late apples and feed the quail. If Lorraine does happen to come back in the house be casual and just pretend she went for a walk. Tell her Mrs. Erickson and Ruth came to visit and brought her school books and inform her they will phone tomorrow and inform her one of you will be coming by after school to see her. I'm going down to the basement storeroom and get a can of wheat and then I'll go to the orchard and whistle up a storm. If we can all be nonchalant we will probably calm Lorraine's fears."

"I should have called or had someone call for me," apologized Maria, "I just didn't think of the repercussions." Her thoughts were still swirling around the fact, THIS WAS MARGO'S CHILD!

"Oh Maria, don't blame yourself you had so many things to tend to during your brief lunch, I just regret I wasn't thoughtful enough to call," added Marguerite Erickson, "Of course we had no idea there would be such a reaction.

And perhaps we should go now while there is still daylight for Rolf to feed the quail."

"By all means," agreed Ruth standing, "Thank you for coffee and for showing us the unique classroom of dolls."

"Oh, that is the sweetest idea," agreed Marguerite, "I'll be thinking of you tomorrow, and thank you for the delicious coffee."

Walking out the back door with their guests, Dagne called after them,

"Thank you for coming and please come again Marguerite."

"Thank you I will be back, and thank you for coffee, Dagne."

"Ruth, thank you for bringing the books, and please come often," invited Maria.

"Thank you, it will be a pleasure to come again, and thanks for the goodies," replied Ruth.

There was much waving, tooting of horns and "goodbyes" as the two cars left the yard.

Rolf paused on the back steps and surveyed the sky with the observation, "It's going to be another beautiful evening." and with that he stepped off the porch and started whistling as he strolled along the path.

Maria and Dagne returned to the kitchen busying themselves with preparations for supper and found it difficult to curb the urge to go to the back door to see if Lorraine was anywhere to be seen. Going by the barn Rolf noticed a door stood part way open but he ignored the obvious and kept on whistling as he headed for the orchard where he stopped to check the late fruit and note the condition of the other trees. He slowly scattered wheat and watched as little brown camouflaged bodies moved among the fallen leaves coming closer to the human they had learned to trust. Rolf softened his whistle then began quietly talking to his feathered friends, standing still so as not to startle his visitors. Then he heard dogs running through the grass. Taking a few slow, short steps backwards away from the feeding quail, Rolf quietly said, "Stay," and used a hand sign for them to lie down. In a moment a little child was standing by his side. Retracing his steps back to where the birds were feeding, he took another handful of grain and cast it before them talking all the while.

Then holding the can down where the child could reach Rolf asked, "Would you like to feed our little Bobwhite Quail?"

"Uh-Huh," and a timid hand grasped a handful of wheat and cautiously threw it in the direction of the quail. All the while Rolf was talking in a reassuring way so these little creatures wouldn't scatter like leaves before the wind. Lorraine threw a second handful, and then a third emptying the can.

"There, now our forest friends have had their supper, and I think it is time for us to have ours. They will be going to roost in a tree pretty soon because the sun is setting," explained Uncle Rolf, "and look at that big moon coming up over the mountains." "What is roost?" asked Lorraine.

"Well," explained Uncle Rolf, "birds roost in trees to sleep but we lie in beds to sleep. Understand?"

"Uh-Huh."

Uncle Rolf walked to where the waiting dogs were lying and petted them then released them from his command with, "Let's go."

"Come on Snow White, let's see who can get to the house first."

*****

Good News

In the big, friendly house Dagne and Maria went about the kitchen in slow motion, not quite sure where to begin because their thoughts weren't really focusing on the task at hand. Dagne opened the oven door to check the Lasagna, closed the door and then absent-mindedly went back and opened the oven door again. Maria stood with a handful of silverware in her hand, staring at the table where the utensils should be placed. Finally Dagne realized it wasn't the oven she needed to open but the refrigerator where the salad makings were and so she filled her hands with lettuce and other greens...

Maria took a deep breath and as she laid the smooth silverware beside the blue and white plates began to speak, "I saw Lorraine's enrollment card today and learned her identity, but I can't hardly believe what I read.

This is too much of a coincidence things like this rarely happen in real life, they are reserved for story books, and then what publisher would accept it? I almost wish I didn't know now. Can this be real? Is it true? Is it the same person? How do I handle this? Where has she gone?" and then her voice broke."

Dismayed Dagne looked up from the sink where she was washing the salad greens. The last time she heard her dear friend so emotionally distressed was when Maria had told them of the plane that went down over Korea. Taking the towel with her as she dried her hands Dagne put her arms around Maria as she sobbed. "Rolf will find Lorraine, I am sure, and we will walk hand in hand with you through every difficulty, you know that. Now who is our little girl?"

But that question only triggered more uncontrollable tears.

"There, there we will talk about it later," comforted Dagne, "You better go splash cold water on your face."

Dagne began to sing a Swedish hymn and when Maria returned to finish setting the table she found the tune soothing and though she did not understand the words, she appreciated the feeling conveyed.

A breathless child's voice announced, "I won, I won, I got here first."

Then the sound of footsteps on the back porch punctuated by the bark of an excited dog catching the spirit of the game, preceded the return of the "quail feeding party," but Dagne continued to sing until Lorraine burst into the kitchen, "We fed the little bobs."

Maria put her arm around Lorraine, and asked, "Were there very many tonight?"

"Uh-Huh."

"Did you count them?"

"Uh-Uh."

"Did Uncle Rolf tell you why they are called Bob White Quail? asked Aunt Dagne.

"Uh-Uh."

"Well, you will have to have him tell you during supper, we can eat just as soon as you wash your hands."

"Okay."

Rolf entered the kitchen as Lorraine hurried to wash her hands.

"Well, girls how was that for a successful quail feeding adventure? It's amazing what kind of little birds show up."

"Very well done, my dear," responded Dagne, "You are a fantastic detective, we shall keep you."

"Keep me, indeed, try and get rid of me!" joshed Rolf. Then looking at Maria's face he knew that tears sat close to the brink and was relieved when Lorraine returned to the kitchen with the question she couldn't wait to ask.

"Why do you call the birds Little Bob's?"

"Oh because those little fellows go around telling everyone their name," and Uncle Rolf pursed his lips and mimicked the Bob White's whistle. They are saying '*Bob White Bob White*' "Can you do that?"

"Uh-Uh."

"Can you whistle?"

"Uh-Uh."

Lorraine's glance followed Rolf's to where Dagne was cutting a chocolate-cherry pie.

"Do you want to trade your piece of pie for a lesson in whistling?"

"Uh-Uh."

"Well, I don't blame you, I wouldn't either. Aunt Dagne's chocolate-cherry pie is too good to trade for anything."

After everyone had been seated and served, Aunt Dagne said, "Flicka, while you were out for a walk with the dogs Mrs. Erickson and Ruth came and brought your books. They plan to come again tomorrow evening to see you."

"Where are my books?"

"Up on your desk."

The mention of her books brought a smile, which quickly faded as she asked, "Are they going to tell my Daddy where I am?"

Maria's face registered the pain of grief as she spoke ever so softly to the child caught again in the turmoil of fright, "LoRie honey, no one is going to tell your Daddy where you are, they don't know where your Daddy is, besides all of us, including Mrs. Erickson and Ruth, want you to stay right here with us, so don't you worry your pretty head anymore. After supper you may go get your books if you want to."

"O.K." And the child began to gobble her food.

Maria reached over and gently touched Lorraine's hand, "Careful you will get a tummy ache. Maybe it would be better if you wiped your fingers on your napkin and went up and got your books now and put them where you can see them while you finish eating. Would you like to do that?"

"Uh-Huh."

"Flicka, how would it be if I helped you carry your books so you don't trip and fall on the stairs, one bandage is enough don't you think?" prompted Aunt Dagne.

"Uh-Huh."

"Excuse us please, teacher and pupil will be right back."

As soon as Dagne and Lorraine were out of earshot, Maria sighed and asked Rolf, "Could you and Dagne stay and look at something special tonight while I read a bedtime story to Lorraine, it really is very important to me."

"I thought you were going to ask me to wash dishes for my supper," twinkled Uncle Rolf, "of course we can stay. Is there anything else we can do?"

"Help me think logically."

"We shall do our best."

Lorraine and Dagne returned with the books and laid them on the corner of the table.

"Snow White, are all those books yours?"

"Uh-Huh," beamed Lorraine and touched the top book with a caring hand.

Dagne unfolded a table for the books and placed the treasures where Lorraine could see them.

"Can we have school again tonight?"

"Well, Flicka, I think you have had enough school for today, but how would it be if you showed the books to Uncle Rolf while Tia and I clear the table and clean up the kitchen? And don't forget you have spelling words on the blackboard to share also."

Each person at the table was eager for the passing of time but for each it was a different reason. Of course Lorraine was excited over her books and so eager to open them and share with someone the marvels of words and pictures not to mention her pride in the correctly spelled words on the blackboard in her class room; Rolf was mildly curious about what Maria wanted them to see; Dagne's thoughts kept racing to the door Maria had almost opened to reveal Lorraine's identity; and for Maria she longed to share with her dear friends the burden of knowledge she carried and then there was a long distance phone call to be made, how would she handle that?

When Maria hung up the dish towel Lorraine slid off of Uncle Rolf's lap where she had been showing him her cherished books and took Maria by the hand and led her upstairs to see her perfect spelling lesson. That trusting hand felt so comfortable and natural in hers, she willingly followed the tug of the enthusiastic child at the same time feeling a stronger tug on her heart.

Lorraine reached up and flipped on the light switch and without a word pulled Maria over in front of the blackboard, glancing from blackboard to Maria's face she waited as Maria began reading aloud: "snow, rain, melt, sled, cold". . . and when she finished pronouncing the twenty words she put her arm around the little girl and commented, "not only did you spell all those words correctly, you wrote so beautifully. I see your teacher gave you a big star, well I shall give you one for correct spelling and one for neatness," and as she promised Maria picked up a piece of colored chalk and made two large stars beside Dagne's original one.

While Lorraine and Maria were upstairs in the classroom, Rolf took advantage of the private moment to inform Dagne of Maria's request to stay. . . . "and I am sure there are tears ready to fall," observed Rolf.

"Oh, indeed there are," agreed Dagne, "Maria has information on Lorraine's identity but though she tried to tell me she couldn't get past the flood gates. It seems very painful to her."

"We must just give her time and all the space she needs when she needs it," counseled Rolf, "in the meantime let's go enjoy the music and look at the evening paper.

Lorraine had quietly led Maria upstairs but she ran ahead on the way back down, rushing to Dagne, she announced, "Tia gave her two more stars on the blackboard."

"Two more? How's that?"

"One for good spelling and one for neat writing."

"Can I save the words for Mrs. Erickson to see tomorrow?"

"You most certainly can Flicka - three stars are something to be proud of."

Lorraine's imagination awakened again, "Uncle Rolf, I want you to see my blackboard," and grasping his hand she seemingly pulled the big Swede to his feet.

In the classroom Uncle Rolf scanned the blackboard and whistled, "Snow White that deserves more than three stars. . . . that is a four star accomplishment." So Uncle Rolf picked up a piece of chalk and drew a large star at the bottom of the blackboard and initialed it. "There now that's official! and from now on I think your teacher better have you do your spelling on paper so you can collect a basket full of stars. Don't you think that would be a good idea?"

"Uh-Huh."

And again Lorraine raced down the stairs to inform Aunt Dagne about the progress of the stars.

Following behind Rolf pondered the magic morale builder found in simple chalk stars drawn on a blackboard. He had no doubt but what this little student would be an outstanding speller the rest of her life.

Carrying two large books Maria caught up with Rolf as he descended the stairs, "This is what I would like to have you and Dagne look at while I read to Lorraine," she said handing Rolf the two leather bound books.

Lorraine and Maria snuggled up on the davenport in front of the fireplace. Maria opened the book and began to read, remembering again when she had sat beside her Mama on the leather davenport in front of the fireplace in the her Papa's study and read this same story. Often her sister, Margreta who was younger would fall asleep leaning against their Mama's arm. Then they would look across to where her Papa was sitting with the evening paper and see him with bent head napping also. Maria could remember looking up into her Mama's smiling face, her Mama winked at her and kept on reading.

When Mama came to the end of the chapter she would clear her throat and Papa would lift his head and comment "I was resting my eyes," Maria remembered how Mama would gently gather up Greta and her Papa would pick her up and carry the girls upstairs, and what a sad day it was when they were too tall to be carried up to bed any more.

Maria could almost hear the wind sighing in the pines outside their stately old home in New Orleans and how glad she was that Greta and her husband had kept the dear home-place with it's rich, comfortable furnishings.

Lorraine's comment about a picture brought Maria back to the present.

Dagne and Rolf sat side by side on the love seat close to the stereo which was turned down to almost a whisper. A photo album was open on Rolf's lap and a second book rested on the end table. Silently the two looked at houses, places, and people, reading carefully the caption beneath each. Nearly half way through the first book Dagne laid her hand on Rolf's and looked at each other without saying a word. They looked across the room and back to the photo before them and then back to the child absorbing a story. Dagne took a piece of paper from the coffee table and marked the page and so they continued their unescorted visit back to Maria's origins, treading silently on the sands of time through the second album also, marking pages as they went, then returning to the first album and began again to assess what they were seeing.

Maria had finished reading the chapter and was explaining the pictures before putting the book mark in it's place and setting the book on the end table to be continued tomorrow night.

Lorraine picked up her Teddy Bear and Strawberry Shortcake Doll and walked over to Aunt Dagne, I'm going to dream about school tonight."

"I bet you will Flicka," Aunt Dagne gave Lorraine a good night squeeze. "Snow White I bet you dream of a blackboard full of colored stars."

"Uh-Huh."

"And if you dream about our Bob White's, call them for me, look, like this: pucker up your mouth and blow 'Bob White...Bob White' you try it." Lorraine puckered and blew.

"That a girl, pucker more and do it again."
The results were a faint whistle.

"Good start, we will practice some more tomorrow."
And Uncle Rolf gave his little bird-watching friend a good night hug. "See YOU tomorrow Snow White."

"Uh-Huh."

Maria had her arms full of schoolbooks to be returned to the upstairs classroom and Lorraine tightly clutched her soft friends as they headed for the stairs.

"Are Lady and Laddie going to stay in my room tonight?"

"Do YOU want them to?"

"Uh-Huh, so my Daddy doesn't get me."

"LoRie your Daddy isn't going to get you. But if you would like to have Laddie and Lady stay in your room that is fine. I'll have Uncle Rolf bring them in while you are taking your bath."

When Lorraine's bath was finished, Maria changed the bandage on her forehead and noticed with satisfaction it was healing nicely. Now she was snuggled in her pink bed with Teddy Bear and Strawberry Shortcake on the pillow and the "two guardians" of the ranch settled on the floor beside the bed.

Maria bent over the pillow and laughingly asked, "Do I kiss every face on the pillow?"

"O.K." and a pair of blue eyes danced at the thought.

"I tell you what, This kiss on your forehead is for you, and this one on this cheek is for Teddy and this one on the other cheek is for Strawberry Shortcake and you can pass them on. OK?"

"O.K."

Maria gave Lorraine a final good night hug and Lorraine turned over with a contented sigh, to watch the aquarium full of fish, the dogs sighed with resignation as Maria instructed then to "Stay", and as Maria descended the stairs to her waiting friends, she sighed with anxiety.

Dagne moved over and patted the space between Rolf and herself as an invitation for Maria to sit between them, knowing it would be more convenient as well as adding moral reinforcing as they looked at the old family album. Maria picked up the album and gently rubbed the cover as one would rub the hand of a dear old friend. Before opening it she commented, "After LoRie had her bath I rebandaged the wound and I am satisfied with the healing process, hopefully the scar will be minimal. Fortunately she can comb her hair low to cover any mark. And the scales registered a generous one-pound weight gain in three days which is a step in the right direction. I don't know if I am imagining it or if her skin is really clearer and cleaner after every bath, there is even a hint of pink returning to that little face, of course wardrobe reflection could be a contributing factor. I wish that was the only concern we had."

Turning to Dagne and then Rolf, Maria asked, "Do you suppose we can contrive a way to make LoRie feel safe to leave the house with me? I would like to take her on evening rounds at the hospital so you aren't so tied down all day and every evening, and also to help her gain confidence?"

"We Swedes are pretty good schemers," replied Rolf, "And Dagne has plenty of smart ideas inside that pretty head. I wouldn't be surprised if we can come up with some kind of solution in short order."

Dagne laid her hand on Maria's and added confidently, "Just let me sleep on this request. But now, let's open this book. You have postponed the pain long enough. The wound can't be treated until it is exposed."

Opening the album, Maria sighed, "I know, how well I know. But this pain is not mine alone."

Turning to the first page Maria began. "This is Grandma and Grandpa's wedding picture, and their first home in Baton Rouge where they lived while Grandpa was finishing his studies at the University Hospital. And this is their Sighing Sycamore Plantation in New Orleans that Grandpa had built after he established his medical practice there. And that is my Dad when he was little ... the pride of Grandpa's heart, as you can tell by all these growing up snapshots. Already Papa graduated from the University. Then Papa met Mama and Grandpa and Grandma were so pleased with the beautiful, talented golden blond Papa had chosen. They really loved Mama. This is my folks wedding picture, and their first little house in the country. Next is little chubby Maria... Grandpa really wanted a grandson but be accepted me and spoiled me wonderfully." "This is my little brother, Thomas Pierre, who was born with a defective heart and he died before he was two years old. Hopes, and dreams, shattered and buried."

"What an adorable, handsome child," commented Dagne, "A blond like you and your Mama."

"This is my little sister, Margreta. I wish this could have been in color because Greta has always had gorgeous golden red hair, which I openly envied."

There were many pages of little girls growing up. Birthday parties, ponies, and playmates.

Finally the page was turned to where Dagne had placed the marker.

"That is Margreta on her seventh birthday," explained Maria "She looks just like our little Lorraine," commented Dagne

"Indeed she does! And I kept saying I had seen this child before. Lorraine is Margreta's grandchild."

"Margreta's grandchild? Your family? How did this ever come to be?" pondered Dagne.

"Life's devious paths are strange paths," observed Rolf. "It is doubtful if Lorraine could ever tell us where all she has been."

"Maybe, little by little, she will recall places but we dare not make her feel pressured or insecure," replied Maria, "but how am I going to tell Margreta that her grandchild is asleep in my upstairs bedroom? Or that her grandchild has been so dreadfully mistreated by her parents? Or that she has apparently been abandoned?" Looking at her watch Maria concluded, "It's too late in the evening to call, Margreta rises early so she doubtless is already asleep and if I were to awaken her with this news she probably wouldn't go back to sleep tonight, not only that she would call Max's folks to tell them and there would be two households distraught. I am inclined to wait until early tomorrow morning to talk to them so they will have the day to adjust to the news."   "That is a thoughtful, sensible approach," agreed Dagne, "Besides now that you have exposed the wound, sleeping on the few facts that you have will give you more control when you have to give your family information that will break their hearts."

"Yes, it's heart breaking, and I am so glad I have you to share this with," replied Maria shaking her head in disbelief.

"Let me fix you a mug of hot milk, before we leave," suggested Dagne.

"Hopefully with a warm shower and a warm drink you can sleep."

"This doctor is going to take two aspirins with the hot milk and go to bed," replied Maria, "And I'll call my dear Sis in the morning."

"That sounds like a good idea," agreed Rolf, "Remember something good has to come from all this. But one thing I will never cease to marvel at is the mystery of coincidence."

The doctor swallowed herself-prescribed aspirin with the very warm milk, and bid her dear friends good night.

"See you both in the morning."

"Oh, you betcha," replied the big man with a bigger heart.

Before Maria turned out her bed light she re-set the alarm clock for 3:30 which would be 5:30 in Louisiana - she needed plenty of time to talk and Margreta needed much more time to get control of herself before her busy day began. It wasn't going to be easy at any time, for any of them, but it had to be said.

Maria groped her way to consciousness as the alarm incessantly obeyed it's preset instructions. Grabbing her robe she dashed to the bathroom to splash cold water on her face, then hurried downstairs to make a cup of tea. It was important, very important that she be fully awake and in control when she called Margreta whom she loved so much and her sister who had suffered dreadfully and deeply wondering where her daughter Margo was. Maria thought, "I've known pain and loss but at least I know where Warren is and why there is a white tomb stone marking the end of our dreams and hopes." But we are all wondering why Margo turned her back on a family that had loved her so dearly. And now this phone call would doubtless add an immeasurable weight to the already crushed couple. Loving, laughing, loyal Margreta and gentle, generous Tom. Lorraine would be a bittersweet element, she could be the jewel in their crown of joy and hope that lay discarded in the dust of disappointment. Maria carried her cup of tea into her library and locked the door. Even though Lorraine was asleep upstairs Maria wanted the security and privacy that only a lock can give — the added assurance that her conversation would not be overheard by an innocent, frightened child, should she awaken and wander about the house.

Before Maria reached for the phone on her desk she bowed her head and prayed for wisdom, then she dialed the number she knew so well.

On the third ring there was a soft, "Hello."

"Good morning Greta, did I catch you in the shower?"

"Oh Hi Sis. No, Tom is in the shower, I'm dressed and have half of my face on."

"Well, if you didn't put any face on you would be beautiful."

"You just say that because we look so much alike. By the way did you call me at this hour of the morning just to flatter me and boost my morale?"

"Taint flattery, honey child, 'tis the truth."

"Thank you, I love you too. And how is everything in the beautiful state of Oregon? And how is the Director of The Children's Hospital faring?"

"The state of Oregon is cool, green, and lovely. Winter could blow into the mountains any day. And the Director keeps unbelievably busy and loves every minute of it. It's wonderful to see kids helped and given hope."

"Well, no one could have a doctor with a more tender touch."

"It's that love for our fellow man that was born into us."

"Maria you have an extra special degree of caring that sets you apart."

"Thank you, but you should say we have. Greta I have something special and important to talk to you and Tom about."

"I hope it's good news."

"It's both, good and bad. Is Tom out of the shower? I want him to be on the line when I tell you."

Oh Maria, what has happened?"

"I'm not altogether sure what all has happened but I will tell you what I know."

Maria could hear Greta speaking to Tom, "Honey, it's Maria and she wants to talk to both of us."

"Tom is on his way down to the den. Do you still plan to be with us for Thanksgiving?"

"I'd sure like to be there, but I dare not promise."

"Good Morning Maria," Tom's rich, southern voice interrupted Maria's sentence.

"And a good morning to you Tom," replied Maria with a gentle voice that had lost much of it's southern accent.

"You sure sound like a northerner," teased Tom. "We were going to call you tonight, it has been a couple of weeks since we heard from you and you have been very much on our minds."

"Y'all been talking about me again?"

"Y'esm."

"Greta and Tom something most unusual has happened and I want to tell you all I know."

150

"We're listening," acknowledged two voices as one.

"Four days ago, on Friday night, my big Laddie brought a wounded child to my front drive. We know that Laddie brought the child because my neighbor Rolf Nielson saw drag marks in the gravel all the way up my lane from the county road. This little person had a nasty gash on the forehead, was dirty, poorly clad, and was in a state of shock and panic lest her father find her. Because of the clothing I thought at first the child was a little boy but she is a beautiful girl. When I suggested taking her to the hospital she attempted to bolt and run... so I showered her here, Rolf and I sutured the wound, fed this little one who could or would only tell us her first name, and put her to bed with two guard dogs in the room for her peace of mind."

"Saturday I had a friend at Penney's select a wardrobe using given measurements. I have talked to the Chief of Police regarding a missing child, and there has been none reported. I also spoke to a judge friend and have a temporary custody. Little Lorraine is beautiful and bright but has been dreadfully neglected and mistreated."

"Because the thought of leaving the shelter of the house was too traumatic I went to the school yesterday to get her school books. The principal was very helpful and cooperative and with the description I gave he knew exactly which child I was inquiring about, and let me see her enrollment card. Her name is Lorraine Hamilton. Her father's name is Max Hamilton and her mother's name is Margo Hamilton."

Maria heard a gasp from two voices on the phone, "Margo's child."

"MARGO'S CHILD!" Tom repeated.

"Margo's baby, our baby," breathed Margreta.

"Maria where is she? Is she alright?" begged Tom.

"What does she look like? Where is Margo?" queried Margreta.

"Should we come?" inquired Tom, not waiting for any answers from Maria.

"Did you say her name is Lorraine?" continued Margreta.

"She must be eight years old because it has been eight years since we last heard from Margo," calculated Tom.

"Yes, her name is Lorraine, but I call her LoRie because Lorraine is such a big name for such a little honey, and you are right she will be eight years old next month. She is asleep upstairs in the pink bedroom with Lady and Laddie lying by the door giving security to this frightened babe. And when I say frightened, I mean she lives on the brink of panic. We are going to have to be very careful, move slowly, and constantly reassure. She looks just like you Greta; she's beautiful, sweet but a fragile bit of humanity. We have no idea where Margo and Max are, but now I can give more information to give our police department so they can intensify their search.

"Should we come?"

"Of course you should come! However, I think it would be best to wait just a little to give us opportunity to introduce the thought to Lorraine that she has grandparents, and let her adjust to this concept that she has someone else special that loves her and someone she can safely love and trust. Perhaps we will need a week, and that will give you opportunity to make plans," Maria paused.

"Could you send us a picture right away?" begged Margreta.

"Of course I can mail some pictures today, the ones we took last Saturday when Lorraine modeled her new clothes."

"Maria continued, "She calls me Tia but as yet she is not aware that the name belongs just as she belongs. I just have a difficult time taking all this in. By the way, I must tell you, Lorraine has a severe case of scoliosis which must be taken care of very soon."

"Oh Maria, I was so in hopes our family plaque would be consumed with time," countered Margreta.

"Honey, that can be the least of the scars, and we know where to get the best surgeon in the country," assured Tom.

"You are right," agreed Margreta, then addressing her question to Maria she asked, "How do you manage when you arc at work?

"Dagne comes and stays each day. She brought her lovely, red, antique school desk and put it up in the doll room and she has school for Lorraine and the dolls. Not only that Dagne prepares all our meals, so we are making out very well. Dagne and Rolf are so quiet, wise, and loving I couldn't have found better neighbors if I had personally shopped the world over."

It's wonderful you have someone so helpful and trustworthy and caring," agreed Margreta.

"They are compassionate and understanding from tip to toe," assured Maria, "priceless people."

"We must call Max's folks right away - they have been so thoughtful and loyal keeping in constant touch with us. Sharing a common pain gives us a special bond. They are remarkable people, they have never blamed Margo, nor condemned Max but have recognized there was a problem out of control and grieved that he could not nor would not seek help. It is also unusual that they haven't groveled in self-inflicted guilt because they knew in their hearts they had done all they could, and given their best to their family. They will want to see Lorraine too."

"Greta, they are most welcome! Just as soon as I pave the way... and I will call you as soon as I get a new progress report on the search for our missing kids."

"Thank you Sis, your phone call certainly put a new light on our day!"

"What is it going to be like being called Grandma and Grandpa?"

"Just wonderful!" assured Tom, "Just wonderful!" We'll be talking to you later, goodbye Honey Child."

"Good bye y'all."

Maria's hand rested on the phone after she had returned it to the cradle... then glancing at her watch she realized it was only 4:15 and much too early to call the police station.

The thought of a leisurely shower and a little time to sit and read was most appealing as she unlocked the library door and turned out the light.
Going by the pink bedroom Maria couldn't resist the urge to stop and look at the sleeping child and contemplate the joy her sweetness would bring to four individual grandparents and to her own hungry heart. Would she be able to recall the past? Looking at the delicate face, soft hair, and little hands Maria wondered what wretchedness this wee soul concealed.

Maria methodically made her bed before going in to shower and dress for the day... she disliked an unmade bed almost as much as unwashed dishes left on a table... Attitudes and standards passed on from her fastidious Grandmother.

While coiling her long braid of blond hair on top of her head it occurred to her she hadn't made any entries in her diary for several days.

"I must make some notations before the events become a blur of memory, and before I indulge myself in any entertaining reading." She resolved, and sat down at her desk at the west window. Opening the lavender, velvet drape the new moon looked her right in the eye. Reaching over Maria turned off the brass, desk lamp so she could appreciate the early morning sky. Venus twinkled beneath the moon as the thoughtful woman contemplated the beauty and enormity of the heavens and thought,

"If I could begin to understand the complexity of the wondrous creation I see, maybe I could understand the miracle of coincidence that has occurred in our family... how can it be?"

Sighing she turned the light on again and began writing intensely lest she forget or omit a single, important detail of the most unlikely events of the last five days. When Maria had finished she closed the diary and returned it to the top left drawer of her desk and reached for the photo album on the cedar chest at the foot of her bed. Turning to the page Dagne had marked she once again studied the pictures of Margreta and marveled that Lorraine looked more like her Grandmother than her own Mother.

The sound of an approaching car interrupted Maria's perusing and she suddenly realized she was extremely hungry, after all she had been up three hours and the energy from the orange and cup of tea had long ago been consumed by the psychological and mental exertion of the preceding hours. She welcomed the arrival of Dagne and Rolf and was eager to share with them the reaction of her phone call.

Back in Louisiana Tom dashed from the den and up the stairs two steps at a time. Margreta met him at the door of the bedroom smiling through her tears.

Throwing his arms around her, Tom exclaimed, "Can you believe it? Can you believe it? We have a granddaughter and maybe we will find our Margo too!"

Greta laid her head against Tom's chest and wept tears of joy and sorrow interwoven; tears of relief and tears of hope.

"Lorraine."

"Tom repeated, that is a lovely name and she looks like you Greta, that means she is beautiful."

Greta smiled through her tears and wistfully added, "I not only hope we find Margo, but that we can bring her and Lorraine home with us. I miss Margo so and love her so much."

"My dear, we both love our girl, regardless what she has done, she is still our daughter and we will never stop loving her. And I am sure that is the way George and Rose Ellen feel about Max." "We had better call them right away before time gets away from us."

"Tom, you make the call and I will stand by on the other line."

"No my dear, I think it would be best if you made the call and talked to Rose Ellen, after all it was your sister that called you. Of course George should hear what you have to say.... all right, we will call. You can start dialing while I run back down to the den."

Margreta picked up the phone and dialed. On the fourth ring Rose Ellen's soft, southern, "Good Morning" made Margreta's heart beat a little faster as she thought of the news she had to share.

"Good Morning, Rose Ellen, this is Margreta, I hope I didn't interrupt your breakfast."

"Oh Good Morning, Margreta, No, you didn't interrupt breakfast. I am sorry it took me so long to answer the phone, I was just taking muffins out of the oven and moving the skillet of sausages off the burner." Tom interjected, "You can move those sausages and muffins right onto my plate, Rose Ellen. I can smell them from here, and I am hungry."

"Well, come on over, I have plenty to go around."

"Thank ya, y'all I better pass this morning but it sure is a temptation."

Rose Ellen, We have a little news to share with you but George should be on the phone too. Is he available?"

"Yes, Margreta, he certainly is. He just came in with the morning paper." It will only take George a minute to go down the hall to the library."

During this brief interchange, Tom's gaze fell on the gold-framed pictures of Margo and Max on the desk. Their high school graduation pictures were on either side of their engagement picture. These pictures were taken ten years ago...what had ten years done to those two? What had ten years done to their Margo? She looked so happy in those pictures. The promise of everything wonderful before her.

George's deep, "Good Mawnin' y'all" brought Tom back to the present.

"Good Morning, George" Tom responded, "How is everything with you folks?"

"Just great, Tom, but a bit concerned by this early call."

Margreta took a deep breath and began, "My sister Maria called from Oregon just a few minutes ago with some very unusual news that concerns all of us."

"Margreta, is Maria ill?" inquired Rose Ellen.

"Oh no Maria is fine, but let me tell you what she told us. Maria said last Friday evening her big Search and Rescue dog Laddie brought a child to her door step in the pouring rain. The child was wounded, weak, and very wet. Because of the clothing Maria thought this poorly clad child was a boy but she is a beautiful but terrified girl. There was a nasty gash on her forehead and when Maria suggested going to the hospital for care, the child attempted to bolt and run...so Maria showered and swathed this little one in her own sweat shirt and robe. Her veterinary neighbor Dr. Rolf assisted with the suturing and his wife prepared hot food and the comfort of a teddy bear. She would only give her first name and was tucked into bed with two guard dogs lying by the bed for the child's peace of mind.

Saturday the clerk supervisor at Penney's selected a wardrobe for this mystery child using given measurements. Maria talked to the Chief of Police regarding a missing child, and there has been none reported. She also spoke to a judge friend and received temporary custody."

"Because the thought of leaving the protection of the house was too traumatic Maria went to the school yesterday to get her school books. The principal was very helpful and cooperative and with the description she gave he knew exactly which child she was inquiring about and let her see the enrollment card. Her name is Lorraine Hamilton. Her father's name is Max Hamilton and her mother's name is Margo Hamilton."

There was a stunned silence then Rose Ellen and George whispered, "MAX AND MARGO'S CHILD!"

George's eyes instantly turned to the photos on his desk, Gregory Monty's high school graduation picture; Gregory Monty in his air force uniform; George Maxwell Jr's high school graduation picture; Margo's high school graduation picture and in a separate frame their engagement picture. George's vision dimmed with tears as he tried to focus on the images before him.

"Where is Lorraine now? Can we see her?" asked Rose Ellen.

Lorraine is with Maria and we can plan to go see her in a week or so," answered Margreta. "Maria needs time to introduce the thought of grandparents to her. Why don't you two come over for supper tonight so we can talk about this?"

"That is a splendid idea," agreed Rose Ellen.

"We have a child again, we have a grandchild." concluded George with a quiet, unbelieving voice."

The October moon over the big ranch house was reluctantly retreating towards the Cascade peaks. Maria swept the drapes aside for just one more admiring glance at that magnificent orb from which she derived so much comfort before going down to greet Dagne and Rolf, who had already let themselves in. Dagne had just finished pouring three steaming mugs of coffee when Maria appeared in the doorway of the kitchen.

"Did you see my beautiful moon?" smiled Maria.

"Woops, remember half of that moon is mine," chided Rolf.

"Oh all right, in fact when my tax statement comes you can claim ALLLL, of it." responded Maria.

"Oh no, half is half."

"If I could have reached that "Wheel of Cheese" this morning I would have eaten all of it... I am starved!"

"I anticipated that," interrupted Dagne, "So I came prepared."

"Wonderful, I'd gladly trade my half of the moon for a plate of food."

"That won't be necessary, though I'll agree that moon surely casts it's spell on me too.

But enough of this, we are anxious to know if you were able to make your phone call and how was your news received?" inquired Dagne as she put the veal chops in the big, cast iron skillet.

"My mission was accomplished and the news accepted enthusiastically and Greta and Tom were going to call Rose Ellen and George. I am sure as the day progresses and they contemplate our conversation they will be moving up to bigger and brighter clouds. It is such a pleasure to share such exciting and happy news! I wish I knew exactly how to tell our Lorraine."

"Well, just let time take you by the hand — there will be a thoughtful and satisfactory way," advised Dagne. "In the mean time I think maybe I have a workable and satisfactory way to get Lorraine to go with you on evening rounds."

"Great, what is your suggestion?"

"Do you mind if we make it a surprise, then you can really test it's effectiveness?"

"Sounds wonderful, and I will have something special to look forward to," replied Maria as she finished setting the table.

Warmth was already radiating from the little fire Rolf built in the Franklin Fireplace, the crackling kindling adding it's own punctuation to the atmosphere. Rolf glanced up from the grapefruit he was pealing and surveyed the dancing flame on the alder log with satisfaction.

Maria had finished her morning rounds with the Head Nurse and was both pleased and relieved that there were no emergencies and she could view the progress of her patients with satisfaction.

Going into her office, Maria closed the door and sat down at her desk. Opening her attaché case she took out a sheet of paper with two names and an address written across the top. Reaching for the phone, she took a deep breath and dialed. The call was answered on the first ring.

"Good Morning, this is Dr. Maria Goetche, may I please speak to Chief Bennett?"

"Certainly, just one moment please."

"Chief Bennett, speaking."

"Good Morning Chief, this is Maria Goetche."

"Well, good morning, and how are you?"

"Just fine thank you, just fine and how are you?"

"When a doctor asks me that I find it wise to say, all is well."

"Tish, how you talk! One would think I had a giant hypodermic in my hand."

"A fella never knows."

"Brad, I have a little information regarding the child-guest at my house, which I would like to have you check out."

"Oh good. Every little bit of information helps. It surely is strange that we haven't had any inquiries, clues, or leads on this case."

"Well, I hope what I have will help fill in the puzzle. The child's name is Lorraine Hamilton, and her parent's names are Max and Margo Hamilton. The address on the school records is: Happy's Trailer Park, 27292 River Road. That address should be current because Lorraine was enrolled on the 11th of October. Hopefully the Trailer Park manager can give you more information - maybe even a description of their car. It so happens I know the parents of this child, though I had never seen the child before, so my interest in finding the parents has increased considerably."

"Maria, you beat me to it! I was going to the school today to see what I could uncover. I'm curious, what prompted you to go to the school?"

"Lorraine was petrified at the thought of leaving the house to go to school, so I went to the school to get her books."

"Fantastic. As soon as my assistant comes in I will personally go out to the Trailer Park and see what Mr. Howorth can tell me, then I will let you know."

"Thank you Brad. I appreciate your help."

"Hey doctor, we are in this thing together, and I'm glad for your info."

"O.K. I'll talk to you later. Good bye."

Dagne poured Rolf and herself another cup of coffee, and refilled Lorraine's mug with hot chocolate, while Lorraine contemplated the design on her mug... on one side was a little boy and girl sitting on a fence and on the other side a child sat in a swing. Rolf's eyes followed Lorraine's concentrated stare and noticed the swing, and put the image in his memory for future reference.

Lorraine slid from her chair and went to get her coloring book and scribble pad. Climbing back into her chair she began sketching the scene from her cup. Rolf noticed but remained silent except for clearing his throat so Dagne would look up from the shopping list she was preparing. Both adults watched the child drawing, looked at each other with eye brows raised in surprised satisfaction but neither broke the magic spell ... Rolf pretended to read the paper and Dagne feigned concentration on the list before her.

Finishing her drawing Lorraine timidly slid her tablet towards Rolf who looked up from the paper. "Well say there, Snow White, that's a really good picture you drew. You better show that to Aunt Dagne."

"Let me see, Flicka, bring your tablet to me," drawing the child close to her she surveyed the apparent talent then the little expectant face. "That is an exceptional picture, do you want to color it and give it to Tia tonight?"

"Uh-Huh."

"Tia will be so pleased and surprised. How would it be if we go sing some songs before Uncle Rolf leaves?"

"The enthusiastic child quickly set aside her pencil and sketch pad, the anticipation of singing appealed to her, especially now that a little song was awakening in her heart.

*****

Candy Clown

Uncle Rolf sat at the keyboard limbering his fingers with long, deep runs, humming the scales as he played. Aunt Dagne motioned for Lorraine to sit on the end of the long bench next to Uncle Rolf and she pulled up a little chair next to the piano and sat down as Uncle Rolf began singing in his deep bass voice.

"Ohhhh what a beautiful morning, Ohhhh what a beautiful day. I have a wonderful feeling, everything is going my way."

Aunt Dagne opened the big song book to "God Bless America" and placed the book in front of Lorraine so she too could see the words to sing. Then they sang "America the Beautiful" and "Somewhere Over the Rainbow."

"Flicka, let's trade places for a minute," suggested Aunt Dagne, then Aunt Dagne and Uncle Rolf played a duet while Lorraine sat enraptured because this was an entirely new experience for her.

Rolf glanced at his watch and commented, "We have time enough to walk down to the orchard before I have to leave, what about it Snow White, shall we all go see who might be having breakfast under the trees?"

"Uh-Huh."

"We will need our warm jackets 'cause it's nippy out there." And each bundled into a wrap as they headed for the back door.

Uncle Rolf called the dogs to him and put then inside so they wouldn't alarm the little, wild, woodland folk.

Lorraine hesitated at the door and looked around cautiously.

Aunt Dagne observed the apprehension and distracted her fear with, "Look at the glow over the mountains, that sun will be popping up pretty quick. Let's watch and see where it comes up."

So Lorraine's rising fears were displaced by the rising sun.

"Flicka, would you like to hold my hand so I don't slip on the steps?" inquired Aunt Dagne extending her hand.

"Uh-Huh."

And Lorraine took the preferred hand with childish concern.

"We better help Uncle Rolf too."

"O.K."

And the frail child forgot her fright as her attention focused on the supposed need of another.

Uncle Rolf whispered as the three walked hand in hand with Lorraine in between the two protective adults, "remember we must walk and talk very quietly."

"Will the Little Bobs be there?"

"Well, maybe. The Bob White and the Ruffed Grouse and even the deer could be there, if they haven't already eaten and left."

They hadn't taken a half dozen more steps when there was a whirl of wings next to the path, followed by another burst of fleeing feathers.

Lorraine screamed with fright and pulled her hand from Aunt Dagne's to retrace her steps in flight but Uncle Rolf quickly and deftly picked her up into his arms and held her close as he explained, "We startled Mr. and Mrs. Ringneck Pheasant they weren't expecting us to come and we weren't expecting them to rush away with so much noise. But they will forgive us. It really does surprise and startle us when they fly up right next to us."

"I want to go back."

"All right, we will go back. Shall we whistle for the Bob White and see if they answer our call?"

"Uh-Uh, let's go back."

Holding Lorraine secure in his arms Uncle Rolf and Aunt Dagne returned to the big, safe house.

Uncle Rolf hugged Lorraine before he set her down, "I'll see you tonight at supper time, and maybe we can practice Bob White calls tomorrow, O.K.?"

"O.K."

Aunt Dagne gave Uncle Rolf a hug and kiss before she handed him his lunch pail, "Take care and I will see you tonight."

Turning to Lorraine, Aunt Dagne suggested, "Let's wave from the dining room window."

"O.K."

Uncle Rolf's pick up was scarcely out of sight when Lorraine asked, "Can we have school now?"

"Sure, we can have our first class in the kitchen while I plan supper, and tidy up. How would it be if you wrote a story for Tia about the pheasants startling us this morning, and then you can color the picture you drew for her."

Aunt Dagne knew fears had to be aired and there was no better way then to write it all down where they could be looked at. When the time came to go up to the classroom Lorraine carried her tablet and Aunt Dagne carried a very large sack of fabric.

Before Lorraine settled down to do her arithmetic Aunt Dagne took her tape measure and quickly took more measurements of her student, then Aunt Dagne unfolded her collapsible cutting table and spread out the fabric she had carried in the sack . . . there was pink and white polka dot; pink and white check; and pink and white stripe. Lorraine had watched Aunt Dagne make dolls the day before and knew something magical happened between the cutting board and the sewing machine. Aunt Dagne cut a few large pieces and many smaller pieces before folding up the table and setting down to her machine.

Arithmetic was finished, a geography lesson read aloud, and a science workbook assignment completed when Aunt Dagne suggested they go get some exercise before lunch. Aunt Dagne was certain going outdoors would still be a fearful experience so they went down to the basement recreation room and jumped on the huge trampoline until they were both out of breath. After a hearty lunch and a restful story Aunt Dagne asked Lorraine to inspect the sewing project.

"Do you think you would like to try this on?" inquired Aunt Dagne holding up a garment.

"Oh! Uh-Huh."

"Slip off your dress and let's see how this fits."

"O.K."

Helping Lorraine fasten the snaps up the front, Aunt Dagne poised Lorraine in front of the mirror and asked, "What are you?"

"A Clown," she whispered.

"Candy the Clown," agreed Aunt Dagne, "And look at this," picking up two clown dolls and tucking one under each arm, "shall we call them Gum Drops?"

"Let's see, you have a clown suit but now you need a clown face, right?"

"Uh-Huh."

Aunt Dagne sat Lorraine on a high stool in front of the mirror and began to draw big white circles around her eyes and mouth; funny, high, blue eyebrows; and a red nose. Then she placed a pointed cap with a tassel on her head and stood back to admire the effect. "We have a new student in the class room - a brand new person. What happened to Lorraine?"

"She is hiding," concluded Lorraine.

"You are so right, she really is hiding. I bet neither Tia nor Uncle Rolf will recognize you, we shall see."

"Can I wear this for class?"

"Absolutely, but do you think Candy the Clown can spell all the words correctly?"

"You are right clowns are smart people too. And after I give you your spelling words you may practice your penmanship while I make some more Gum Drops."

As the afternoon progressed Lorraine became more and more anxious for Maria's return finally the sound she had waited for so expectantly. The back door opened, but self-consciousness robbed Lorraine of her resolve to run and greet Maria at the door instead a little clown stood frozen in the center of the kitchen with her arms full of Gum Drops and her heart full of doubts.

Maria's quick eyes took in the loveable little clown creation before her with pink and white ruffles framing the sweet face, encircling the wrists and ankles and noticed the feet shuffle and one foot came to rest on top of the other. The down cast eyes were riveted to a spot on the floor. "We have a visitor. What a cute costume!" exclaimed Maria as she knelt before the child and hugged her. "Do you have special name?"

"Uh-Huh."

"What is your new name?"

"Candy the Clown."

"Of course, you look like a candy cane."

"Where is my little LoRie?"

"She's hiding."

"Ah, so she is! And no one can see her."

"Do your dolls have a name?"

"Uh-Huh."

"I thought so, what is it?"

"Gum Drop."

"Very nice and can you describe a gum drop?"

With the focus of attention being shifted to the little dolls, Lorraine's feet settled comfortably to the floor and her eyes surveyed the painted faces of the cloth magic in her arms.

"Well a gum drop is a soft, sweet candy. Some are as small as a large pea and others are as large as walnuts. And they come in all different colors. We will have to get some so you can see and taste for yourself."

"O.K."

"Did Aunt Dagne make any more Gum Drops?"

"Uh-Huh."

"How many?"

"I dunno."

"Where is Aunt Dagne?"

"Up stairs."

Lorraine and Maria entered the doll classroom to find Dagne painting the face on the last of several Gum Drop dolls, which were dressed in miniature clown suits identical to Lorraine's.

"What a clever idea Aunt Dagne."

"Did you recognize our girl?"

"Goodness no, I thought we had company."

"Well, we do. We have a clown at our house."

"I know some sick children that would like to see our Candy Clown and have a little Gum Drop Clown to love."

"Where are they?"

"They are in a Clinic for sick children."

"They can have mine," volunteered Lorraine handing her dolls to Maria.

"Oh thank you LoRie, that is very sweet of you, but I think Aunt Dagne made enough so you can keep the ones she gave you and there will be enough to share."

"O.K."

Aunt Dagne set the last doll aside all complete with a contagious smile.

"Supper is all ready, all we have to do is set the table."

"O.K. LoRie and I will wash our hands so we can set the table."

When Lorraine entered the kitchen she could smell something good but there were no pans on the stove. So when Aunt Dagne opened the oven she was surprised and relieved to see meat loaf, baked squash, baked potatoes, and baked apples.

Then the back door opened again and Uncle Rolf came in exclaiming, "Man, oh man, this hungry Swede just had to follow his nose." Then catching sight of Lorraine he remarked, "Well, we have company."

"Where is my Snow White?"

"She is hiding," volunteered Aunt Dagne. "Uncle Rolf I want you to meet Candy the Clown."

"Well, glad to meet you, I'd like to shake a clown's hand," he replied holding out his own.

Lorraine being unaware of the custom of shaking hands held out both of hers which Uncle Rolf took tenderly in both of his. Then he lifted the little clown up into his arms and hugged her.

During supper Maria asked Lorraine, "Would you like to go with me to visit the sick children, and show them your clown suit?"

"Will my Daddy get me?"

"Remember Lorraine is hiding and NO ONE can see her. And NO ONE has ever seen Candy the Clown before."

"Can I give the children a Gum Drop?"

"You most certainly can," assured Maria

"Who has gum drops?" asked a puzzled Uncle Rolf.

"I have two Gum Drops," replied Lorraine pulling her new clown dolls from off the chair behind her.

"Those look like Jelly Beans," teased Uncle Rolf

"Uh-Huh."

"Where did you get those little fellows?" questioned Uncle Rolf as if he didn't know.

"Aunt Dagne made them."

"Aunt Dagne can do just about anything, can't she?"

"Uh-Huh."

When supper was finished Aunt Dagne brought down a basket filled with the extra dolls and Maria asked Lorraine "Shall we go now?"

"I want Aunt Dagne and Uncle Rolf to come too."

"That's a nice idea," responded Maria sensing Lorraine's fear and the need for reinforcement. So everyone put on their warm coats.

Uncle Rolf suggested, "How about letting Aunt Dagne carry the basket and I will carry our clown to the car."

"O.K."

Lorraine clutched Uncle Rolf about the neck and cried with fear. Aunt Dagne got into the car on one side and Uncle Rolf set Lorraine on the back seat between them. She sat as far back on the seat in the darkened car as possible wanting to be invisible from all danger.

Maria pulled into the Staff basement garage and the four entered the Children's Clinic by the back door. Inside the warm building Dagne removed Lorraine's coat and gave her the basket of dolls to carry. Maria took Lorraine's hand and together they made evening rounds. At every bedside Lorraine held her basket high so each child could choose their own Gum Drop.

Candy the Clown certainly was not aware of the healing properties in each Gum Drop she shared but she did see the smiles on the children's faces and was warmed by their happy smiles. Neither was this little clown aware of the healing that was taking place in the depths of her own being as she shared herself.

It goes without saying that had Lorraine known she was in a hospital she would have panicked, experiencing traumatic fear. However, the kindly deception, protecting her from the facts served as a very valuable tool for her own therapy and entrance to a normal, healthy life.

Lorraine had visited the last child and paused momentarily for Maria to finish making notes on the chart she held in her hand when the little dark haired boy asked Lorraine, "Will you come again?"

"Uh-Huh"

"When?"

"I dunno"

"How about tomorrow night?" interjected Maria.

The little patient and little clown simultaneously echoed, "O.K."

"Thank you," he repeated admiring the Gum Drop clown held at arms length.

"Welcome," responded Candy the Clown

"Luf you," called the little lad as his two visitors turned toward the door. Lorraine looked up into Maria's face wondering how she should answer.

"We love you too Derek," assured Maria as she stepped back to the bed and gave Derek a warm hug.

As Lorraine observed this little good night ritual she could identify with Derek and knew he felt good inside just as she had felt warm and happy when she had been hugged. She waved to him as she left the room, and felt at peace though she couldn't identify nor explain the emotion.

Lorraine held the empty basket in her left hand while her right hand sought Maria's and loved the reassuring little squeeze she felt as they made their way down the hallway.

Aunt Dagne and Uncle Rolf had followed quietly and unnoticed at a distance observing as they went past each door the special joy each child displayed. Even older children were touched by the simple shyness of the child-clown and the sweet message the Gum Drop doll sent directly to their hearts. Most impressive of all was the silent change being wrought within Candy's costume. Parents and visitors smiled at Candy and made appreciative comments. This kind of attention was similar to that she had been receiving at Maria's but still this new appreciative audience caused her to duck her head with shyness.

Turning the corner of the hallway Lorraine was startled to see a Father holding a little girl who was crying inconsolably, "take Sissie home, I want my Sissie."

Holding her breath, Lorraine stood riveted to the spot watching to see what would happen next.

To her amazement and relief the Father gently explained, "Sissie will come home next week when she feels better."

"But I want my Sissie now," wailed the worried tyke, as her Mother emerged from Sissie's room.
"Shhhhhh Babe, Sissie isn't crying and you mustn't cry either, everything is going to be all right," comforted the Mother.

"But Mama, I need my Sissie and my Sissie needs me," the little one lamented.

Because Lorraine was holding Maria's hand with a "vise-like" grip Maria looked down at the worried and perplexed clown beside her, and their eyes met for a moment. Looking back to the sobbing child and then up at Maria again Lorraine asked, "Can I give her my doll?"

"Do you want to?"

"Uh-Huh."

"That would be a nice thing to do," assured Maria as they walked together closer to the sorrowing sister.
Speaking to the Father, Maria said, "There is someone special here to see your little girl.

At that instant the Father noticed Candy the Clown, "Annette look who is here to see you," and the Father knelt down so the clown and child were face to face. "What is your name?" He asked.

"Candy," and grasping the doll in her basket she handed it thoughtfully to the wee girl with the tear stained face, and both of them smiled.

*****

Unresolved Anger

Down a stately lane, in a stately house, in the beautiful state of Louisiana, a stately man with premature gray hair about the temples, bowed his head and begged, "Oh, God of heaven, help," George sat thus for several minutes before he joined Rose Ellen.

When George entered the kitchen Rose Ellen was still standing in the nook, staring at the phone with mixed feelings of hope and fear, joy and anguish, belief and disbelief. Old "heart wounds" began to bleed again and an exciting anticipation took root somewhere in her toes and grew rapidly until it reached the base of a brain that had been bruised by brutish, uncontrollable forces. When George walked in, love transformed Rose Ellen's face and her eyes were like glowing candles in a dark night.

"We have a family again," whispered George with a husky voice as he embraced Rose Ellen.

They dried each others tears and smiled. Rose Ellen mused, "We have a little Lorraine. I wonder what color her hair is?"

"It has to be golden," chuckled George, "With two Grandmothers that look like sisters that child doesn't have much choice."

"Oh, sure she does. She could have your dark brown hair, or Tom's blondness, or she could be her own person."

"Well, whatever she looks like, whatever color hair she has she will be beautiful because she is ours," concluded George.

"It's going to be a long week of waiting," sighed Rose Ellen.

"Well, yes, but we have a lot of shopping to do this week Grandma Rose," chuckled George.

"Oh, you know what? We will have to call Maria because we have no idea what size our little doll is."

"That's no problem," assured George, "but it will sure be a switch shopping for dolls instead of trucks, and pink frills instead of jeans and cords."

"I can easily teach you Grampa, but let's eat before our breakfast gets cold and we don't have enough strength to do anything."

Though the Hamilton's and the Boesche's were very close friends and visited often there was an element of excitement, anxiety, and anticipation which surrounded the planned visit for the evening. The day seemed excessively long and difficult to endure. Longer than any wait any child ever had for a birthday or Christmas morning!

Before George's extended hand reached the doorbell button, the front door was flung open wide and Tom's words voiced the feelings of each person, "Come in, come in, today seemed to last forever."

"You better believe it did," acknowledged George as he warmly shook Tom's extended hand.

Rose Ellen and Margreta hugged and cried wordlessly - conversation seemed so needless and impossible.

As they hung their wraps in the front hallway, George observed, "Something smells fit for kings!"

"More than that," countered Tom, "Fit for grandparents!"

Wiping away tears that represented many emotions, Rose Ellen said wistfully, "I hope we are eating in front of the kitchen fireplace tonight."

"How would it be to sit on cushions on the hearth?" asked Margreta.

"Sounds perfect," agreed Rose Ellen

"Martha made lasagna and fresh French-bread and that shouldn't be too hard to handle from the coffee table," continued Margreta.

"Oh, you know Martha's cooking wouldn't be hard to handle from any place," and the two grandmother's laughed.

The men had joined the ladies in the spacious, warm kitchen and instinctively knew what to do to help serve the meal. Margreta thought of the many changes that had come to pass in the stately old house since Margo had left the nest. In fact drastic changes began to be made at onset of World War II with many of the hired help taking defense jobs and some joining the service, and with each succeeding war it seemed another change was made. Of course the biggest change that the old plantation had undergone was when the slaves were freed but that was more than one hundred years ago and there was none living in the area that could recollect those bygone days. Now days, Margreta dismissed the cook when she arrived home and after all those years of house servants they were adjusting to doing for themselves. And so it had been for George and Rose Ellen and they too had graciously adjusted to the change and the new found "aloneness".

Time and tide waits for no man, and to prove this point the banjo clock beside the fireplace ticked in unison to the baton of father time. The only other sound in the hushed kitchen was the occasional protesting crackle of the pine log on the fire.

Each of the four grandparents had silently served themselves and were privately contemplating George's thought provoking words in Grace: "Father help us to be grateful for all our natural blessings, and may we be thankful for blessings we don't even recognize. Teach us to accept the clouds with the sunshine."
Tom took a sip of the hot coffee Margreta had poured for him, then set his cup down in a very positive

manner before speaking, "It is good to realize that clouds come in varied shapes and sizes."

Rose Ellen smiled sadly when she commented, "Some of those clouds have been dreadfully black, and have hung over-head for such a long time."

Sympathetically Margreta replied, "Indeed they have, fortunately you have a faith that helped you to be flexible and bend with the storms."

"And our love that drew us even closer together," sighed Rose Ellen as she gently laid her hand on George's.

"If anyone ever tried to analyze and understand the pain and sorrow of a child's heart, we did," said George shaking his head with disbelief at his failure. "We could see the pattern of what happened and what was happening but Max built an impenetrable defense around himself at a very young age - his disposition was so different from Gregory's."

"Both of the boys dearly loved Baby Jane but Max seemed more possessive, whereas Greg was protective, of course the boys were only three and six, just babes themselves. How could we have warned the boys that our little girl had a defective heart and may not live? The adjustment to her death was more difficult for Max. We cuddled him continually to comfort him as well as ourselves, but he so often had that far away, lost look in his eyes. Greg cried and loved us and we cried and loved him. We thought time would help Max forget but there was a lasting scar which we were aware of afterwards."

"Max was four and Greg seven when Doctor Miles made his daily house calls to visit Great Grandpa Mondon during Grandpa's final illness. Those two little boys stood outside the closed bedroom door holding each others hands, and when Doctor Miles came out, their frightened inquiring eyes searched the doctor's face for answers and comfort. Fortunately Doctor Miles was an observant, compassionate man and he understood their worried countenance. He set his black case on the floor, sat down in the big rocker and took a boy on each knee. "Grandpa says you are his special boys, is that really so?"

"Yes, sir," they whispered in unison.

"Well, I can see why, you look like mighty fine boys to me, and your Grandpa must be a very special Grandpa to you."

"Yes, sir," they again answered.

"Boys, your Grandpa is comfortable, he is just awfully tired. But I am sure he would enjoy having you go in to visit him after breakfast, lunch, and supper for a few minutes. Now don't you worry because his nurse will always be with him. I'll see you boys tomorrow. From then on Doctor Miles always invited the boys to go in with him so they could watch the doctor take Grandpa's blood pressure and listen to his heart with the stethoscope. Then came the evening Grandpa asked the nurse to lift the boys onto the bed, with one on either side of him."

He held a child's hand in each of his failing, frail hands and said,

"Good bye my little men, I am old and tired and I must go."

"Go with Bumpa?"

"Go be with God and baby sister Jane."

"Don't go Bumpa, won't we see you anymore?"

"Someday, now give me a kiss and be good men for me."

"When we put the boys to bed that night Greg cried in our arms but Max just clung to me,

"Don't leave me Buddy," "So I held Max until he fell asleep. The next morning we had to tell the boys Grandpa had indeed gone to be with God.

"At the funeral Greg cried with us but Max just looked angry as though he had been deserted," observed George.

"Doctor Miles even came and talked to the boys, I remember his kindly, wise words as he again took them on his knees," added Rose Ellen.

"Boys, I know you miss your Grandpa, he was a good grandpa and a fine man, but your Grandpa was very old, and very tired, and he didn't feel well anymore. It was hard for him to walk, and hard for him to use his hands, hard for him to see, hard for him to hear, nothing tasted good - he just wanted to go to Heaven. Your Grandpa loved you, now you must remember the happy times you spent walking in the meadow watching the colts; when you picked apples and peaches together; when he played his harmonica for you; the times you sat in the big swing under the willow tree and he told you stories and you laughed."

"Great Grandpa Randolph Mondon was the best Bumpa in the whole world," summarized Max, "And I want him to come back and see me."

"Bumpa is in Heaven talking to Baby Jane, telling her about us," concluded Greg, "but I miss him."

Doctor Miles continued, "You boys will always remember your Grandpa loved you and you can keep that love safe in here," indicating his heart."

"And as if that wasn't enough," said George picking up the thread of their memories and shadows, two years later the boys' Nanny Beulah got the flu with pneumonia and died so suddenly. She had taken care of them from the day they were born, in fact she was present when they were born, holding them closely and tenderly when they were only minutes old - talking and humming to them, forming a permanent bond. After that Max carried on badly, refusing to let Nora help him as his Nanny and became fiercely independent. The boys were inseparable buddies but so different."

Rose Ellen went on, "Of course Max was beside himself when Greg volunteered at the beginning of his junior year at the University to become a helicopter pilot during the Korean War. Max wanted to go too but he was too young. Max took flying lessons, joined junior ROTC, pushed himself to get the best grades, and impatiently waited for the day he would be old enough to also volunteer for flight duty. But when we received word that Greg had been shot down, was missing in action and presumed dead, then later confirmed dead, something inside of Max snapped or died. And though he saw our tears and heard our voices of mourning I don't think he recognized the fact that we grieved and hurt as much as he did."

George began again, "We tried to talk to him, reason with him, remind him we loved him, and assured him this was all in God's hands and we had to accept it as such, and though he was courteous and respectful he still stood aloof and distant with unresolved anger within. I have tormented myself asking what I should have and could have done differently. Why did this sensitive, tender life develop so differently? Rose Ellen and I have known more pain from Max's rejection then we have from the loss of our other two children though we loved them all equally. The bond of our love has been tested and strengthened. But this last cloud is one we all share and now it appears it has a beautiful silver lining."

*****

Puppies

At Maria's request Rolf and Dagne had come early. Rolf had just put another log in the Franklin Fireplace and was pouring himself a cup of coffee when Maria and Lorraine entered the kitchen.

"Good Morning kids," was Uncle Rolf's teasing greeting.

"Good morning Dagne, good morning Rolf, good morning world," was Maria's bouncy greeting, as she stopped in front of the fireplace to savor the friendly warmth.

"Good morning," Dagne responded.

Lorraine went directly to the range to watch Aunt Dagne bake pancakes on the steaming griddle and was fascinated as the bubbles in the batter rose and burst. Setting the bowl of batter on the counter Aunt Dagne put her arm around Lorraine and gave her a gentle squeeze, "How's our girl this morning?"

Lorraine's answer was a faint smile as their eyes met.

"Would you like to have a bunny pancake for breakfast?"

"Uh-Huh," replied Lorraine not really knowing what that would be, but if Aunt Dagne was making it then it was all right.

Lorraine watched with special interest as Aunt Dagne ladled a large spoonful of batter onto the griddle and announced, "This is bunny's body," then another spoonful was placed above the body which was labeled bunny's head, a drizzle of batter formed two pointed ears, "And this is his tail," concluded Aunt Dagne.

"Tia, look," begged Lorraine as Maria finished pouring orange juice and coffee refills.

"Isn't that clever, you lucky little girl."

Lorraine looked admiringly at the baking bunny, "You can have it Tia."

"Oh LoRie thank you but that was made just for you. Aunt Dagne made big brown moons for me."

Lorraine watched apprehensively as the pancake bunny was transferred from the griddle to her plate, this was a very special moment.

After grace was said, Uncle Rolf teased, "You better watch that bunny it might hop right off of your plate."

The thought amused Lorraine and a smile seemed to hop around the edge of her mouth.

"What do you want on it?" asked Aunt Dagne.

"I dunno."

"Would you like some fresh black berry jam? asked Aunt Dagne.

"Uh-Huh."

Maria passed the butter and jam and helped Lorraine put a generous coat on Mr. Bunny.

"Are you going to eat his ears or tail first?" asked Maria curiously.

"His ears."

"I think I would start at the top too," agreed Maria.

It was so hard to actually cut into this masterpiece which actually captured the imagination.

"You better eat him quick before he runs away," encouraged Uncle Rolf again.

So first one ear and then the second ear disappeared, but the third bite of jam-covered pancake slid off the fork and slid down the front of Lorraine's new blue blouse and landed jam side down in her lap.

Her hands covered her mouth in horror and she looked down and surveyed the catastrophe, then tears of embarrassment and fear ran down her cheeks, and over her hands, as she remembered past accidents.

"I didn't mean to," she sobbed not able to lift her eyes.

"LoRie, we all have accidents sometimes," comforted Maria as she took a paper napkin and gathered up the offending pancake and jam. "After breakfast you can go put on a clean dress, a little soap and water will take care of this just fine."

"Snow White, that bunny hopped right out of your plate, and you thought I was spoofing, didn't you?"

"Uh-Huh."

"As soon as we are through with breakfast, I have something special to show you," announced Uncle Rolf changing the subject.

Curiosity and excitement shone through the tears as she lifted her head to meet Uncle Rolf's grin. Pulling her chair over beside his, he suggested," I'll cut and you eat. In fact, I need another pancake myself, and here's two sausages for you and two for me and I bet I can finish before you do."

The challenge erased the self-consciousness and fear and the pancakes vanished.

"Good girl, you beat me by two bites. Let's give the cook a hug and then everyone can come with me.

Excitement and anticipation tingled down Lorraine's back as she followed Uncle Rolf down the hallway, looking back to make sure Maria and Aunt Dagne were really coming.

Uncle Rolf opened the utility room door and went to the corner where Lady was lying. He reached down and stroked her head and she thumped her tail in response. Then Lorraine saw the six sleeping puppies snuggled beside Lady. Without a word Lorraine knelt and laid her head against Lady's then Lady licked her cheek.

Uncle Rolf reached down and picked up one of the soft puppies and gently placed it in her waiting hands.

Nothing but ecstasy registered on Lorraine's face as she cradled the tiny puppy in her hands.

"What's wrong with its' eyes?" she asked with concern.

Uncle Rolf explained, "All puppies and kittens are born with their eyes closed but they will open in about ten days."

"How can they see where they are going?"

"Well, they aren't going very far until their eyes are opened, but they can smell and feel their way to their mother. Now let's set the little fellow down by Lady and see what she does."

Lorraine laid her cheek against the soft fur of the sleeping puppy, then cautiously set it down by Lady, who immediately began to lick it as the little creature nuzzled his way up to her warm side. Then Lady licked Lorraine's hands as the delighted child continued to kneel by her side.

Maria sat at her office desk, taking a break between morning rounds and the ceaseless office calls and dialed Judge Spencer's number. On the third ring Judge Spencer answered the phone himself.

"Good Morning Steve, this is Maria Goetche. I'm sorry to disturb you before regular office hours, but as you know sometimes it's early or not at all."

"You are so right, Maria. It's good to hear from you. Any clues or leads to your mystery?"

"As a matter of fact, yes we have one excellent clue as to who the child is but nothing yet as to the whereabouts of the parents."

"Indeed, what is the clue?"

"According to the school registration records this child's parents have the same name as my niece and her husband. . .who broke contact with the family approximately eight years ago."

"Maria, what are you saying?"

"I am saying this is the most unlikely turn of events that one could imagine!"

"Well, I guess so! What a coincidence! What a fantastic coincidence!"

"Steve, please do me the favor of keeping this quiet for now."

"Absolutely, Maria, I agree. Does Chief Bennett know about this?"

"Not yet, he is next on my list of calls to make."

"Thanks Maria, this is a first for me and it really is exciting. Please keep me posted."

"I certainly will, thanks for your time."

"Thanks for the good news doctor."

Maria dialed Chief Bradley Bennett's number and waited. . . "Good morning, this is Dr. Goetche, is Chief Bennett in please?"

"Certainly, I will connect you."

"Good morning Chief Bennett, this is Maria Goetche."

"Good morning Maria, how does the day look from there?"

"Well Brad, there is a sunny sky with clouds the shape of question marks."

"Very good, I concur with that description. Armed with a search warrant, Mr. Howorth took me into the trailer to be sure there was no foul play, and he was able to give me a good description of their car so we have that added bit of information in the system."

"Brad I have a little bit more to add to your file."

"Yes?"

"The other day when I told you I had gone to the school and got her name and address from the school registration records, I was too much in shock to tell you the rest of my discovery."

"Good news, I hope."

"Yes good, but distressing and amazing."

"How's that?"

"The name of Lorraine's parents is identical to the names of my niece and her husband who broke contact with the family approximately eight years ago."

"Maria, are you saying the same name? Are you sure? Do you think? I guess I would be in shock too."

"It is very likely, it is very probable, but please don't release this information to the news media."

"You have my word Maria, and I agree this is not the time for stories. But what a story! What a coincidence. In the meantime the search goes on."

Lorraine could hardly wait to finish her lessons so she could run to check on the puppies. In fact watching the puppies was even more important than eating. Kneeling beside them she would stroke their tiny velvet coats and count them to be sure they were all there. She was most delighted when Uncle Rolf came home and would pick up one of the sleeping bodies and let her hold it. Then came the wonderful morning when she went to visit Lady's family and discovered they had their eyes open.

"They can see me, they can see me," Lorraine exclaimed, and went racing to the house to share the good news. "Aunt Dagne, Tia, the puppies can see!"

That evening when Maria returned home Lorraine took her out to the room known as the nursery to admire the squirming, squeaking miniature Search and Guide dogs.

Petting and evaluating each one Maria asked Lorraine, "LoRie, which one do you like best?"

"I dunno."

"Well, you think about it and whichever one you like best you can have for your own."

"To keep?"

"Yes, to keep."

"A puppy of my own?"

"That's right."

"Will my Daddy take it away from me?"

"Absolutely not! said Maria.

"Oh Tia," and Lorraine slid her hand trembling with excitement into Maria's.

"LoRie, have you ever held a puppy before?"

"Uh-Uh."

"It's fun, isn't it?"

"Uh-Huh."

This was changing the subject but Maria HAD to ask this next question, days had stretched to over a week and the waiting was unbearably painful for everyone. She knew the answer but had to begin somewhere. "LoRie have you ever gone to your Grandmother's house?"

"Uh-Uh."

"Do you know where your Grandmother and Grandfather live?"

"Uh-Uh."

"Have you ever seen their pictures?"

"Uh-Uh, I don't think I have a Gramma."

"Flicka, do you like to eat fish?"

"I dunno."

"I like fish, we'll make a first class Swede out of you yet because Aunt Dagne is baking fish for dinner."

Maria read a longer story than usual with a back ground of lively music; added extra bubble bath to the tub; and discussed plans for a picnic to the park and Lorraine responded on the surface but when she pulled the covers over her the weight of silent worry laid heavy on her stressed body.

The still of the night was shredded with Lorraine's screams as the hideous nightmare engulfed her. . . "Don't let my Daddy get me!"

Lorraine's eyes embraced the puppies as they slept - she loved them all and one of them was going to be hers. She shivered with excitement at the thought, but somehow she wasn't really seeing them as clearly as before.

"Do I have a Grandma?" she asked herself. "Where is my Mama?" "Is Daddy going to get me?" Then she thought about her little brothers, she had loved them dearly but the nightmare events of the past weeks had pushed all thoughts from her mind except the need to flee, the need to hide, the strong instinct to survive had predominated. But now she remembered and waves of longing and lonesomeness swept over her mixed with stabs of fear and pangs of doubts. She felt sick and scared as waves of nausea swept over her little body.

Maria heard Lorraine gag and saw her hands cover her mouth. "Are you sick?"

"Uh-Huh."

As Maria scooped Lorraine up in her arms and took her to the bathroom as she realized their conversation had touched a nerve.

"Let's go get a glass of apple juice, O.K.?"

"Uh-Huh."

Maria poured two glasses of juice then held Lorraine on her lap while the child sipped and sighed deeply.

Maria heard the deep sigh and gave Lorraine a tight squeeze.

Maria reached to turn off the alarm, it was four A.M. Methodically she slipped her feet into her slippers and snuggled the velour robe about her still half asleep body. Automatically she buried her face into the cold, wet washcloth then hastened downstairs to the library, locking herself in. Then grasped the phone as one would grasp a tiger's tail and began dialing. A deep sigh escaped her body as she waited for an answer.
On the third ring there was a "Good Morning."

"Good morning Margreta, how are you doing?"

"Oh Hi Maria, I'm so glad you called. This waiting is difficult, our hopes and anticipation are racing away with all of us."

"Margreta, I know it is painful being so far away and wondering what is going on."

"No clues?"

"None! And when I tried to suggest the possibility of grandparents it brought a negative response and more nightmares, terrible nightmares."

"Dear little babe."

"Margreta when you do come, don't expect Lorraine to accept you right away. It will take time, a lot of time, and in her own time and way."

"That is understandable."

"Lorraine will probably feel very threatened by your presence and try to run, but you mustn't be offended because it will certainly not be anything personal."

"This will be a different experience for all of us, yet somehow familiar."

"Margreta please don't consider Lorraine's fear as rejection, because it isn't. It is a fear of the unknown stimulated by a fear of the known."

"Very well stated."

"If you give her lots of space, gain her confidence and let her come to you, you won't be disappointed and she will be less apprehensive."

"That is sound and sensible counsel for most relationships. Maria, we have been having a ball shopping."

"I bet you have, but don't clean out the stores all at once, there will be a birthday and Christmas isn't all that far away. It would probably be more therapeutic to have little surprises often then an overwhelming amount all at once."

"I am with you all the way on that."

"Margreta will you share our conversation with Rose Ellen and George, and of course handsome Tom?"

"Handsome Tom has been eves dropping," chuckled a masculine voice.

"Oh Tom, you conceited clown."

"I'm not conceited, you said I was handsome and I believe you."

The laughter that followed was the needed antidote for the stress they all felt.

"Well, after that I think I need a cup of coffee, and I'm really glad Margreta doesn't have to fill you in."

"Yup, it's nice to hear things first hand; now handsome Tom has to get ready for work."

"No one is going to be able to stand that man today," chuckled Margreta, "And we will be waiting so anxiously for the call that will propel us toward the meeting of our little granddaughter."

Rolf frowned into his cup of coffee after Maria recounted the nightmare episode of the night before. Rubbing his chin thoughtfully he stirred the coffee silently.

Dagne mixed fresh blue berry muffins to cheer Maria, knowing they would be enjoyed by everyone, but her reflections and contemplations were secret.

Maria was fixing a sandwich for herself. Brown bagging was the most sensible way to have lunch today because she planned to go out to the school and talk to Ruth and Mrs. Erickson during her noon break. Her heart was sad...

Except for the occasional snap of the wood on the fire and the simmer of the teakettle there were no sounds, yet the room was alive and filled with love for a child.

Lorraine and Aunt Dagne were engrossed with the giant world globe in front of them. All of the lessons of the day had centered around the fascinating subject of geography. Aunt Dagne had cleverly included reading, spelling, math, science, and now a little history using the embossed globe as a springboard for discussion. With a tiny wooden pointer she had traced the area in

Sweden where her Mother and Father were born and where her Grandparents had lived and repeated the stories she had heard as a child, always coming back to the fact her parents and grandparents were special people.

"Tonight you will have to ask Uncle Rolf to show you on the map where he was born, and where his mother, father, and grandparents lived," hoping to instill the thought that everyone has grandparents. . . .but before Lorraine could make conversation the phone rang.

"Hello."

"Hello Dagne, this is Ruth."

"Oh hello Ruth, nice to hear from you."

"Will it be convenient for Mrs. Erickson and me to stop by after school tonight?"

Turning to Lorraine Aunt Dagne asked, "Would you like to see Mrs. Erickson and Ruth tonight?"

Lorraine's reply was a sparkling of eyes accompanied by a timid nodding of the head.

Continuing her conversation, Aunt Dagne replied, "We would be delighted to have you visit our classroom this afternoon. We will see you later."

Lorraine absent-mindedly ran her hands over mountains and oceans on the globe while addressing Aunt Dagne, "Can I save the words on the blackboard to show them?"

"Oh absolutely Flicka, I want them to see the words you learned today, do you want to read them to me again before we go for our walk?"

"Uh-Huh."

All right, slowly and clearly because they are big words."

Lorraine took a deep breath and began, "River, valley, ocean, land, mountain, prairie...." until she had read twenty solid words.

"I'm so proud of you," exclaimed Aunt Dagne and gave her student a big hug.

"Can I show them the puppies?"

"That would be fun, wouldn't it?"

"Uh-Huh."

After their walk, Aunt Dagne suggested, "Wouldn't it be nice to have a little tea party in the class room when Ruth and Mrs. Erickson came?"

"Uh-Huh."

Aunt Dagne set down the silver tray and a new doily, "You may put the doily on the tray and fill it with cookies and coffee bread while..."
Aunt Dagne's sentence was interrupted by the sound of a car in the driveway.

"Is my Daddy going to get me?"

Not waiting for an answer Lorraine fled to the bathroom and locked the door.

Aunt Dagne met Mrs. Erickson and Ruth at the door with a cordial,

"Come in, it is so nice you could come."

"Thank you," acknowledged Mrs. Erickson, "It is such a restful drive coming out here, and this house just seems to smile."

"Well, maybe the house doesn't smile, but we surely do at the prospects of our visit," interjected Ruth.

"Would you ladies care to join me in the kitchen for a moment so we can chat while I check on the progress of the coffee?"
When they reached the kitchen, Aunt Dagne seemed to raise her voice imperceptibly.

"Lorraine will be here in just a moment, she hurried to rinse the stickiness from her fingers. She was fixing a tray so we could have a special little tea upstairs."

Aunt Dagne's ploy was effective - the bathroom door opened.

*****

New Friend

Uncle Rolf sat rocking in the rocker by the kitchen fireplace while the little girl on his lap gave a detailed account of "the tea party" held upstairs in the special classroom. Then without hesitation Lorraine asked, "Do you have a Grandpa and Grandma?"

"Well Snow White, I most certainly did have. Everyone has a Grandpa and Grandma. My Grandpa was tall and straight, with white hair and sparkling blue eyes. He was a school teacher and he loved to teach me all kinds of interesting things. My Grandma was soft and warm and made the most wonderful breads and cakes. She was a dressmaker and tailor and made clothes for the rich folk and she also made warm coats for me. I loved to go to my Grandma's and Grandpa's house and have them come visit us."

Lorraine sat silently contemplating all this then inquired, "Where are they now?"

"Little girl, they are dead now. They lived a long time and became very old and tired but I still remember all the nice things they did and the fun we had."

"What kind of fun?"

"Oh, ice skating in the winter and riding in the big horse-drawn sleigh."

"Um, are you going to die?"

"Someday, everybody dies sometime."

"I don't want you to die."

Gusts of wind splashed rain against the windows making the warmth of the Franklin Fireplace most welcome as Aunt Dagne and Uncle Rolf shared the evening paper. The fragrance of freshly baked bread filled the kitchen and a big kettle of lamb stew simmered on the back burner as supper waited for Maria who had been detained at the hospital because of an emergency.

Bits of laughter and the soft tones of an one-sided conversation drifted down the hallway. Aunt Dagne's eyes met Uncle Rolf's over the top of the paper as they listened appreciatively.

After savoring the sweet sound of the child's gleeful giggles Uncle Rolf observed, "Isn't it marvelous how those tiny, four legged creatures could accomplish what we couldn't?"

They wisely let the magic of the puppies work a miracle without interference. After a few minutes Lorraine entered the kitchen cuddling one of Lady's babies close under her chin.

With thoughtful eyes she scanned Aunt Dagne's face then Uncle Rolf's countenance as she knelt close between them, "This puppy wants me."

But do you want that puppy?" asked Aunt Dagne?

"Uh-Huh."

"Why do you want that little sleepy head more than any of the others?" questioned Uncle Rolf.

"Cause it's so little and needs me."

"I see, just the same reason I need you."

"Uh-Huh."

"Well, have you thought of a name for that little fellow?"

"Uh-Huh."

"Very well, what name have you chosen?"

"Ruth."

With raised eyebrows Uncle Rolf met Aunt Dagne's gaze.

Aunt Dagne winked at Uncle Rolf and concluded, "Lady Ruth's Rowdy sounds like real canine royalty."

Maria marveled at the gentleness of the clown-child with the tiny puppy snuggled in her arms as they moved from room to room and bed to bed visiting with each little patient. The healing effect the little animal had on the children couldn't be ignored nor denied. And the joy revealed in Lorraine's eyes was effective in changing her whole countenance.

Then thirteen year old Bernie looked at Lorraine and asked," What happened to your head?"

Lorraine's hand went instinctively to the bandage letting her finger explore the dimension of the covering, but she didn't answer.

"Well, why are you wearing that patch on your head?" he insisted.

"I dunno," fear and tears mingled in the blue eyes.

"Aw, come on, you know. What's the matter with you, can't you stand up straight?"

Lorraine's eyes frantically searched for a place to hide or a way of escape.

Maria interrupted her conversation with Bernie's parents and asked Lorraine, "would you like to go to the Nurses Station and wait for me?"

"Uh-Huh," and the adults opened a path for her to reach comfortable ground.

After evening rounds had been completed Maria asked, "should we go down to the cafeteria for a milk shake?"

"Uh-Huh."

"We can't take your puppy to the lunch room, so let's make a little bed for him in a deep desk drawer. He can keep the nurse company until we get back."

"What flavor of milk shake are you going to have?

"I dunno"

"Vanilla, strawberry, or chocolate?"

"Chocolate."

As they approached the counter Maria said, "Good evening Mickey, we would like one chocolate and one strawberry milk shake, extra thick please."

"Right away, Doctor Goetche, it's nice to see you, and who is your clown friend?"

"This is Candy the Clown."

"Well, I would say she sure looks like a candy cane."

But Lorraine stood with mouth and eyes open looking at Maria in horror.

"LoRie, what is wrong?" asked Maria reaching for Lorraine's hand.

Lorraine shrunk from Maria's touch, "Are you going to kill me too?"

"Of course not, LoRie, I make children well."

"Are you a real doctor?"

"Well, yes I am, but I don't hurt anyone, I make them feel better. Didn't I make your head feel better?"

"Uh-Huh."

Putting straws in their shakes Maria chose a table off by themselves. After taking a long sip Maria asked, "Pretty good isn't it?"

"Uh-Huh, are you going to send me back to my Daddy?"

"Absolutely not!" "Why would I do such a thing as that?" "And I have no idea where your Daddy is."

"Is that boy upstairs going to tell my Daddy?"

"Honey girl, Bernie doesn't know who you are nor who your Daddy is or anything about you. He was just being a bratty kid."

"Will he hurt my puppy?"

"No way, he doesn't know where your puppy is, and besides the nurse wouldn't let him."

"Oh."

"Remember everything is all right when you are with me."

"I have bad dreams at night and my Daddy is chasing me."

"I'm so sorry little one, but remember it's just a dream, and after while those bad dreams will go away." "Now you can start dreaming about your puppy."

"I'm scared."

"LoRie, come sit on my lap while we finish our shakes, I want to tell you a secret."

"What is it?"

"I love you little girl."

"Love you too."

"LoRie, I have an idea to help chase the bad dreams away at night."

"How?"

"Every night when you go to bed, after you say your prayers, you can say, "Happy dreams, fun dreams, sweet dreams tonight...and I bet pretty soon all the good dreams will chase those nasty, bad dreams away. Shall we try it?"

"Uh-Huh."

"Great. Let's finish our shakes, go get your puppy, and go try our dream magic."

"O.K."

Lorraine sat snuggled on Maria's lap, ignoring her milk shake. Maria's cheek rested on top of Lorraine's head, and responded to the child's snuggle by hugging her tightly. Maria knew that this hideous fear of doctors had to be aired before there could be any healing of heart, mind and soul, and the sooner the better but oh she dreaded touching this painful wound but she must care for this hidden injury and hopefully it would also help with the nightmare problem.

In all her years of practice this was a first and she searched her mind for a gracious, gentle way to help this haunted child.

Maria took a deep breath and asked, "Are you still a little bit afraid of me?"

There was a slight hesitation, "Uh-Uh."

"Can you tell me why you are so afraid of doctors?"

"Cause they kill people."

"Why do you say that?"

"Cause they killed my little brothers."

"Are you sure?"

"That's what my Daddy said."

"What happened?"

"I dunno."

"What were your brother's names?"

"Randy and Clay."

"How old were they?"

"Randy was three and Clay was tiny."

"Did they both die the same time?"

"Uh-Uh, Randy died when we were in Texas"

"And what about baby Clay?"

"We were in California."

"What did your Mommy do?"

"She cried and Daddy hit her."

"Did your Daddy get unhappy when Randy or the baby cried?"

"Uh-Huh."

"When your Daddy was unhappy did he hit your brothers?"

"Uh-Huh."

"What did your Mommy do then?"

"She cried and Daddy hit her too."

"What did you do?"

"I hid under my bed."

"Did your Daddy drink lots of beer?"

"Uh-Huh."

"LoRie, sometimes people have been hurt so bad in accidents or got so sick with a bad disease that the doctors can't help them even though they want to and try very hard. I think that might have been the problem with your little brothers. Maybe your Daddy hit your brothers so hard the doctors couldn't do anything to help, to make them live, but that doesn't mean the doctors hurt them or made them die."

"Randy and I played in the sand pile together."

"You miss him, don't you?"

"Uh-Huh."

"Baby Clay used to hold my fingers and laugh, he was so little."

"You will always remember those tiny fingers and that sweet laugh."

"Uh-Huh."

"Did you ever see your grandparents?"

"I don't think I have any."

"Oh, I am sure you have grandparents."

"I dunno."

"Would you like to have me find them for you?"

"Will they take me away? Will they hurt me?"

"No! No! No! No one is going to take you away! I want you to stay at my house with Aunt Dagne and Uncle Rolf. O.K.?"

"Uh-Huh."

"And no one is going to hurt you at my house, remember?"

As Maria drove toward the hospital she was relieved that Lorraine finally knew she was a doctor so she could be open and relaxed, no longer fearing a traumatic scene. Now she needed more information regarding the little boys who had died so she could help Lorraine cope with that black part of her life. But she was going to deal with yet another immediate problem this morning.

She felt anger and sadness as she thought of Bernie's taunts the night before and his parents had totally ignored the cruelty and rudeness of the situation. Just because he was an only child and had been indulged on account of a chronic asthmatic condition didn't excuse his thoughtlessness. Maria considered the statistics which indicated that patients who were self disciplined as well as having the security of parental discipline had fewer attacks. She marveled that the element of control was a healing factor.

Ordinarily Maria made her rounds accompanied by a nurse, but this morning she was going to alter her schedule and stop by Bernie's room unaccompanied - she was early and had plenty of time for this change in routine. Dropping a stethoscope into the pocket of her jacket, she gathered up her patient's chart; a new

198

magazine she had purchased on her way in that morning; filled her cup with fresh, hot coffee and headed for room #312.

Bernie was eating his breakfast and watching cartoons on TV - Maria smiled, waved a greeting, turned a chair around and sat down with her coffee to watch the remainder of the cartoons with her patient.

When the program ended Maria said, "That's a fun way to start a day, isn't it?", "Well how is our future aviator this morning?"

"Better."

"O.K. let me listen to your lungs. I have a nice cold stethoscope to give you goose bumps."

Bernie grinned and grimaced.

"You're right, you sound lots better. How was breakfast?"

"O.K ... I guess. I don't like wheat bread 'n prunes."

"Aw, but it's good for what ails you."

"I don't care, I don't like it."

"I bet if you close your eyes and ate that toast you wouldn't know the difference."

"Do I have to?"

"Yes, you really should. Eat the bread with the prunes, close your eyes, chew and shiver like sixty, then I have something special for you."

"But I don't like it."

"Bernie there are lots of things in life we don't like to do, but we do it anyway because they have to be done. And getting you well is one of the things we are going to do."

Bernie's curiosity about the something special prompted him to make short work of the offending food.

"Well, if I had a star I'd paste it on your forehead," teased Maria.

Bernie replied with a sheepish, half-smile.

But when Maria handed him the newest issue of Aviation News his face glowed, "Gee thanks."

"You're welcome Bernie, and don't loose your dream to fly."

"I won't, my Dad flies, and he's teaching me."

"Yes, I know. What about your Mother, does she fly also?"

"Yep, she has her own two-seater."

"That's great, Bernie. Do you know how lucky you are to have parents that care about you and give you the best things in life?"

"Ya, I guess."

Maria took a long sip of coffee, then spoke again, "Bernie, do you remember the little candy-cane clown that came to visit you last night?"

She is wearing that bandage on her forehead because her Dad hit her with a tire-iron and threatened to throw her in the river."

"Wide eyed Bernie replied, "really?"

"Really, then her folks went off and left her and no one knows where they are."

"They did?"

"And she doesn't stand straight because she was born with a diseased spine and she is going to have to have surgery to straighten her back."

"Will she live?"

"Oh yes, she'll live. But she will always have nightmares of her Dad chasing her. And bad dreams about her two little brothers that died and she doesn't know why. It is going to be rough living with all those memories."

Bernie was thoughtful for a minute, then observed, "She really is a cute little kid."

"You should have seen her the first time I saw her, she was wet, cold, dirty, ragged and scared silly. And she is still scared."

Bernie laid back and pulled up the covers obviously ashamed. . . . "Her folks went off and left her?"

"Exactly."

"Will she come back to visit?"

"I really don't know. She wasn't very comfortable with all the questions."

"Yea, I know. Her folks didn't come back for her?"

"No one has seen them."

"Jeepers, no wonder her eyes looked so dark and sad."

"There are lots of kids that need a good friend Bernie."

Another long silence was followed by, "I'm going to give my Mom my allowance money to buy her a big stuffed animal."

"That's flying high fella, thank you." Maria gave her patient a friendly wink and left him anticipating righting a wrong.

Maria felt pleased and gratified that a little seed of kindness could take root and grow so fast. She was anxious to bring her Candy Clown again but feared the reluctance that she would doubtless encounter.

"But don't fret now, you have other pressing problems to solve," she reminded herself.

At breakfast, Mr. Howorth informed his wife that he had the sheriff's permission to prepare the empty trailer for rent again.

"If you help me put away the dishes then I'll help you clean," suggested Mrs. Howorth.

"You have a deal," he replied. "I'll get the cleaning supplies – this should be a quick job."

Mrs. Howorth gathered up the half dozen boxes of pitiful possessions. When reaching under the big bed Mr. Howorth's vacuum bumped something and reaching under he removed a suitcase as well some boxes of stuff. Handling the suitcase with unexplained care and was relieved to give the Sheriff control. Chief

Bennett thanked Mr. Howorth and reached for the phone.

Glancing at her watch Maria noted that she had twenty minutes before her nurse was free for scheduled rounds. Opening the large envelope from radiology she drew out a set of x-rays and switched on the viewer and was deep in concentration of the problem before her when the phone rang.

"Dr. Goetche speaking."

"Good morning Maria, this is Brad from the Sheriff's Office."

"Oh, good morning Brad, anything good to report?"

"I'm afraid not."

"Oh no, what?"

"Mr. Howorth has gathered up the possessions left at the trailer. At your convenience please stop by and claim these items."

"Sure, what has happened?"

"The Sheriff's Office in Crescent City, California just replied to our inquiry stating the body of a man tentatively identified as Max Hamilton and the body of an unidentified woman are being held in the morgue pending positive identification and someone to claim the remains."

"Oh Brad."

"I'm so sorry Maria."

"Who is qualified to make the identification?"

"Probably only the child."

"Unfortunately, you are doubtless correct. After so many years and hard living no one else would recognize them."

"This is bad business."

"It is terrible! Brad, if you were to go and make your own identification with whatever information is available would the authorities release the bodies to you to be brought here to a mortuary and prepared for viewing before further identification?"

"Perhaps."

"Could you, would you do that for me, for us?"

I certainly would Maria, and I agree with your thinking that the trauma of a child seeing the bodies of their parents is terribly tough anytime so any cosmetic work that can be done would be."

"Exactly, but how, oh HOW do I tell this child?"

Sounds of a child repeating Raggedy Ann drifted out from the little upstairs classroom. Aunt Dagne was amazed to hear such feeling of expression as Lorraine first read the well-known poem, and then she encouraged her to start memorizing it, which she did with ease and eagerness.

"Just wait until Tia hears you recite that poem tonight. That will be a special surprise."

Lorraine's eyes lighted with anticipation as she responded,
"Uh-Huh."

"You have all of your assignments finished already, would you like to have a sewing lesson this afternoon?"

"Uh-Huh."

"That will be fun, but let's go have lunch first. I'm getting hungry, what about you?"

"O.K."

"While Aunt Dagne heated the beef barley soup she had made the day before and sliced generous pieces of the fresh wheat bread, Lorraine put the place mats on the table and set out the silver ware.

"What are we going to make?"

"How would you like to make a cobblers apron for yourself like the one I am wearing?"

"O.K." was the eager response while smoothing Strawberry Shortcake's dress.

After the satisfying lunch had been tucked tidily into their tummies, tot and tutor returned up the winding stairs to the room where surprises were made.

Holding up a folded piece of blue fabric with tiny white elephants, Aunt Dagne asked, "Do you like this piece of material?"

"Uh-Huh."

The sewing lesson went well and time sped by quickly, so thrilled was the little seamstress with her new learned skill.

Aunt Dagne tried the finished garment on Lorraine, facing her before the antique oval mirror as she fastened the back neck button and tied the large bow. Twirling Lorraine sideways so she could get a view of her back, "there Flicka, what do you think of that?"

Lorraine could only run her hands down the front and try out the large pockets for size as an answer.

"You did a lovely job, it won't be long and you will be making all of your clothes," speculated Aunt Dagne.

"And do you know there is enough material left to make an apron for your doll, do you want to?"

"Uh-Huh."

Lorraine looked up into Aunt Dagne's face with wonderment and anticipation of the new found activity.

"That will be another surprise for Tia tonight."

Lorraine clasped her hands and scrunched her shoulders in a shy but excited gesture of anticipation.

After the dolls apron had been made and modeled, "Aunt Dagne suggested, "how about saying the first verses of the poem for me again before we go start supper?"

So Lorraine took a deep breath and began reciting the introductory verses of Raggedy Ann.

"Beautiful Flicka, just beautiful, now let's go make chicken and dumplings."

The prospect of two surprises charged the child with such enthusiasm and excitement she took off skipping down the hall, hopping down the winding stairs to find her puppy so she could tell him about the secrets.

Lorraine paced from window to window watching for the arrival of Uncle Rolf and Maria then over to Aunt Dagne to ask, "how long before they come?"

"Uncle Rolf should be here in about 20 minutes and Tia might not be here for another hour."

"Oh."

"Would you like a cookie and glass of milk while you are waiting?"

"Uh-Huh."

"That means puppy goes back to his box, and washed hands."

"O.K."

Aunt Dagne hoped this diversion might relax the nervous energy pulsing through Lorraine's body.

"Do you want to keep the poem a surprise until Tia comes?"

"Uh-Huh."

"I think that would be nice."

There was the sound of tires crunching on gravel and Lorraine literally flew down the hallway and posted herself by the back door waiting for Uncle Rolf.

It seemed forever before she heard the storm door squeak open then the wooden door was flung back and in stepped the gentle giant, "there's my Snow White, and where is my Lady Dagne?"

"In the kitchen."

Uncle Rolf whispered, "What's she fixing tonight?"

The whispered reply, "chicken and dumplings."

Uncle Rolf winked and laughed.

"How was your day?" he greeted Aunt Dagne.

"We had a super day, didn't we Flicka?"

"Uh-Huh."

"See Lorraine's new apron, she made that in class today."

Uncle Rolf whistled, "You made that yourself?"

"Uh-Huh, Aunt Dagne helped me."

"Well, of course my dear, the teacher has to help when you are just learning, but you followed the instructions very well."

Lorraine glowed with pride and thrust her hands deep in the apron pockets in anxiety waiting for Maria to come. Having a secret was a totally new aspect for her and keeping a secret was a wondrous experience but it almost hurt trying to keep it all inside.

Uncle Rolf turned Lorraine around and around to admire her workmanship then sat down in the rocker next to the fireplace to look at the paper. "Do you want to read the funnies to me?" he invited.

"Uh-Huh."

"Good, I need your help reading all those pictures."
Lorraine surprised herself with a giggle and picked up her Strawberry Shortcake doll to share the funnies.

After the serious reading had been finished, Lorraine slid down from Uncle Rolf's lap and went to talk to Rowdy again.

Picking up her puppy she whispered, "I've gotta tell you about Raggedy Ann."

During her recitation Maria stepped in the back door and saw this sweet child sharing wondrous things with a doll under one arm and a puppy tucked under the other.

In Maria's years as a surgeon and physician she had many times faced the heart breaking task of telling parents that there was nothing more medical science could do and the child they cherished could not survive. With compassion, gentleness, and sorrow her tears always flowed with those of the heart broken parents. But now her tears were dried and sorrow seemed to swallow her as she considered having to tell Lorraine about her parents.

Laying her purse and gloves on the floor, Maria knelt in the hallway beside Lorraine, and put her arms around the excited child. "Well, look at you, if you don't have an apron just like Aunt Dagne's."

"I made it."

"You did? When?"

"Today, and her's too," holding out the doll with the miniature apron.

"Fantastic! You did a beautiful job LoRie, a beautiful job!"

Lorraine ducked her head and perched one foot self-consciously on top of the other.

Maria gave her a light squeeze and asked, "What smells soooo good?"

"Chicken 'n dumplings."

"Dumplings' indeed!"

Maria stroked the puppy's head, gathered up her purse and gloves and rose to her feet, following Lorraine into the kitchen.

"I hear we are having chicken and dumplings tonight! It smells too good to be true."

"It better be true," responded Uncle Rolf, "This Swede is plenty hungry."

After Uncle Rolf had said grace and everyone had been served a generous portion and then Aunt Dagne asked, "Tia, did you notice Flicka's new apron?"

"I most certainly did. LoRie told me she made it and the doll's apron too, it looks perfect. That's a lovely color for our blue eyed girl."

"It is an ideal color and I was so proud that she followed my instructions so carefully. But Flicka has another surprise to share tonight.

"You're going to tell us she made the supper?" asked Uncle Rolf, winking at Lorraine.

"She helped, but that isn't her surprise. Tell Tia and Uncle Rolf what you learned today."

Lorraine took a deep breath and began releasing the secret of Raggedy Ann line by line as far as she had memorized.

As Maria saw the pleasure on this little girl's face she writhed within thinking of the tragic news she carried in her heart for this innocent babe.

Everyone had laid their silverware down and was listening with rapt attention and when she had finished they applauded with genuine admiration.

Lorraine was so relieved to have at last unlocked her secret, she confided, "I never had a secret before."

"But it was fun having a nice secret, wasn't it?" asked Maria.

"Uh-Huh."

"Well, I have a secret too," continued Maria. "What?" asked Lorraine with eager eyes wide with anticipation.

"Oh, I can't tell, you will find out when we visit the kids tonight."

"I don't wanna to go."

"Because Bernie smart-mouthed last night?"

"Uh-Huh."

"Bernie said he won't get smart again, and he wants to see you."

"I don't wanna to go."

"It will be O.K. if I hold your hand won't it?"

"Snow White how would it be if Aunt Dagne and I go with you and we each hold a hand, and if you get scared I'll hold you. Wouldn't that be O.K.?!!

Lorraine's troubled eyes traveled from face to face in wordless anxiety.

"We want you to have your surprise, and we want to see your surprise. Remember no one can hurt you when you are with us."

The doubtful child swallowed hard, but formed no words.

Aunt Dagne smiled, "Shall we give it a try, Raggedy Ann?"

"O.K."

Later when they were putting their coats on Maria handed Lorraine a small box wrapped in blue paper with airplanes all over it. "That's for Bernie."

"What is it?"

"It's a surprise gift from you to him. O.K.?"

"Uh-Huh."

Walking through the tunnel from the parking garage to the hospital Maria dropped back and spoke quietly to Aunt Dagne while Uncle Rolf and Lorraine counted their steps and listened to their echo in the tunnel.

"Could you and Rolf stay for awhile? I need to talk to you - I need your help."

"Your voice says the news isn't good."

"It isn't."

Maria went directly to Bernie's room. Outside the door she turned to Lorraine and said, "You can give your gift to Bernie anytime."

Lorraine didn't realize she wasn't holding onto anyone's hand, so intent was she, holding the mystery box. But as they entered the door Lorraine pleaded, "hold me."

Uncle Rolf scooped her up into his arms and followed Maria into the room.

"Hi, Bernie."

"Hi, Dr. Goetche."

Turning to Bernie's parents Maria greeted the pair, "Hello Mom and Dad."

"Hello doctor."

"Folks, I want you to meet my helper, Candy the Clown, and Uncle Rolf and Aunt Dagne. This is Bernie Butler and his parents Mr. and Mrs. Butler."

There were handshakes all the way around and the usual, "It's nice to meet you."

"Bernie, I gave Candy the message that you wanted to see her tonight."

And without further ado Bernie addressed Lorraine, "I have something for you." And he held out a beautifully wrapped package with Care Bears all over it tied with a rainbow colored ribbon.

For a moment all she could do was look in astonishment at the lovely gift and then at Bernie. Suddenly she remembered she had a gift in her hand which she extended to a very surprised Bernie, and silence hung expectantly in the air.

As the gifts exchanged hands, Lorraine whispered, "Thank you."

"Hey thanks," acknowledged Bernie with a big grin.

"Oh thank you," whispered Lorraine again.

Lorraine was so awed by the size and beauty of the package all she could do was touch the ribbon admiringly, while Bernie watched and waited.

"Oh, little Flicka, isn't that gorgeous?"

Lorraine could only nod her head as she caressed the ribbon wondering if this was just a fleeting dream, but yet she remembered the cruel taunts of the night before. It had all brought back the nightmares of the schoolyard.

Uncle Rolf whispered in her ear, "You better open it and see what's hiding inside."

"I can't."

"Do you need some help?"

"Uh-Huh."

"O.K. let's sit on this chair and see what we can do."

Uncle Rolf showed Lorraine how to slip the satin ribbon off the corner of the box without tearing it, then he took his little pocketknife and carefully slit the tape, "there now, I think you can take the paper off."

"Uh-Huh," and ever so carefully the clown-child lifted the paper off. It was apparent the wrappings were as important to her as the gift itself.

Holding out her hand, Aunt Dagne asked, "Do you want me to hold the paper for you?"

"Uh-Huh."

Under the paper was a white box with more tape which Uncle Rolf cut, then Lorraine lifted the lid.

Whatever was in that box was carefully hidden under tissue paper.

Color began to creep into her cheeks and her hands experienced a slight tremble of anticipation and Bernie watched with satisfaction as the suspense grew.

Timidly she separated the tissue; her eyes grew wide and turned deep blue. "OHHH" formed on her lips but never reached an ear.

Tenderly she stretched a finger to touch something pink and plush. Maria had been watching both Lorraine and Bernie, noticing the play of emotions and the changes of attitudes.

"If all human rifts could only be healed so simply," she thought, catching Bernie's eye she winked.

"Take it out and show us what you have," begged Aunt Dagne.

Lorraine lifted out an adorable eighteen-inch elephant all soft and smiling adorned with ribbons and lace and she couldn't resist peeking under the huge ears.

"How adorable," exclaimed Maria, "I wouldn't mind having a friend like that to ride to work with me, with wonderful large ears to listen to all my problems."

"Dr. Goetche, someone might send you to the funny farm if they saw you driving along the highway talking to a pink elephant," chuckled Bernie, and everyone laughed at the preposterous thought.

Lorraine did not understand the conversation and secretly wondered what the joke was about. Humor had been an unknown factor in her life.

Uncle Rolf leaned forward and whispered something in Lorraine's ear and she quickly responded with, "Thank you."

"Aw, that's O.K." responded Bernie obviously pleased with the pleasure that radiated on Lorraine's face.

"Hey Bern, hadn't you better open your package?" asked his Dad.

"Oh yeah, I sorta forgot."

Now it was Lorraine's turn to watch with curiosity and fascination, even flinching as Bernie ripped off the paper with enthusiastic abandon.

"Oh neat!" exclaimed Bernie when he discovered he had an airplane model, "can I work on it now?"

"I don't know why not," replied Dr. Goetche, "Just as long as you don't glue yourself to the bed."

"This is great, thanks."

Lorraine and Bernie's eyes met briefly confirming that the subtle message in the exchange of gifts was well understood though never mentioned: Bernie was saying he was sorry for his bratty thoughtlessness and Lorraine was saying you are forgiven. A load of guilt was lifted from Bernie's shoulders and he sighed with relief that the burden had vanished. Now he could breathe easier and a sense of well-being warmed him. Lorraine no longer felt fearful and slid from Uncle Rolf's lap with her pink treasure clasped in her arms.

Going to Aunt Dagne she whispered, "Look, the ears have hearts on them." And Lorraine admiringly stroked the huge, soft ears.

Aunt Dagne asked, "do you know why those hearts are on the ears?"

"Because your new friend will listen with love when you share all your secrets."

Lorraine's eyes danced with anticipation.

"What are you going to call your pink friend?" questioned Maria.

"I dunno."

"How about naming it Bernie for me," suggested the patient.

Lorraine's face brightened with approval, and carefully lifting one big ear she whispered,

"Your name is Bernie," then lovingly patted the ear back in place. This little christening ceremony brought smiles to the faces of everyone in the room.

Maria turned to Bernie and commented, "I'm sure glad to see you feeling better," as she felt his forehead and patted him on the shoulder. "I better see how the other kids are doing. See you tomorrow fella. Thanks for being such a good guy.

Bernie blushed and mumbled, "Thank you, doctor."

Aunt Dagne whispered to Lorraine, "You better thank Bernie again, love."

"Thank You."

Bernie waved and Lorraine self-consciously buried her face in the elephant's trunk as everyone said their farewells and left.

Addressing Maria, Uncle Rolf chuckled, "Aunt Dagne and I will wait down in the lounge while you girls take that elephant on tour."

Sounds good to me," replied Maria. "Come on Clown girl let's go."

On the way home from the hospital Lorraine sat in the front seat with Maria but was oblivious to anyone or anything because she was busy telling her new companion about Rowdy the puppy and the Strawberry Shortcake doll.

"Please join me with a cup of hot chocolate," begged Maria

"Chocolate, you would serve a Swede chocolate?" teased Rolf.

"Yes chocolate, or anything that promises sleep tonight."

"Can you guarantee there is something in the cookie jar?" pursued Rolf

"If there isn't we will pretend with cinnamon toast or rice cakes and peanut butter," countered Maria.

"That's good enough, you have a deal."

After Lorraine and doll and elephant had been snuggled into bed Maria eased herself into a chair at the kitchen table between Rolf and Dagne. She sipped the foam from the top of her cup of chocolate and shook her head,

"Life bends bitterly sometimes."

"Yes indeed," agreed Rolf, "but friends are to keep the bending from breaking. What can we do?"

"Well, I'm not sure but probably an awful lot! Chief Bradley called me this morning to say that a man and woman are in the morgue in Crescent City, California, and is assumed they are Lorraine's Mommy and Daddy. A long expired driver's license tentatively identifies the man as Max; but there was absolutely no identification on the woman. Because it has been so many years since any of the family has seen Max and Margo, Lorraine is the only one who can make positive identification. I requested Chief Bradley to make arrangements for the bodies to be brought here to the mortuary and prepared for viewing. But how am I going to tell Lorraine? How am I going to tell her?"

*****

Bumpas are Coming

Next morning Maria was up before dawn to call Margreta and hoped as she dialed the number that she would be able to keep her composure - tears were so close to the surface.

"Hello Greta."

"Oh hello Maria, we didn't think you were ever going to call."

"I know, but I wish I didn't have to call, it's not good Greta."

"Maria, what is it?"

With trembling voice Maria whispered, "Dear girl, they are both dead."

"What happened?"

"Car accident."

Miles apart, the two sisters wept. Finally with trembling voice Greta broke the silence, "We will come right away. I'll have to call you back regarding our schedule."

"I'm so sorry Greta, I'm so very sorry."

Then Maria had to repeat the painful process and call Rose Ellen and George.

George answered with an anxious "Hello."

"George this is Maria."

"Maria, your voice tells me you don't have good news."

"I don't, oh, I don't."

"Do we dare hope?"

"No dear heart."

"Our sons are both gone!"

"But you have a precious granddaughter."

Nearly two hours later Maria sat with Dagne and Rolf around the kitchen table contemplating their steaming cups of hot coffee and watching the steam rise as though somehow a genie would emerge from the coffee vapors and give them the magic approach whereby they could break the shattering news to Lorraine.

Maria took a sip from her cup, traced a line in the tablecloth with her fingernail then commented, "Of all the years I have worked with tragic and devastating situations this is the most difficult experience yet."

"No doubt it is dear girl, because your heart is so completely involved," empathized Rolf.

"Let's just take one step at a time… remember you have Dagne and me on either side to support you."

"Maria, I'll fix breakfast while you get Lorraine up. I'm sure it would be best for her to eat first because I'm certain she couldn't eat after hearing such traumatic news."

"Good starting place," agreed Maria.

"And let's give her the good news first, that way she will have something positive to balance the emotions," suggested Dagne.

"I need a good breakfast myself to stabilize my churning stomach and galloping heart," admitted Maria as she headed for the stairway.

While Aunt Dagne busied herself with French toast and sausage, Uncle Rolf set the table; poured the juice; put another log on the fire. Next he took a long piece of string and tied a paper butterfly at the end, then wrapped the string around the paper and tucked it into his shirt pocket.

Laddie came down stairs, Rolf opened the back door to let him out and brought Rowdy in. Stroking the puppy's nose and ears Rolf confided to the plump little animal, "We should give you a "wagging tail degree" for making our little girl so happy."

When Rolf heard Lorraine and Maria coming down the stairs he took the string and paper gadget out of his pocket and pulled it across the floor in front of the curious puppy and anything that moved needed to be investigated. Rowdy chased and barked and Lorraine quickened her steps to see what the commotion was about. Giggling with delight as she watched the little game from the doorway. Uncle Rolf put the end of the string into Lorraine's hand and down the hallway she skipped with curls bouncing as the excited ball of fur barked and chased the elusive piece of paper.

Uncle Rolf observed aloud, "Isn't it amazing how much joy such a simple thing can bring to both child and pet?"

"Simplicity has a way of being beautiful and satisfying if we don't try to complicate it with improvements," replied Maria.

"Breakfast is ready, Flicka babe, put old 'Roughhouse' outside and wash quickly," called Aunt Dagne.

Lorraine picked up her puppy-friend and whispered, "We'll play some more after breakfast. I'll hurry and you wait for me, O.K.?"

Hurrying to wash her hands she felt happy with the world as she gathered up her pink elephant from her chair where she had left it and laid it across her lap as she sat down.

Seeing the French toast and sausage on her plate and the bowl of peaches with cream Lorraine hugged her elephant and whispered in it's ear, "I like French toast the 'mostest'."

After the last bites had been relished and coffee cups refilled, Uncle Rolf turned to Lorraine and said, "Snow White, we are going to have special company tomorrow."

A frown creased her forehead and her eyes searched Uncle Rolf's face but she couldn't ask "Who?"

"Remember I told you about my Grandmother and Grandfather and how much I loved them."

"Uh-Huh. Are they coming to see us?"

"I'm afraid not, they died a long time ago. But your Grandparents are coming to visit."

"I don't have any Grandma and Grandpa."

"Oh, everyone has two Grandmas and Grandpas, and both of your Grandmothers and Grandfathers are coming to see all of us."

"Are they going to hurt me?"

"Absolutely not!" replied Uncle Rolf as he lifted Lorraine onto his lap.

"Are they going to take me away?"

"No one is going to take you away. You are going to stay right here with us."

"Are they going to tell my Daddy where I am?" Maria reached over and took both of Lorraine's hands in hers, "LoRie baby, no one is going to tell your Daddy where you are. Your Daddy isn't going to come get you; your Daddy isn't going to hurt you; your Daddy is dead. And so is your Mommy."

"Did Daddy hurt Mommy?"

"I don't think so."

"Why are they dead?"

"They hit a big tree with their car and they died."

"Where are they now?"

"Their bodies are down town in the mortuary."

"Are they going to heaven to be with my little brothers?"

"Yes dear."

"Where is heaven?"

"Up above the moon and the sun and the stars."

"Am I going to die too?"

"Sweetie, we all must die someday. But you have a lot of living to do and many, many things to accomplish. You probably won't die until you are a very old lady."

"Are you going to die?"

Someday, but I have a lot of work to take care of first. Your Daddy had been drinking and was not driving carefully so he ran into a huge tree."

"Was he mad?"

"Maybe, but we don't know."

"Can't he talk anymore?"

"No, he can't talk anymore."

"Can't he walk anymore?"

"No, he can't walk anymore."

"Can he see me."

"No sweetie, he can't see you." The perplexity on the child's face wrenched Maria with pity and as she hugged Lorraine to herself huge tears spilled from her eyes. "Oh! How does one explain the finality of death?!"

For a few minutes only the sound of the ticking clock and the soft crackle of the fire could be heard as Lorraine snuggled in Maria's lap silently sorting facts and feelings. Wisely the adults respected the necessity for this bruised bud to contemplate and comprehend these sudden changes in her life in quietness and without interruption. So they sat with bowed heads as if in prayer considering the impact of these deaths on all their lives but most especially the pain and trauma this little girl was feeling deep in her soul. Individually they considered how suddenly their lives had all been touched and changed by the unexpected arrival of this nighttime visitor.

Finally Lorraine looked up into Maria's eyes and asked, "Why didn't my Daddy and Mommy like me and want me?"

"LoRie, I don't think your Daddy disliked you but I would guess he had a disease called alcoholism caused by drinking too much. In reality he probably didn't like himself because he didn't have any control of his feelings and his life and took out his anger on you."

"He hit Mommy too."

"It sounds like he was mad at the whole world and your Mommy was sick and paralyzed with fear."

"Will I be sick too?"

"Absolutely not! You will be healthy and happy and learn how to talk about your feelings. It is very important to talk and ask questions, and you can talk to

Aunt Dagne, Uncle Rolf and me just anytime you want to. O.K.?"

"Uh-Huh."

"Give me a hug. I love you little one. We all love you."

"Can I go play with Rowdy?"

"You sure can. He needs to go for a walk out to the orchard, in fact why don't you see how fast he can run?"

While Lorraine was out playing with her puppy, Aunt Dagne poured hot coffee in the three cups and commented, "One thorny hurdle taken care of. You did very well my dear."

"I just had to plunge into the icy waters and go with the current."

Uncle Rolf patted Maria's hand, "Lorraine really led the way and you provided the needed support. You know, I've been thinking about when the grandparents arrive perhaps it would be best for all of us to go to the airport so she will be on neutral ground and feel in control when she meets them for the first time. Whereas, if she were to wait here at home she would be apprehensive and doubtless feel threatened."

Aunt Dagne picked up the conversation where Uncle Rolf left off, "Perhaps between the two of us we can persuade Lorraine to go shopping with you for some little gifts for her grandparents. It would be a positive action to strengthen her sense of control and change her anxiety to anticipation."

"Your idea sounds good," agreed Maria, "and I am wondering if she would feel fortified if she invited Ruth and Mrs. Erickson to also go to the airport. That would give her five of us, that she knows to meet four she doesn't know. Because I know that regardless of how hard we try to reassure and calm her there is going to be a moment of horrible panic."

"Sounds good," observed Uncle Rolf.

"We must keep her busy planning in a positive, productive way so time doesn't become an enemy," suggested Aunt Dagne, and when all else fails she and I can bake cookies by the jillion."

"It sure helps to have a plan of action," sighed Maria with relief, "Now   I must go make rounds."

Lorraine was coming in as Maria was going out, "See you later LoRie," whispered Maria as she squeezed the breathless child.

Uncle Rolf put another log on the fire, then emptied the coffee pot into his cup, which he set on the counter top so he could dry the dishes while he drank his coffee.

"Flicka, shall we start some dough for fresh bread and a coffee ring and some cinnamon rolls before we have class this morning?"

"O.K."

"I need your help, if you want to wash your hands and get your apron."

"O.K." Being needed was a new feeling, and it felt warm and comfortable somewhere inside her little bent body.

"While you girls play in the flour, I think I'll go wash and vacuum the car," announced Uncle Rolf, putting on his jacket.

Lorraine stood on the step stool with a large wooden spoon in her hand helping Aunt Dagne count and stir each addition made to the crockery bread bowl.

"You know Flicka, I think it would be nice if we got a surprise gift for your Grandmas and Grandpas, what do you think?"

"Uh-Huh."

"Shall we ask Uncle Rolf to take us to town this afternoon after the bread and rolls are all baked?"

"Will my Daddy get me?"

"No Flicka, remember your Daddy is dead."

"Will you hold my hand?"

"Absolutely, now let's go have class while this dough rises."

Some of the new spelling words added to the impressively long list were: dough, surprise, cinnamon, airplane, and suitcase.

After class was finished; the bread baked and the cinnamon rolls sampled, Uncle Rolf asked, "Snow White, are you girls ready?"

"Uh-Uh, I'm 'fraid."

Uncle Rolf picked Lorraine up into his arms and asked, "Now you aren't afraid are you?"

"Uh-Uh," but big tears splashed down her cheeks.

Settled on the front seat between the two adults Lorraine snuggled as close to Aunt Dagne as she could get.

Uncle Rolf parked in front of the Golden Goose Gift Shop and opened the car door for Aunt Dagne and lifted Lorraine into his arms.

Inside the store Lorraine looked in awe at all the sparkling crystal; pewter; silver; porcelain, and an attractive display of silk and dried flowers. She had never seen so many beautiful things in one place.

Aunt Dagne walked to a display of nice coffee mugs and teacups.

"Maybe something like this would be nice Flicka and it would be easy to pack in a suitcase."

"Uh-Huh."

"How about flowers for the Grandmas and animals or birds for the Grandpas?"

"O.K."

"Which ones do you like best?"

With her hands folded behind her back, Lorraine's eyes surveyed the vast assorted display. Finally she pointed to a mug with a wild goose for one Grandpa and one with an eagle for the other Grandpa; a porcelain mug with yellow pansies for one Grandma and another with red roses.

"Those are lovely choices," agreed Aunt Dagne, "Just right."

"Look at this," called Uncle Rolf from the next isle. "A surprise to put in the surprise." He was holding a miniature pewter figurine of a mouse and a bunny. Seeing Lorraine's perplexed expression, he explained, "You can hide one of these little fellows inside a mug."

A smile of comprehension spread across the child's face. Uncle Rolf set the figurines back on the shelf and lifted Lorraine so she could see the higher shelf. The mouse and bunny had caught her fancy too so she retrieved them, then found a wolf and a tiger. She was obviously pleased with her selection and silently admired the articles on the counter. Then there was the selection of gift-wrap and ribbons, gift cards were going to be made in class the next morning. The purchases were beginning to work the magic of anticipation because on the way home Lorraine was so absorbed in the gift-wrap and ribbons she forgot to be afraid.

At home the kitchen table soon became the center of preparation and excitement. Aunt Dagne showed Lorraine how and why to remove all price tags; then they folded the four boxes and lined each one with a sheet of tissue paper. Next they took another sheet of tissue paper and wrapped each figurine and hid them in the right mug. Then came the wrappings of pink, lavender, blue and green... with a temporary tag on each so they would know who each gift was intended for. Then each box was carefully set on the coffee table in the living room.

Lorraine stood with hands clasped admiring her handiwork and a shiver of excitement escaped her tense little body.

"Flicka, would you like to invite Mrs. Erickson and Ruth to go to the airport with us tomorrow to meet your Grandparents?"

Without hesitation she replied, "Uh-Huh."

"Would you like to call them?"

"Uh-Uh, I can't."

"Shall I do it for you?"

"Uh-Huh."

The phone calls had the desired settling effect and the elated child busied herself with sharing her secrets with Pink Elephant and a Rowdy puppy.

Maria made one last phone call, "Margreta, I just want to remind you not to rush Lorraine lest we have a runaway on our hands - this is such a sensitive situation, and please don't feel rejected if she ignores you, there will be many years for closeness and loving."

"Oh, we understand Maria." "That babe must be terribly frightened about all this."

"We can talk about the terror that is evident, but it's the fright she covers that I fear," concluded Maria "see you tomorrow evening love. Good bye."

Maria would like to have had Margreta pass the last minute message on to Rose Ellen but she knew her own personal voice contact and care at this point was very essential. Everyone was hurting; everyone had their own personal doubts and apprehensions; so there just couldn't be too much concern for the hearts of others. In closing Maria said, "And don't be afraid to cry, perhaps tears will help bridge the gap. I love you little Grandma . . .Good bye."

The next morning when Maria went into Lorraine's room to call her the usually soundly sleeping child lay motionless with her blue eyes wide open staring at the shadows the aquarium made on the ceiling. Laddie thumped out a welcome with his tail and yawned.

Maria scratched his ear appreciatively and smiled at the huge blue eyes peering back at her from the pillow, taking notice of the tenseness she asked, "shall I tickle your toes?"

"Uh-Uh." and a little smile stole across Lorraine's face.

Maria extended her hands and the child responded by sitting up as Maria sat on the edge of the bed, "your Grandmas and Grandpas should be just about ready to leave for the airport. I know they are excited about their trip, and I think they are a little bit afraid too because they are going to meet someone they have never met before. Are you a little bit afraid too?"

"Uh-Huh."

"Being afraid is alright LoRie, everyone is afraid at different times for different reasons."

"Are you 'fraid?"

"Not today, but sometimes I am. After you are dressed do you want to look at your Grandma and Grandpa's pictures again?"

"O.K."

"And then we will eat some breakfast, are you as hungry as I am?"

"Uh-Uh."

When Maria and Lorraine entered the kitchen, Uncle Rolf chuckled, "wait 'til you girls see what we are having for breakfast. Look at those pancakes Snow White and the strawberries and whipped cream - good enough to feed a pink elephant or a puppy dog, eh?"

Lorraine nodded her head and wasted no time sitting in her chair, and ate her share of the pancakes as well the as pink elephant's portion.

When everyone had been served and Aunt Dagne had finished eating she asked, "may I please be excused so I can start stuffing this turkey?"

"Certainly, my dear," replied Uncle Rolf, "but how would it be if I stuff that bird for you while you girls do up the dishes?"

"You have a deal," replied Aunt Dagne, "then Flicka and I have a special art project to work on."

Lorraine's eyes traveled to the counter top where a huge plump turkey lay in the roaster pan. She had never seen anything like it.

"Uncle Rolf saw the astonished look on the little girl's face and asked her, "do you think you can eat all that turkey?"

"Uh-Uh."

"Am I ever glad, because I would hate to miss out on my share of the good eating."

"Me too," chimed in Maria, "Uncle Rolf makes the best turkey dressing that ever was made!"

"But you do like turkey don't you?" continued Uncle Rolf?

"I dunno."

"Have you ever eaten turkey?"

"Uh-Uh."

"Well now, you have a real treat coming .... there is nothing more delightfully delicious than Aunt Dagne's roast turkey," advised Uncle Rolf.

"Just wait 'til you smell it cooking in the oven," concluded Maria. "But now I had better go to work. I'll see all of you at the airport at four."

"We will be there," assured Uncle Rolf, "I hope you have a good day."

"Fortunately, I will have a very busy one. See you all later." Maria hugged Lorraine and was out the door.

Lorraine went to the dining room window to wave to Maria and felt part of her security leaving though she couldn't define the feeling. The anxiety, doubt, excitement, curiosity, and fear all seemed to have gathered in the pit of her stomach at once but of course she couldn't diagnose the ill feeling that crept over her.

She whispered to Pink Elephant, "I'm scared, I don't know any Grammy and my Daddy might get me."

Maria's car was well down the driveway and the silence from the dining room echoed through the house. Aunt Dagne recognized the foreboding stillness for what it was and intercepted the stealthy enemy, "Flicka, shall we start making the cards?"

"Uh-Huh."

Aunt Dagne had already seated herself at the table with a sketchpad and pencil and her artistic fingers were skillfully outlining little animals and flowers when Lorraine came to stand at her elbow to watch and admire. So absorbed was the child in the magic that was created by each pencil mark that a sigh soon escaped, hardly realizing that fear had temporarily lost it's painful grip.

Uncle Rolf interrupted with a soft whistle when the turkey was all stuffed and in the pan. Lorraine pushed the step stool to the counter so she could climb up for a closer look.

"All right Snow White you can put the lid on the roaster and I'll pop Mr. Turkey into the oven, how about it?"

"O.K."

When the turkey had at last been put into the oven and the controls set, Uncle Rolf stopped to admire Aunt Dagne's artwork and asked, "how come you got all the talent?"

"Your art work is in the oven."

"Snow White, will you let me see all the cards before you seal them in their envelopes?"

"I'm going to go feed the horses and check on Nick's cow and see how Mr. Morris's pigs are doing while you gals do your school work."

"See you later Farmer Brown," chuckled Aunt Dagne.

Lorraine carefully colored, cut, and pasted the pictures onto craft paper.

"You do lovely work Flicka! I'm so proud of your carefulness and good choice of colors. Uncle Rolf will be pleased and your Grandparents will be very surprised. Do you want to write something inside the cards?"

Lorraine shrugged.

"You could write, 'I love you Grandma."

"Uh-Uh, I love you."

"Oh I know you do sweetie, and you love Uncle Rolf and Tia, but our love grows and can be shared with other special people too."

"I don't know any Grandma 'n Grandpa."

"You are right, you really don't know them, you have just heard about them. How would it be just to write 'Welcome'?"

"What does that mean?"

"That's a word we use when we are happy to see someone and want them to feel comfortable with us."

"I'm 'fraid."

"I understand dear, it is natural to be a bit nervous - I am sure your Grandparents are feeling the same way. Do you just want to write 'From Lorraine'?"

"Uh-Huh."

Aunt Dagne showed Lorraine how to fold the large sheets of paper to make envelopes and so thoughtfully the cards were tucked in with a mixture of anticipation and dread, and placed with the gifts. Lorraine helped Aunt Dagne do up the dishes and tidy the kitchen and all the while Aunt Dagne was tossing out oral spelling words and math problems. Then they mixed up a double batch of cowboy cookies and when the cookies were all baked and the baking dishes washed and put away Aunt Dagne poured two glasses of milk and put some cookies on a plate and picked up a storybook and began to read while they enjoyed their snack.

Uncle Rolf came back while the story was being read so he quietly poured himself a glass of milk and sat at the table to sample cookies and listen to the story too.

When Aunt Dagne finished reading the chapter Uncle Rolf suggested, "Let's go for a walk down to the pond and see how many wild ducks and geese are there. It is such a lovely day and we have plenty of time before lunch and getting ready to go to the airport."

Lorraine clutched Pink Elephant tightly as she realized the awful hour was fast approaching and it was an unnerving anticipation.

"Some fresh air sounds great," agreed Aunt Dagne, "but first you must see the lovely cards Flicka made. We have a real little artist."

Lorraine was glad for a diversion of thought and hurried to get her handiwork which Uncle Rolf genuinely admired, "did you do all that coloring, cutting and printing yourself?"

"Uh-Huh."

"How about that! Now we have two artists in the house," and Uncle Rolf gave the beaming child a rewarding squeeze.

At the pond Uncle Rolf identified the different kinds of ducks, counted the geese and was astonished to see a Trumpeter Swan. "I bet that beautiful bird has an interesting story to tell," commented Uncle Rolf as he filled Lorraine's hands full of grain to throw on the shore for their migrating friends.

After lunch was over and the dishes done Aunt Dagne suggested, "Flicka would you like to take your crayons, scissors and art supplies up to the cupboard in our classroom before you take your bath and change your clothes?"

"Uh-Huh."

"I'll be right up to help you."

Lorraine headed up the stairs with a folder of art paper, scissors, and crayons in her hands and she whispered to Pink Elephant clasped to her body as she went, "I don't wanna go, I'm 'fraid, my Daddy might get me."

A few minutes later Aunt Dagne went upstairs to help with the bath water but every room was empty.

"Flicka, Flicka, where are you, Flicka?"

Aunt Dagne went back to the class room to see if Lorraine was sitting playing with the dolls or was looking at a picture book which she loved to do but the only response she had was the doll's sweet, but silent smiles. Then she went to Lorraine's bedroom - perhaps she was watching the fish in the aquarium, hypnotized by the guppies acrobatics. These little creatures opened and closed their mouths continuously with silent messages, but no spectator. Maybe Lorraine was in the bathroom getting ready for her bath but that room was also silently empty!

It would never do to show alarm or an undue amount of concern, so Aunt Dagne began to sing one of her game songs knowing a relaxed, playful atmosphere would cause the least resistance and embarrassment. Thus Aunt Dagne went from room to room searching in every closet, peering under every bed, and checking every window to be sure they were still locked all the while her voice rose sweet and clear, hiding the frustration growing in her heart.

When the last bedroom had been searched to no avail Aunt Dagne spoke aloud to herself, "Flicka wins the game, she hid so good I can't find her. If I hurry I can shower and change my clothes and be the first one ready."

So Aunt Dagne went down the hall and stairs chanting, "I'm going to be first, I'm going to be first." But that challenge didn't bring a response either.

Uncle Rolf was coming out of the downstairs bathroom freshly showered and dressed when Aunt Dagne announced, "I can't find Lorraine anyplace."

"What?"

"I've searched every closet, looked under every bed, checked every window to be sure she didn't climb out on the porch roof, I even pretended this was a game and sang our fun songs but nothing!"

"Is the front door locked?"

"I'll go see....yes, it is."

"Let's get Laddie," suggested Uncle Rolf, "I'm sure he will find her."

Soon Uncle Rolf came in whistling with Laddie at his side - Uncle Rolf continued to whistle as Aunt Dagne and the dog accompanied him up the stairs together.

At the top of the stairs Uncle Rolf stroked Laddie's head and said "Go find Lorraine Laddie, go find our girl."

Sniffing quickly from room to room the dog led the anxious adults past the last bedroom. In Maria's room Laddie began to wag his tail and ran to the big window overlooking the mountains, and nuzzling behind the draperies he gave a little bark followed by his "victory speech" which consisted of a low, *"awoo" "awoo"*.

Uncle Rolf pulled back the heavy satin draperies and said, "Boo you rascal," and looked into the enormous blue eyes of a terrified child pressed tight against the wall.

Grasping Lorraine's hands he lifted her out from her hiding place and knelt to hug her... "Little girl, we know you are very worried about going to the airport and meeting strange people today, we understand. But we are going to hold your hand all the way and if you want I will hold you in my arms and no one is going to touch you. No one is going to hurt our girl. No one is going to take you away. Do you believe me?"

"Uh-Huh."

"All right, into the bathtub quick. When you are ready you and I can play a game of Old Maid while we wait for Aunt Dagne to get ready."

"O.K."

Finally, dressed in pink and her beautiful hair brushed into soft ringlets and tied with ribbons Lorraine joined Uncle Rolf at the kitchen table for the promised game, but not before Aunt Dagne had stood her before

231

the mirror to reassure her how nice she looked, "You are a beautiful little lady" beamed Aunt Dagne holding the child at arms length."

Beaming with victory over winning two games, reluctant smiles spread across the child's face and then Aunt Dagne appeared with coat and purse in hand.

"Aha, it looks like we better get our coats on, but first I am going to peek into the oven to see how old turkey is doing - Snow White do you want to look too?"

"Uh-Huh," and for the first time she was aware of the tantalizing aroma that was beginning to permeate the whole house.

"Tell Rascal goodbye," instructed Uncle Rolf, "and you had better bring Pink Elephant for the ride."

Once on the road Aunt Dagne marveled aloud at the beauty of the deep blue sky and the brilliance of the autumn leaves.

Uncle Rolf observed, "There is going to be a full moon tonight - I bet the stars will be magnificent."

And so the forty-five minute drive was filled with appreciation for the natural beauties around them and the passing landscape.

Inside the terminal Mrs. Erickson and Ruth were already there and Lorraine let go of the hands she held to run greet them. Both were amazed at the dramatic change in Lorraine's appearance. Each hugged their little friend and had they not known, they would never have suspected she was the same child that had so recently enrolled at their school.

"How are classes going?" Mrs. Erickson asked of Lorraine.

"O.K."

"You certainly have a beautiful classroom."

"Uh-Huh."

"I think it's the prettiest school room in the whole wide world - even prettier then little princesses have."

"She looks like a princess," interjected Ruth "that is such a pretty dress and your hair is beautiful."

Lorraine smiled with shy pleasure, savoring the praise and attention.

"She is our princess," confirmed Aunt Dagne who then turned to Lorraine and asked in a whisper, "Did you tell Ruth about your puppy?"

Eyes dancing with remembering, Lorraine announced to Ruth, "I have a new little puppy and I named him Ruth."

Smiles lit the faces of the adults and Aunt Dagne coached again, "but what is his full long name?"

"Lady Ruth's Rowdy and I call him Rowdy."

Ruth chuckled, "that is a real honor chickadee, thank you. Shall I name one of my kittens Rainey for Lorraine?"

"Uh-Huh."

"That's a promise."

"Here's Tia," interrupted Aunt Dagne, as Maria came rushing up a bit breathless from her long walk from the parking lot.

"Don't you look gorgeous!" beamed Maria as she hugged Lorraine and touched her soft curls and then the arrival of the long awaited flight was announced.

As promised Uncle Rolf took Lorraine's hand and he suggested, "Let's watch the plane land." And he walked closer to the window to watch as the giant bird touched down on the runway. While Uncle Rolf and Lorraine walked away to watch the landing, Aunt Dagne quickly filled Maria in on the events of the afternoon and the missing child. Each adult tried to imagine the thoughts and feelings this child was having... when in reality her head and heart were blanked with fear.

As the passengers began to enter the lobby Lorraine pleaded, "Hold me!" and Uncle Rolf quickly lifted her into his protective arms. Aunt Dagne stood on one side and Maria on the other as Mrs. Erickson and Ruth gathered close in a defending circle. Suddenly four passengers stopped mid-stride and gazed in awe at Margo's child.

"Greta," cried Maria running forward to embrace her sister, "I'm so glad you're here!"

"Oh Maria, it has been such a long, agonizing wait!"

Lorraine grabbed Uncle Rolf in panic and opened her mouth to scream but no sound came and that was her Mama's voice she heard, but she couldn't see her Mother.

Uncle Rolf knew from the desperate hold Lorraine had on his neck that the situation was extremely tense, as he had expected it would be, but he could not fully understand because he had not heard what Lorraine had heard.

Lorraine watched as Maria greeted each one with a hug and wondered why they were all crying.

Stepping a bit closer Aunt Dagne greeted Margreta and Tom with a hug and Uncle Rolf shook hands commenting, "what can I say dear hearts?"

Followed by Maria's introduction of Rose Ellen and George to Aunt Dagne and Uncle Rolf; Aunt Dagne was just as warm and gracious in her greeting to them though she had never met the Hamilton Grandparents before. Uncle Rolf extended a sincere and caring handshake to this grieving family also. But new terror was added to the mounting trauma because that last man looked like her Daddy and none of the adults knew what the child saw. Then Maria carefully focused her attention on the last introductions to be made, hoping by now Lorraine had opportunity to assess the visitors and perhaps lost some of her fear.

"LoRie, this is your Grandma and Grandpa Boesche. They are your Mother's parents."

Through flowing tears and with trembling voice they greeted their grandchild with, "Hello darling, we love you."

But Lorraine could only hear her Mommy's voice, but those weren't her Mama's words - she gazed with silent unbelief.

And LoRie, this is your Grandma and Grandpa Hamilton. They are your Daddy's parents."

Unashamed their tears mingled with their smiles, "We love you sweetheart, you are a beautiful honey bee."

With all color drained from her face, Lorraine's dry mouth couldn't even utter the cry her heart wanted to make when she looked into the likeness of her Daddy's face.

Uncle Rolf tightened his hold, sensing that this little injured bird would fly to goodness knows where if she had opportunity to get free.

Turning to leave, Uncle Rolf saw Mrs. Erickson and Ruth standing discreetly aside, "Oh wait, wait, such terrible manners! We haven't introduced Lorraine's very special friends. "This is her teacher, Mrs. Erickson, and the School Receptionist, Ruth Haynes, Mr. and Mrs. Boesche and Mr. and Mrs. Hamilton."

"How do you do, and thank you for coming," was the grandparents greeting.

"Lorraine invited us to come for this special welcome and we were happy to accept because she is a most special little lady," responded Ruth.

"Thank you for allowing us to share this dramatic moment and we shall see you again," concluded Mrs. Erickson, bidding farewell to the family.

Sensing that Lorraine had reached the breaking point, and replied, "We are going to go downstairs and watch the luggage get dizzy on the carousel, find an ice cream cone, and we will see you all at the house later."

Having finished their tour of the terminal, and their strawberry cones, they were finally on their way home when Lorraine began to sob, "My Daddy's going to get me!"

Aunt Dagne cast a despairing glance at Uncle Rolf as they drove the quiet back roads towards home.

"Honey girl, your Daddy isn't going to get you, remember he is dead," comforted Aunt Dagne.

"That man looks like my Daddy."

"Flicka, perhaps your Grandpa Hamilton looks like your Daddy, after all he is your Daddy's father, but Grandpa Hamilton is gentle and kind and he loves you. He is never going to hurt you." Again the adult's eyes met with a deeper comprehension, and with a warning of the struggles that lie ahead.

"When we get home would you like to put on your new apron and help me?"

"Uh-Huh."

"I'll have you set the table while Uncle Rolf puts the chairs around and helps carry your grandparent's suitcases upstairs."

"I bet the house smells like turkey from the attic to the cellar" speculated Uncle Rolf, "just you wait and see."

"After everyone is in and settled but before we eat let's give your Grandmas and Grandpas their gifts — that will help make them feel welcome," suggested Aunt Dagne.

"A fresh, hot cup of your good coffee will make me feel really welcome and comfortable," interjected Uncle Rolf, "that stuff they sell at the airport sure wasn't made for Swedes to drink."

As they drove into the yard Aunt Dagne deliberately planted a challenge, "Do you suppose we can get the table all set before Maria and your Grandparents get here?"

"Uh-Huh."

And so the race was on. Uncle Rolf turned on soft background music to blend with the fireplace's warmth and the turkey's tantalizing aroma — there was even a whisper of fresh apple pie scent to tease the senses. He then joked and kept up a steady stream of banter hoping to keep Lorraine's thoughts occupied and distract her swirling fears.

When Aunt Dagne heard Maria's car come into the drive, she exclaimed, "Well you won the race little girl! Would you like to put the celery sticks, pickles and olives in a dish for me?"

"Uh-Huh."

Lorraine was so busy with her little tasks and the happy experience of being needed as Aunt Dagne bustled behind her she was scarcely aware of people arriving. This was a wonderful new world to be included in where you were given tastes and samples and errands running to the refrig for more butter and cheese.

At last everything was ready except taking the turkey out of the oven. Aunt Dagne fixed a silver tray with coffee cups and a plate of fresh fruit slices, and another tray with creamer, sugar bowl, teaspoons, and napkins.

Placing the tray with sugar and creamer in Lorraine's hands Aunt Dagne picked up the tray with the steaming hot coffee and one cup of hot chocolate and said, "O.K. Flicka let's surprise everyone."

Following Aunt Dagne with the tray Lorraine felt warm and comfortable until she heard her "Mother's voice" again and she froze in her tracks. Uncle Rolf was closest to Lorraine and saw the transformation of expression and rigid posture and taking a cup of coffee from Aunt Dagne he spoke gently and nonchalantly to the child, "Little girl may I have some of your sugar and a spoon please?"

The request saved the moment and Lorraine moved close so Uncle Rolf could serve himself. Slowly she moved around the half circled group, standing almost at arms length from each as they served themselves from the tray but never did she raise her eyes from the tray or where her next step would be.

After everyone had been served, Lorraine followed Aunt Dagne's example and also set her tray on the massive round coffee table. Aunt Dagne knelt casually on the carpet next to the coffee table and invited Lorraine to join her by silently patting a place beside her. It was a much easier place for Lorraine to handle her mug of chocolate and she felt so much more secure close to Aunt Dagne.

"Thank you," whispered Aunt Dagne and Lorraine managed a hint of a smile as she looked admiringly into her eyes.

Lorraine took a cautious sip of the warm chocolate and gave a little relieved sigh but couldn't raise her eyes. When the last sip had been taken from her cup Aunt Dagne very quietly suggested, "This is a good time to hand out your gifts."

Without a word Lorraine stood up and reached for the closest gift but when she read Grandpa Hamilton's name on the card she didn't know who he was, and looked at Aunt Dagne in perplexity. Understanding the dilemma Aunt Dagne smilingly indicated where he was sitting and Lorraine stood at a distance and reached to hand the gift still without raising her eyes.

"Is this for me?" asked Grandpa Hamilton and the reply was an almost indiscernible nod of her head.

And so the remaining gifts were distributed as Aunt Dagne quietly pointed to the person whose name had been carefully printed on the envelope. The delighted grandparents unwrapped their gifts through a haze of tears with genuine pleasure savoring the joy of receiving their first gift from their grandchild. Lorraine snuggled close to Aunt Dagne shyly enjoying the praise and appreciation as each one unwrapped and showed off their gift with such dignity and sincerity. Maria had known nothing of the plans for this little gift giving ceremony and was thrilled at Aunt Dagne and Uncle

Rolf's foresight, and mouthed a silent "thank you" when she caught their eyes.

Then Grandpa Hamilton reached under his chair and brought out a beautifully wrapped box, "Lorraine, now I have something for you," and he extended the box to her. She hadn't seen where the box came from and was amazed that this gift all of a sudden materialized, and she could only stand looking at it in disbelief.

"Well Snow White, let's open that box and see what it is all about."

And so Lorraine turned to Uncle Rolf. Having so slowly and carefully unwrapped the box she lifted the lid and felt faint. There was the most beautiful big doll nestled in the tissue paper and it looked just like the one in the store in Klamath Falls that she had pointed out to her mother. Gingerly she reached to touch the face and hands not sure if this was real or not.

"What do you tell your Grandpa?"

"Thank you," she murmured. It was so beautiful she couldn't believe her eyes.

Then Grandma Hamilton produced a box from behind her chair, "Honey girl, this is for you."

Lorraine's eyes grew wide with wonder as she saw the large box wrapped just as beautifully as the first one. Again she took her treasure to Uncle Rolf and painstakingly unwrapped as he slit the tape with his little penknife.

She held her breath when she lifted the tissue paper to reveal a dress that little girls dream about - the same blue as her new doll's dress.

"Let's see Flicka," asked Aunt Dagne and Lorraine handed the box to her. "Take it out of the box Flicka, so we can all see."

Doing so she held it up in front of herself.

"That will look lovely on you," commented Maria.

But the awestruck child could only look down at the tucks and lace and touch the soft fabric caressingly.

"Did you say thank you?" whispered Aunt Dagne.

"Thank you whispered Lorraine."

"Well, Lorraine this Grandpa has something for you too," commented Grandpa Boesche holding a chunky box in his hands.

When Lorraine took the box it was heavier than she expected and she almost dropped it, surprised by the weight she involuntarily looked up to the smiling face and almost smiled back. This box was a pretty one too and the happy excitement of the moment almost had her trembling.

"Do you suppose that's a box of rocks?" teased Uncle Rolf as Lorraine came back to his knee for more help.

A self-conscious shrug was her only reply but her questioning, dancing eyes met Uncle Rolf's.

When the lid came off there lay a pair of shiny roller skates....Lorraine clasped her hands with delight and looked across to Grandpa Boesche, her eyes saying what her lips couldn't utter.

"Do you like that?" he asked.

A nodded reply was enough for that Grandpa's pleasure.

"One last box, darling," announced Grandma Boesche as she handed Lorraine the final gift.

Lorraine hadn't seen any of these gifts behind the chairs and was just as amazed at. the last one as she was the first. This box was a different size, and big and heavy. Her curiosity was running high but she was just as patient and careful in unwrapping the last box as the first one.

Uncle Rolf teased again, "I think this should be mine since I am helping here."

Lorraine shot a quick, amused glance at Uncle Rolf and kept right on unwrapping, stopping only briefly to admire the attractive paper.

Off came the lid and the tissue pulled aside to reveal a coat and bonnet and muff all in blue to match her dress - just like in picture books.

Lorraine looked up at Grandma Boesche and looked back at her coat and touched it admiringly and that Grandma understood the unspoken words.

But Aunt Dagne pulled Lorraine to her and quietly asked, "Can you say thank you everybody?"

"Uh-Huh."

And the hearts of four grandparents understood.

*****

Finding Hope

In spite of the sorrow and pain the four grandparents were feeling as a result of the death of their adult children, they experienced a deep comfort and satisfaction in the presence of their newly found granddaughter and the joy and pleasure they could give her. It was truly a bittersweet situation! By the time the turkey dinner was finished Lorraine had grown somewhat used to hearing the sound of "her Mother's voice" whenever Grandma Boesche spoke. Of course it helped to be safely seated between Aunt Dagne and Uncle Rolf. She could look at the table and the plates of everyone but it just was not comfortable to lift her eyes to look at anyone.

While the adults visited she found her thoughts traveling to the living room and all those lovely gifts laying on the coffee table.

"Was it really real? Are all those things for me? Do I get to keep them?" The enormity of the surprise was almost overwhelming to a child totally unaccustomed to gifts. "But Tia gave me all those new clothes, soft, warm, and pretty. They are mine to keep, she told me so, and Tia doesn't lie."   "A doll, just like in picture books, just like in dreams, just like in the store that day with Mama. Where is my Mama? Why didn't Mama like me? Will I ever see Mama again? Will I ever see my little brothers again? Can my Daddy hurt me?"

These troubled thoughts were interrupted when Grandpa Hamilton brought his fist down on the table with a bang. Lorraine was startled and her hands covered her mouth to stifle a scream and her eyes searched the face of the man who looked like her Daddy, "Was he angry like her Daddy? What was he going to do?" Lorraine heard talk about taxes, governors, elections, and pensions. Then Uncle Rolf said, "You sound like a man after my own heart, I think you should be nominated for President." Everyone laughed a happy kind of laugh which was so foreign to Lorraine but she knew all was well and she was safe.

Maria suggested, "Why don't you fellows tune up your violins while we gals tidy up this kitchen, then we will join you?"

"You mean you aren't going to make us wash dishes for our dinner?" kidded Tom.

"Music is better payment, thank you."

Uncle Rolf had seen Lorraine's fright moments before, now he bent down and spoke quietly into her ear, "Did Grandpa Hamilton wake you up when his fist hit the table?"

"Uh-Huh."

"Me too, he really rattled the plates." Uncle Rolf looked at her and winked as he slid his chair back from the table and lifted Lorraine down.

"Let's go see how he does with the violin."

Lorraine started to follow Uncle Rolf in to the piano but she had to walk right past where her new doll lay on the coffee table. Carefully picking up the doll she watched the eyes open, then gently tipped the head so the eyes closed again, then lifted the head so the eyes opened. It was so beautiful! Cradling this dream of dreams in her arms she kept asking herself, "What shall I name her? What shall I call her?" She heard one Grandma called Rose Ellen, "that is a pretty name, and the other Grandma is called Margreta, that is nice too. Then there is Maria and Aunt Dagne, they are all happy names." Unconsciously these names were taking a special place in her life. Lorraine slid her finger inside the doll's tightly coiled curls, touched the lace and ribbons and satin. Then she noticed the doll's patent leather buckle shoes. As she ran her fingers over the shiny, smooth surface Aunt Dagne observed as she came into the room and noticed as the fingers admiringly caressed the tiny shoes.

Kneeling beside Lorraine Aunt Dagne put her arms around child and doll, "Your new doll is almost as pretty as you are, what are you going to name her?"

"I dunno."

"We will have to think about names for a few days - she must have a special name, but she is your baby doll so you must name her yourself"

"Uh-Huh."

"Bring her and let's go listen to everyone play."

So child and doll sat on the davenport with Aunt Dagne in front of the great fireplace as the flames danced to the rhythm of the music. Lorraine was entranced as Grandpa and Grandma Boesche played their violins; Grandpa Hamilton played the trombone; Grandma Hamilton played her flute; and Tia played her cello, accompanied by Uncle Rolf on the grand piano. When they had finished playing the song Uncle Rolf turned to Aunt Dagne and commented, "we need the heart of a guitar."

"Come on Dagne," begged Maria, "we need your special touch."

"It's good just to listen and it sounds great," replied Dagne.

"Musicians do more than listen and play, they feel joyful and make others feel joyful too," encouraged Rose Ellen. "And we have lots to be joyful about tonight!" So Aunt Dagne joined in softly strumming her mellow old guitar. Lorraine had never heard such sweet music and felt a strange but delightful tingle run down her back as she listened, sometimes she felt sad and sometimes she felt happy. She looked at her hands, turning them over, stretching them as far as she could and secretly dreamed of a day when her own fingers would make wondrous sounds.

Next morning Aunt Dagne, Uncle Rolf and Maria joined Lorraine as she fed Rowdy and the other puppies. After playing with them and petting Lady,

Maria picked up one of the puppies and stroked it's head.

"LoRie, we all have to do something very difficult today and we want you to know we will all be together and no one is going to hurt you.

Lorraine's big blue eyes were asking, "What?"

"Remember we told you that your Mommy and Daddy were killed when their car hit a tree?"

"Uh-Huh."

"Well, the police want to know for sure if the bodies at the mortuary are really your Mommy and Daddy because the identification on your Daddy was very blurred and your Mommy didn't have any at all, and no one knows where to look for old records. So the police would like to have you go with us and tell us if you know these people."

"I'll hold you Snow White, I'll hold you tight. "And I will be by your side with Tia."

"You were safe with me at the hospital, weren't you?" asked Maria.

"Uh-Huh."

"And you were safe with us at the airport, weren't you?" asked Aunt Dagne.

"Uh-Huh."

"Your grandparents are going too, and you will be safe with all of us today," assured Aunt Dagne, and afterwards Uncle Rolf and I have a surprise for you.

"What?"

"It's a surprise for afterwards," teased Aunt Dagne.

"Oh."

"It's time to get our coats on and go."

Lorraine hadn't been given time nor opportunity to panic but Uncle Rolf held her hand just in case.

"Why don't you bring your new baby doll with you?" suggested Aunt Dagne.

And so Lorraine sat between Uncle Rolf and Aunt Dagne in their car and followed Maria and the grandparents in the other car.

Chief Bennett and Dr. Putnam, the coroner, and Mr. Stephens the lawyer met the family at the mortuary. Small talk followed the introductions and condolences, each adult postponing the painful task ahead, each privately and fervently wishing there was some 'way to circumvent the necessary process of law! Uncle Rolf knew this brief pause was like a rest-stop on the mountain of mourning for the adults, but for the child holding Aunt Dagne's hand at his side as she whispered secret messages to the doll in her arms, these were moments of confusion and perplexity and he knew that all too soon this battered babe would be immersed in soul searing trauma, and he pondered how he could insulate this tiny human from the pain.

Gently leading Lorraine and Aunt Dagne to a davenport aside from the others Uncle Rolf and Aunt Dagne sat down so they were eye level with the blue eyes and strawberry curls of a little girl who had so dramatically won their hearts. "Snow White, do you know how much we all love you?"
A quizzical look was her answer.
"All of us, everyone of us," and the gesture of his hand encompassed everyone in the room, love you dearly and want you to be our special sweetheart and we are not going to let anyone or anything hurt you. Do you understand what I am saying?"
"Uh-Huh."
"Do you believe me?"
"Uh-Huh."
"And Flicka, when we leave here we are going to go get the surprise we promised.
"O.K."
Like a signal, that confirmation prompted Uncle Rolf to stand lifting Lorraine and her doll into his arms. His eyes met the eyes of the mortician and he nodded

affirmation that they were ready for whatever lay behind the closed doors.

In the slumber room two open caskets sat against opposite walls with a large golden candle setting on a stand in between.

Chief Bennett and Dr. Putnam stood at the foot of the first casket and waited as Uncle Rolf stepped close with Lorraine. Uncle Rolf felt Lorraine's body tense as she beheld the face of the woman in the casket.

"Is that your Mommy?" he asked.

"Uh-Huh," grasping the collar of his jacket in her clenched hand.

Then they stepped to the other casket. Aunt Dagne caught the doll when Lorraine's hands flew to her mouth as she screamed and struggled to be free.

Uncle Rolf held her close and asked, "Is that your Daddy?"

An ashen faced child nodded her head then whispered, "Is he going to get me?"

"No, honey girl, no one is going to get you nor hurt you."

Lorraine saw the tears of her grandparents but could not comprehend their meaning. Graciously Chief Bennett, Mr. Stevens and Dr. Putnam stepped out of the room and the mortician closed the door behind him and the four men walked silently down the hallway each privately questioning the traumatic scene they had been witness to. Quickly Uncle Rolf and Aunt Dagne stepped out of the slumber room as Margo and Max's grief stricken parents stood hand in hand by their respective child - still hearing the tortuous scream of their grandchild. Seeing but not recognizing. Feeling the years of stinging, cruel rejection; the fear of the unknown; the uncertainty; the pain of fruitlessness, vain waiting engulfing them again. Now they knew and they were crushed but they had a hope. Empty but not empty, they had the fullness of a grandchild. Alone but not alone, they had each other.

Down the hallway and to the parking lot, Lorraine still clutched Uncle Rolf's jacket collar, tense and poised for flight. After opening the car door, he reached up and gently released the hand from his collar and sat the traumatized child on the seat beside Aunt Dagne.

"Now, it's time for Flicka's surprise," prompted Aunt Dagne hoping to divert the attention of this frightened little one.

In the shoe store Lorraine held her doll on her lap and watched in wide-eyed amazement as the clerk fitted her with black patent buckled slippers just like her dolls. The admiration in Lorraine's eyes as she looked into Aunt Dagne's face, then Uncle Rolf's, and the look of wonder; as she evaluated her shiny shoes confirmed the love that words couldn't express. Patent leather slippers were a far cry from the ragged, worn shoes of days not too far past. Even the pink Keds of the present were soft and flexible so the stiffness of this new footwear made walking a new experience. The delighted child couldn't take her eyes off of her feet to even watch where she was walking. She just trusted the guidance of Aunt Dagne's hand. But a multitude of thoughts were swirling through Lorraine's head so fast she was dizzy and nauseous. The shock of seeing her Mother who didn't see nor speak to her. The horrifying confrontation of her Father and expecting his wrath to explode. "Were they always going to lay there in that room? Are they going to come and take me away? Will Daddy grab me and throw me in the river? Are these new shoes mine to keep always? Will they take my new clothes away from me? Can I keep my doll or will Daddy throw it away and hit me? Will I have to go back to that cold trailer house and be hungry again?" Everything in the store began to go in circles, it got black, Aunt Dagne caught her as she fainted...

Later, Uncle Rolf drove slowly down Broadway contemplating what to do next, when his eye caught the Dairy Queen sign and his driving immediately had a purpose. "Snow White, it's too bad you don't like ice cream," he teased.

"Uh-Huh," was the immediate and emphatic response."

"What kind do you like best?"

Lorraine shrugged her shoulders burdened with worries a child should never have to bear.

Aunt Dagne helped with the big decision by asking, "What shall it be pink strawberry or chocolate?"

Another shrug.

Uncle Rolf volunteered, "Well, I 'm going to have vanilla."

"And I will have strawberry, please." Aunt Dagne added. "Flicka do you want chocolate so we will all be different?"

"Uh-Huh."

"Do you suppose your doll will cry if she doesn't get a cone?" asked Uncle Rolf again.

"Uh-Uh."

Amused blue eyes searched Aunt Dagne's face as a napkin was tucked under a little chin and the doll and lap were also generously covered.

In the quiet that followed, each silently savoring their cold treat, Uncle Rolf knew what must be done and now was the time to do it. With that resolve he turned the car toward the hill over looking the city. Perhaps this would answer questions that had not been verbally asked and take care of fears that had not been expressed.

As they drove through the cemetery gate Aunt Dagne looked at Uncle Rolf and affirmed her agreement by the slightest nod of her head. While Aunt

Dagne helped Lorraine wipe the chocolate from her fingers and mouth.

Uncle Rolf commented as he glanced down at the child, "What about it that was pretty good stuff, wasn't it?"

"Uh-Huh."

Taking a deep breath Uncle Rolf kindly continued, "Little girl, this is the cemetery where your Mommy and Daddy will be buried in a day or two, and this is where I will be buried someday." "This is the last resting place." "Afterwards a marker with their names will be put on each grave so we will always know where they are."

The quietness of the lovely Memorial Park was accentuated by the rustling of leaves under foot as they walked among the trees and shrubs. Uncle Rolf continued, "We aren't sure yet just where their graves will be but someone will prepare the graves for them."

Aunt Dagne pointed to the city way below warmed by the autumn sun,
"Whenever you look up here you will know where your Mommy and Daddy are and know that all is well."

Back at the house, Aunt Dagne and Maria were serving dessert following a lunch that was exceptionally quiet. There was some small talk but each person was really immersed in their own thoughts, and memories. Only the background music kept the meal from being an awkward and uncomfortable experience.

When the big grandfather clock in the hallway struck one o'clock Aunt Dagne used the moment of disturbed contemplations to announce, "Lorraine and I are going to walk down to the pond to see if the Snow Geese have arrived for the winter." Turning to the child Aunt Dagne suggested, "Maybe you should change your shoes and put on a pair of warm jeans, O.K.?"

"Uh-Huh."

After the two had gone down the well-worn trail that led through the orchard and beyond, Rolf gave an account of the mornings happenings finishing by telling of their visit to the Hill Top Cemetery.

"But we are planning on a burial back home in Louisiana in our family plot," explained Max's father, George.

Rolf placed a gentle hand on George's arm as he replied, "That sounds like a logical plan of action, but if Lorraine stays here it probably would be best if her parents were buried here."

"We want to take Lorraine home with us, she is all we have and we want her," replied the grief stricken grandfather.

Maria entered the conversation with, "George, Rose Ellen, Tom, Greta, of course you want to take Lorraine home with you. I know you want her and she is all you have, I agree, however, it may be a mistake to pluck her up and rush off - it may only add to the trauma and prolong the adjustment to the routine of a new family, a new way of life. May I suggest you leave our sweetie here with me, with us, at least for now until her surgery and therapy is completed, and surgery as soon as possible is an absolute must."

Rolf took up the cause with, "knowing that her Mommy and Daddy are buried on the hill, where we can go visit the graves, I feel it will add to her security."

Maria continued, "We can fly down to visit at Thanksgiving, Christmas and whenever, so she can get acquainted with you in your homes. . . .and then see how she progresses."

Greta spoke up, "Oh, I want to take her home so desperately, but perhaps we should wait and then let her decide what she wants to do."

George consented, "My heart tells me you are right. At least now we know we have her, and we know where she is and we can reach out and touch her from time to time winning her love and confidence."

Four grandparents nodded and smiled in agreement.

Rolf took a deep sip from his steaming mug of coffee then continued,
"There must be some definite endings in Lorraine's life before there can be productive beginnings, and there must be healing of emotional wounds before there can be progress and a secure future. It also occurs to me that you will also benefit and the uncertainties of the past will be put to rest if you would consent to what I suggest."

All eyes were fastened on Rolf.

Maria urged, "Go ahead Rolf?"

"These days, the custom in this country is to leave the grave site before the casket is lowered to it's final resting place, however, I've been thinking it would be very beneficial to adopt the European custom this time and respectfully wait until the casket is lowered before departing. This would serve to confirm in Lorraine's mind exactly where her parents are, hopefully also burying a host of her fears. Does that not seem logical?"

Maria was first to respond, "Oh Rolf, if we could bury her terrors, I think it is an excellent suggestion. What do the rest of you say?"

Holding Rose Ellen's hand, George concluded, "If this will help make a brighter future, I am willing."

A murmur of consent from the other grandparents sealed the agreement.

Lorraine and her family sat in the back of the chapel watching as the room quickly filled with Maria's friends; neighbors; and co-workers. Suddenly Lorraine patted Aunt Dagne's hand and pointed as Ruth and Mrs. Erickson' took a seat. Those thoughtful ladies had also taken time out of their busy day to come share their love in support of a hurting child.

It wasn't long until the undertaker and ministers came and led the family to the front row. Lorraine snuggled between Maria and Aunt Dagne where she could hear and observe everything. The two closed caskets were lavishly blanketed with flowers, and as such did not pose a threat to the wary child.

Soft organ music soothed and settled, then a soloist began to sing:

"God hath not promised skies always blue, flower strewn pathways all our lives thru; God hath not promised sun without rain, joy without sorrow, peace without pain. God hath not promised we shall not know - Toil and temptation, trouble and woe; He hath not told us we shall not bear, many a burden, many a care.

God hath not promised smooth roads and wide, swift, easy travel, needing no guide, never a mountain, rocky and steep, never a river, turbid and deep.

But God hath promised strength for the day, rest for the labor, light for the way, grace for the trials help from above, unfailing kindness, and undying love."

One of the ministers read the obituary and prayed. The other minister read some scripture then turned to Lorraine and addressed her personally and individually:

"Little Lorraine, the other day you identified your Mommy and Daddy's bodies. They could not see you, nor hear you, nor touch you but you could see them, and it was very frightening for you. But you were just looking at their dead bodies. The God who created them, and all of us, including you and me, took their soul, their spirit, their life to eternity with Him. This is the most important part of our body. Now their lives are safe in God's care. In just a little while we will put their bodies to rest in the cemetery up on the hill, but remember those are dead bodies now, their lives are in eternity. God has something important for you to do - someone important to be. God loves you and there are lots of people that need your love just as you need the love of your Grandparents and Tia and Aunt Dagne and Uncle Rolf. Someday you may ask, "If God is a God of love why did he let my Mommy and Daddy die?" "I don't pretend to have all the answers, but this I do know, if we are careless with the lives we have been given often we lose the privilege of living." "We dare not blame God for what He allows, after all our lives belong to Him." "Look for the sunshine; listen to the song of the birds; there is beauty all around us to remember God has many precious promises for all of us, and He is true to His word."

Lorraine had listened well because when the caskets were opened she could look without panic, though she held Aunt Dagne and Maria's hands tightly.

At the cemetery Uncle Rolf held Lorraine's hand while a psalm was read and a final prayer given, then Chief Bennett sang The Lord's Prayer as the caskets were lowered into the earth. His deep bass voice lifted to the clouds then drifted to the valley below. Uncle Rolf plucked four carnations from the blanket and gave Lorraine two.

Softly he coached, "now let's drop one flower into each grave." With purpose and gravity she followed Uncle Rolf's example, as did the rest of the family, then she turned and whispered, "Hold me."

Max's parents, George and Rose Ellen, sat side by side at the kitchen table staring at the sealed manila envelope which Chief Bennett had given them after the funeral with the comment, "These are all the personal belongings which we removed from your son's body the night of the accident." Not realizing he was handing them an envelope full of ghosts.

Turning to Margreta and Tom he had said, "Your daughter didn't have anything with her."

"Not even her wedding rings?"

"No there were no rings, nothing, however Maria received Margo's personal belongings from the Sheriff which was left at the trailer. There wasn't much but a few boxes and the suitcase of Margo." And placed a consoling hand on the grieving father's shoulder.

Margreta, with tears, opened the suitcase to find the old Bible of Bumpa Goetche. She opened it slowly, and found the letter written by Margo. She read it. She wept.

Finally George took out his penknife and slit the top of the envelope while the others looked on. Apprehensively he reached his hand inside and as his fingers touched an object he closed his eyes and withdrew what his fingers had claimed. As he opened his fingers he simultaneously opened his eyes and looked at a gold wristwatch, horrendously marred, dirty, and the crystal scratched beyond belief. Turning it over he read again the inscription so familiar to him.

"Our love to Monty. God Bless. Dad and Mom 11-1-50"

As George's mind flashed back to that morning so filled with his anxiety that no one really noticed how blue the sky, nor how crisp the air, he began to recall out loud.

"Monty had volunteered to join the Air Force knowing he would soon be drafted anyway, and this was the day he was to be sworn in. The gift wrapped watch lay beside Monty's breakfast plate. He had burst into the kitchen singing, "Off we go into the wild blue yonder," grabbed his mother and waltzed her around the kitchen exclaiming, "I don't know if I am scared, nervous, or excited maybe a whole lot of all three." Then sitting down to the table he whistled, 'Wow, the Tooth Fairy has been here already. May I open it now?' But without waiting for an answer he unwrapped his gift as rambunctiously as a ten year old, then when he lifted the watch out he turned suddenly solemn as he read the inscription. 'Mom, Dad this is elegant and I shall always cherish it and someday when I am an old man it will be given to my eldest son.' Ellen and I took Monty to the recruiting center and saw him sworn in and then he was whisked away in the throng of would-be airmen."

Then Ellen took up the memory, "We will never forget that evening the Air Force chaplain called at our door to give us that dark, dreaded news that Monty had been shot down and was dead. Then a week later there was another knock as the Air Force Lieutenant who had accompanied Monty's body back to the States came to call, offering his condolences, and returned this watch and his Air Force ring. Now it has been returned again."

George resumed, "Max had asked if he could wear Montey's watch, perhaps hoping he could feel the pulse of the brother he adored and wanting to feel what Monty felt. When those boys were little they were inseparable and that bond seemed to grow as they grew. They both loved sports, especially tennis and football, and how they could swim. There were plans to learn to fly; to travel around the world together on the sailboat they intended to build; and eventually be law partners. Competition was keen even academically yet they were amiable rivals each helping the other to excel, such keen, intrusive minds."

256

Taking the envelope George turned it upside down and only a billfold came tumbling out - an item so worn and tattered it was a marvel that it held anything. Methodically he began removing each piece of paper from the sad bit of worn out leather. He noticed the California driver's license had expired long ago and as he gazed at the identification picture it was like looking at the face of a sullen stranger, but it bore the name and birth date of his youngest son; the son for which he had such great aspirations. It didn't take long to inventory the scant collection which included a few paycheck stubs with pitifully small sums of take-home-pay. A couple of miscellaneous receipts for car parts, even a few dollars but not enough to buy groceries for a week. Tucked way down in a corner was a tightly folded piece of paper worn and yellowed by time. Being careful not to tear the fragile remnant George's eyes fell on a message penned in Max's meticulous printed style on the back of a Latin 201 Exam paper.

No one would ever know that Max had fled to the Library like a wounded animal that day he was given his Latin Exam paper with another failing grade and he was haunted by Monty's death; his drinking had become uncontrollable; the alcohol fanned his anger giving only momentary unconsciousness from the torment. "I should be excelling for Monty's sake - I should be carrying the Torch - I should make a name for Monty - I should make Monty and the family proud" - but the alcohol robbed him of his ability to think, to retain, to concentrate, to control, he had to have more alcohol. He was ashamed, he was driven, he was afraid; he was lost and too proud to ask for help. It hurt so deeply to think about it, how could he ever talk about it, even to Mom and Dad? After all they hurt too, but not the way he hurt. "Monty was part of me. I dream of Monty, I talk to Monty, when I drink I can even feel Monty. I can't stop drinking but if I don't stop I will be a failure - me who has never failed."

He knew he would be called to the Dean's office, he also knew a letter would be sent to his folks. How can I face the embarrassment, the humiliation? I've dishonored Monty's memory. How will Dad and Mom take the disappointment? Margo will be crushed and she will cry. I'll get mad and the hurt will show in her lovely eyes."

Suddenly he felt defiant and rebellious and out of control, rage seethed within! Who cared? What difference if they did care? In his anguish he wrote:

I've lost my Monty,
I've lost Mom and Dad's respect,
I've lost Margo's love,
I've lost touch with God,'
I've lost it all.'"

*****

The Triumphant Spirit

The funeral was over: Quiet, caring, sympathetic, tender words of warmth. Another chapter sealed in the book of life. Unsung tunes of praise, friends sharing their hearts and comfort. At first Margo's family visited the cemetery daily then as the routine and necessities of life pressed close, the visits to the graves settled to a weekend memorial.

Lorraine found something new to do everyday. Aunt Dagne helped Lorraine with advanced spelling words and math. Stretching from third grade to sixth grade. Which meant her enthusiasm was boundless. The visiting grandparents returned to their Southern homes while Aunt Dagne made adjustments in the school schedule and Maria made appointments for SCANS and X-rays to prepare Lorraine for the long-overdue surgery which would require some very sensitive preparation. Gradually Lorraine began to trust Maria. The thought of going to school put her in hysteria, however she did go to town and to Uncle Rolf's farm where the baby colts where trained.

Junior high-school glided along smoothly, even playing the violin in a holiday concert. Participating in the debate team added to Lorraine's confidence. Then there was the victory of riding old Bess, the mare that frightened Lorraine the evening she arrived.

Playing basketball and tennis in high school was a wonderful outlet for stress. Training her buddy, Rowdy was a lesson in authority. Winter swimming in the high school pool with the family was a wonderful chance to out-run fear of water.

Vacations to the sunny south with grandparents was a sweet interlude and they became a happy proud family. While pages of life turned, her big day was fast approaching and Lorraine was even now thinking of graduation from the University. Scholastic honors were accumulating with her success.

Concluding pages reveal a human spirit that triumphed in picking up the pieces and putting them together without a plea for pity and the will and grace to express gratitude and love. May this simple account serve as a reminder and lesson that we humans don't walk alone.

After the graduation there was a reception honoring Lorraine, and she had invited Bernie who was now a respected aviator, to assist Lorraine in dedicating her long, out-grown wheel chair to the display in the hospital lobby, where the chair would be left permanently as a reminder of what determination can do.

As the sun was setting that lovely summer night, Lorraine and Bernie drove to the top of cemetery hill at Grants Pass. Lorraine knelt and placed a white chrysanthemum on each of the four graves. Then she spoke aloud, speaking in memory and love to Baby Clay and Baby Randy.

"Little brothers you were spared much, and I love you so much, you made my life bearable. Now, I shall try to make up for lost time that belonged to you."

"Daddy and Mama, I forgive you. This diploma is granted to Doctor LoRie Lorraine Hamilton. This you should of and could have had. Because someone special loved and cared for me it is mine. I am Margo's Child!"

THE END